MY CHERRY DUET

The Trenton Troublemakers Book Two

ROWAN ROSSLER

For all the bas-ass ladies of rock and the sexy guitar gods.
Thank you for the music.

"It'll only hurt if it isn't you."

GIA BARLOW: THE UNSTOPPABLE FORCE

Equal parts smooth velvet and explosive gasoline, Gia Barlow is the standout voice of this decade. She struts like a sinner, sings like a saint, and has single-handedly reignited the rebellious riot grrrl spirit.

Her band, cheekily named Pop My Cherry, makes a provocative declaration—a bold, in-your-face feminist statement that walks a fine line between risking cancellation and achieving brilliant subversion.

But make no mistake. Barlow isn't here to serve the male gaze or indulge your fantasies. Just because she writhes on stage in fishnets and leather rompers is beside the point. Her music begs you to listen. It smacks you in the face.

Think you've got her figured out? You're already behind. Gia is liquid mercury: impossible to pin down, relentless in her transformations.

And with former teen idol JC Trenton joining her for a sold-out European tour, brace yourself for the potent repertoire of Gia's addictive songs, and for the genius way JC harnesses nuclear melodies from his guitar.

Next-level fandom is about to erupt.

—Pitchfork, Best New Music

Chapter One

GIA

"Regina!" Mom bellows at full volume, Italian mother fury. "You have a visitor. *Spicciati!* Chop, chop."

I wake up tangled in the top sheet and sense trouble right away. My head throbs like a blown-out amp. It hurts to think. It hurts even to squint at the January sun blaring through the curtains I forgot to close.

Sweet hell, what happened?

Last night flickers somewhere on my mental horizon, the truth of it sloshing through the Jäger bomb wasteland of my body.

I croak out a pitiful, "Coming!" and slowly peel myself upright. Whoever's staring back at me from my vanity mirror looks less like Gia Barlow, future legend of rock and roll, and more like the poster child for middle-class suburbia I'm trying to escape. Maybelline mascara smeared under both eyes and hair by Supercuts. Sexy as a used napkin in a thick cotton nightgown.

What was Nonna thinking, buying a twenty-year-old the kind of high-necked shroud only a nun would wear? More importantly, who shows up unannounced on a Sunday? The Lord's Day of rest is sacred, according to my mother. As important to her as the glow-in-the-dark stars on my ceiling are to me—the little reminders to keep aiming high. And that I can shine just as bright.

Just maybe not *this* morning.

As I paw through last night's clothes for my phone, I'm hoping the texts might fill in some blanks. But when I find it, it's out of juice, the screen sticky, like I used it as a coaster.

Wait.

The fog suddenly lifts, and fragments of last night's EP release party creep back in. The bartenders who kept pouring as the evening wore on, and every conversation, along with my manners, blurred around the edges.

Uh-oh.

Please let the mystery guest be another cousin determined to mold me into the perfect Catholic.

Anyone but *him.*

I pad down the hall barefoot and hear Mama talking, which, unfortunately, she does all the time. At the top of the stairs, I pause, peering down into the foyer. For a strangled moment, my lungs forget how to function.

Shit!

It *is* him.

JC Trenton stands beside my mother, all casual about his super hotness. Dreamy as fuck in his jeans and leather jacket. Trouble as hell with dark waves of hair that some chick had her fingers in last night. He has a way of looking at a woman that turns her inside out. And for the past six months, he's been doing just that—playing my heartstrings to the breaking point.

"There she is." His eyes twinkle with that delinquent mischief my heart finds increasingly difficult to ignore. "Keeping rock star hours like a pro. Atta girl."

"Where's your housecoat?" Mama asks, horrified, and at the same time, I mumble at JC, "What are you doing here?"

He smiles, revealing his perfect teeth and kindly ignoring the fact that I must look like a third-rate sister wife. "Checking in on our resident hurricane."

"Jameson dropped you off last night. *Someone* could barely walk." Mama eyes me with all the disdain she can muster. "Or speak an intelligent sentence."

Here we go. Ten to one, I'm getting an earful once JC leaves. About all the novenas she'll be forced to pray for her irresponsible only child.

What can I say?

Musicians and alcohol are the dream duo, until they aren't.

"I stepped in before fists started to fly," JC explains, his smile widening in what feels like respect, but also confirms my worst suspicions. A not-so-pleasant vision percolates through what's left of my brain as I walk down the stairs.

"I could've handled myself." *The weakest protest in history.*

JC winks. "I was more concerned for the other woman."

Right. *Her.*

The insufferable blonde macking on my guitar player while I downed every shot shoved into my hand and plotted her unfortunate death. Diving off bars is new, even for me, but call me territorial or slightly unhinged when it comes to JC, and you'd be right on both counts.

"Would you like a coffee, Jameson?" Mama asks.

"I'd love one," he replies. "And please, call me JC."

"The usual for you, Regina?" Mama stares me down, prepare-to-be-lectured vibes radiating off her like heat.

"It's *Gia*, Mama. Has been for the past five years."

I hate correcting her in front of JC, like I'm a child. And honestly, why name me *queen* in Italian if you treat me like the village idiot?

"I like Gia," JC chimes in, his voice bedroom-soft yet confident. "It suits you."

Mama sniffs, "Both of you should embrace your real names," and swishes into the kitchen, taking her timeless Sicilian scowl with her.

When I meet JC's eyes, he seems to understand my pain. Or at least his "Moms, huh?" comment lands with a degree of solidarity. I rake a hand through my hair, wishing I'd bothered to brush the tangled black mess my BFF Audrie always jokes mirrors my personality.

"Why didn't you just call? I'm not exactly in your neighborhood."

"I promised I'd make an appearance," he says with a shrug. "You had her worried."

A fresh scary thought closes in. "Please tell me *you* didn't drag me into my bedroom?"

JC, raised in a Shaughnessy mansion, has no business witnessing my sad little room with its spinster twin bed and home made curtains. Or the photo of his old band pinned to the wall reserved for all my musical heroes.

"Your mom wouldn't hear of it," he says, killing my fears. "Although I did help both of you up the stairs."

He smiles, and once again, I'm lost in the absolute beauty of his face. At certain angles, his eyes shine teal blue, like the sky after rain. In the dim glow of late-night studio sessions we clocked all winter, they smoldered gray. This morning, they're alive, shining a kind of metallic bluish-gray that defines his entire being: the elegance of a prince with a side order of renegade.

"Have a seat." I gesture at the sofa in the living room we're already standing in, and wish our house didn't look like someone left in a hurry.

JC brushes past me, and I catch that familiar whiff of something citrus and sophisticated. He mercifully says nothing about the plastic-wrapped furniture. Or when he scans the mismatched box-store decor.

"How's the head?" he finally asks.

"Like it has a chainsaw buried in it."

JC cracks up, a deep rumbly laugh I wish I could recreate with an instrument. Instant number-one hit.

"How bad was I?"

"Nothing I couldn't control."

"Did I throw up in your car?"

My giant cringe seems to amuse him. "I'd still be here, even if you did."

I sit at the far end of the sofa, swallowing down a tiny nervous flutter in my throat. Welcome to my current hell. My abominable hair and worse breeding, and JC embraces it all.

What he hasn't literally embraced yet is me.

"You looked great last night," he adds. "Loved the leather pants."

"Thanks. I thrifted them. Major score."

In the silence, I can hear the beat of my own pulse. And JC keeps looking at me until I'm completely frazzled. There's something behind those eyes. They're *lingering,* like the tension in his jaw. Is he second-guessing his decision to join a scrappy, on-the-brink band for our first European tour? I hope not. Today is Sunday, and we leave on Friday.

His head snaps up as Mama reappears with a tray bearing two cappuccinos and a plateful of biscotti hard enough to chip a tooth. She hands us our mugs, smiling tightly. At something.

"Did Jameson mention our discussion last night?"

I choke on the cocoa-dusted foam. I *know* that tone. "No. Why? What happened?"

JC flicks a tight-lipped glance my way. "Group intervention."

Mama sinks into Dad's tartan recliner. In her vintage Pucci robe and battered fleece slippers, she has the air of a fading movie star clinging to her beauty. "Everyone thinks it's best if you have a chaperone on this tour."

"What for?" My voice rises an octave. "I toured last year and survived just fine."

"That was in North America," she reminds me. "You like to think of yourself as a wise old soul, but Europe is different."

"How do you know? You toured there *never.*"

JC dodges my baleful gaze, but I catch the shadows under his eyes and the tiniest flicker of discomfort. For one bewildering second, all the questions pinballing in my thoughts make it hard to breathe. Did Mama unload her sob story last night? Lay on the guilt of her brief cabaret singer dreams going bust? When I decided to pursue music, she had a conniption. All I heard was doom and gloom. The music biz preyed on young women; failure lurked around the corner.

And for god's sake, Regina, you need a backup plan.

Like her "back-up plan" of getting pregnant at nineteen? Even mouthy me understands that remark would slice too deep. But every time she tries to cram me into a square-peg mold, it dances on the tip of my tongue.

And JC must sense the pending crisis because he quietly attempts to right this monstrous wrong. "It's not like I'd be monitoring you."

"Except that's exactly what a chaperone does," I point out.

Suddenly, I feel like a stranger in a strange land. It's wild how fast this is all turning against me. And the last thing I need is our dynamic locked into the friend zone.

For the past six months, JC has treated me politely and professionally. He's shown up on time every day for our recording sessions and offered great crew suggestions for our upcoming tour. I was hoping Europe might shift our vibe, bring us closer to what I'm feeling.

Now Mama unloads this BS?

I lean back, unimpressed. "I'm not agreeing to this."

Mama ignores this, crossing one leg over another in a silent gesture that says I'm screwed. "Jameson has already agreed," she says. "In fact, it was his idea."

My head snaps toward JC. "Your idea?"

He sips his coffee, silently staring at the laminate. Doesn't deny it. "After last night, Sawyer had some concerns," he finally says. "This was the compromise."

The room tilts. Of course, Sawyer Trenton is behind this. JC's older brother. CEO of Trenton Talent Management and fun as a blister. He hooked me and JC up last August after my band's guitar player bailed. Sawyer promised to sweet-talk JC out of self-imposed retirement if I signed with them.

I mean, duh, no brainer.

Who says no to having rock and roll's sexiest enigma join their band? Except I've spent far too many nights thinking about him. And now my first major tour gets chaperoned because I couldn't keep my shit together.

Because of him.

"If you want to be a professional musician," Mama drones on, "act like one. You aren't a soloist, you're in a band. It's not your way or the highway." She reaches for a biscotto and points it at me like a gun. "I think a chaperone is a great idea. And while you live in my house, you play by my rules."

I hold her gaze, my jaw clenched. She's been a formidable dream-crusher, so why am I surprised she's turned up here according to spec? But using JC as her puppet? On the cusp of my band's breakthrough moment?

That's ice-cold.

And so is my voice when I declare, "Maybe it's time I moved out."

Mama, fully aware my bank account hovers at the three-hundred-dollar mark, can't resist one last twisting of the knife. "Once you pay back your father's loan, you can do whatever you want."

Of course. The big leverage. I borrowed money to cut a video and partially fund last year's tour. I'm still thirty grand in the hole. Our European tour will finally get the monkey off my back.

I say nothing and drink my coffee, swallowing down outrage along with it. The immovable glacier can try to hold me back all she wants. I have big dreams for this world. Dad told me I was singing before I could crawl. It's all I've ever wanted to do. There is no backup plan.

JC cuts me a glance, his gaze no longer remote; it's imploring. Both guilty and soft, like the warm brown sin of his hair. Is he trying to apologize? He better be.

What I have in mind for us in Europe will make God blush and run for cover in His favorite cloud.

Chaperone?

Maybe when hell freezes over.

Chapter Two

JC

I weave through traffic on Georgia Street, hands gripping the steering wheel, still replaying the disaster. Gia gorgeously disheveled and upset, her mother firm as an army general, me riding the razor's edge between Chief Unpopular and Mama Antonia's new snitch. It takes the whole drive into Vancouver to organize my spinning thoughts.

Gia Ana Maria Barlow, with her fierce beauty and blinding confidence—no wonder my head is vibrating like a tuning fork. She strutted around the party last night in skin-tight leather, flirting hard with every guy but me. I nursed a drink at the bar, tracking her every move while pretending to care about the blonde-haired woman next to me.

Pathetic? Sure.

But it's why I was paying attention when she climbed onto the bar, eyes shooting daggers at the blonde talking to me, the crowd chanting

Stage dive! Stage dive! When she flung herself straight at us, I caught her, the momentum nearly knocking me on my ass.

Gia, delivered into my arms like a goddamned gift. Any fool knows the drill. Kiss the woman and end the fucking torture of pent-up sexual tension.

But I didn't.

Performance anxiety for the first time in my life.

Still riding that shame twelve hours later.

Out of nowhere, one of those Lycra-clad road bike freaks who think they own the world whizzes past me in the curb lane. He cuts me off, banking wide to turn right. I jam on the brakes, laying on the horn, and he's got the nerve to flip me the finger. Switching lanes to roar past him, my frustration has less to do with a kamikaze cyclist and everything to do with me.

How the hell will I survive a month of forced proximity, me and Gia stacked on top of each other in a cramped tour bus with a dangerous kind of friction hovering? I still haven't forgotten the shimmering warmth that rippled through me in waves when I held her in my arms. All the wrong ways I wanted to tame her fire.

By the time I reach the restaurant to meet my brother Sawyer for lunch, my head is still lost in last night. I stare out the windshield, my eyes charting nothing. There are no easy answers, just tangled emotions.

A sharp knock on my window snaps my focus back.

The smiling valet outside leans in. "Are you valeting?"

I nod and hop out, leaving the engine running. "Thanks, man."

He hands me a numbered chit and the scent of money and grilled steak hits me as I head inside. Lift is Sawyer's favorite eatery. A trendy waterfront haunt where he can indulge in caviar eggs benny while admiring a million-dollar view. I recognize the hostess—blanking on her name, as usual—but she lights up when she sees me.

"Good morning, JC. Sawyer's already here. Follow me."

Her ponytail sways in front of me as she leads me to Sawyer's usual table, but all I see is yesterday—Gia passed out cold in my car, pale skin luminous in the moonlight. I sat there, parked in her parents' driveway, gathering courage to haul Gia inside and face her mother.

The whole time, fighting my urge to weave my fingers into her hair and never let go. Even in a drunken stupor, she was achingly beautiful.

Sitting in a wingback chair facing the marina, Sawyer types furiously on his phone.

"Hey," I say.

"I ordered you a gin and tonic," he replies without looking up. "And put my money on the chorizo omelet."

Typical Sawyer. Arrives early with zero patience, decides on my meal, and will try to stiff me with the bill, guaranteed.

I take a seat and smile politely at the hostess. "Can you add an americano? No cream."

"Of course."

She hesitates a second longer, vying for Sawyer's non-existent attention. My older brother's a good-looking guy—dark-haired, a little broody. A fit, macho business type oozing wealth and authority with the power to make or break careers.

But when Sawyer's uninterested, you feel the chill.

Taking the hint, our hostess marches off. The gray-haired men at the table next to us, lunching with attractive, age-appropriate females, track her departing curves. Will I be one of *them* in my fifties? Midlife Crisis JC, predictably lusting after women half my age? Then I remember I'm already that guy, and thirty-four is around the corner.

God, when did birthdays begin to feel like marking time left on this earth?

It feels like yesterday I was seventeen and invincible.

Sawyer's fingers continue flying across the screen. "Wasn't Tinder supposed to make it easier to get your cock sucked?"

I lean in, angling for a view of his phone. He's messaging some redhead named Sparkle, all big-haired glory and glossy lips.

"You know half those chicks aren't even real, right? A hundred bucks says her name is anything *but* Sparkle."

He huffs a laugh. "Do you even recall the name of the last woman you slept with?"

The blonde from the bar, who insisted I take her number, was for sure a Natalie. Or Nicole. Shit. Maybe Nadine? I should have locked in a system for remembering names by now. But I have no intention of calling, or sleeping with, what's-her-name. My mind barrels down a one-way Gia track, hurtling toward the inevitable crash of disappointment.

"I'm not *that* bad," I counter.

"Not lately." A long, piercing stare follows, as if Sawyer's considering that Gia might be the reason for my dry patch, but his mind can't rationally put us together. "And that is troubling. At this rate, you'll be scrolling through the *Carbon Dating* app at sixty."

"Maybe I've become picky," I say.

He cocks a brow. "Sure. Let's run with that."

Okay, fair. No one ever voted me most selective, but I do have some standards.

Sawyer sets his phone down. "Your issue is commitment. The only thing you ever cared about was performing. Tell me the truth," he says, as if he knows I haven't been up front with him. "Is scoring films and session work in LA doing it for you? Part of your soul had to die with your band."

I fixate on the marina stacked deep with yachts. Sawyer is needling me about commitment, and all I can think of is how I couldn't even kiss Gia after she landed in my arms. I love my brother but hate that he is somehow always right.

Well, *almost* always.

He's clueless about the real reason why I killed the band, and I'm not sure he cares to hear why this late in the game. Besides, I'm not prepared to dig through the ashes of my dreams over a chorizo omelet.

Not when Gia makes me feel like I've spent the last decade majoring in the minors.

"I swung past Gia's place this morning," I say, eager to switch gears. "She's doing okay."

Sawyer hums a sympathetic sound. "You're still in one piece, so I take it she agreed to the ultimatum."

"It's not like she had any choice."

"Someone needs to control that whirling mass of barbed wire," he says, the insinuation clear that the task will never be his. "The last thing we needed was a bar brawl to end the night. Thanks for stepping in and driving her home." His brow furrows. "You okay playing tour chaperone?"

"It's fine," I say. "I thrive on challenge."

Sawyer runs a hand over his tight military-style haircut, blowing out a sigh that sounds oddly defeated. "I'm getting too old to handle the drama of divas half my age."

"She likes to rile you. You know that, right?"

"It fucking works." He drains his bourbon over ice and signals for another. "Makes me wonder if it was all worth it."

"Ticket sales are through the roof. There's your answer."

"No offense to Gia's talent, but *you* are the hot commodity," he stresses. "The returning Messiah."

"Is that how you're selling me?" Leave it to Sawyer to package things up with a preposterous bow. He is that guy—the one selling ice to the folks living in the Arctic, selling things that might be better off gathering dust on the shelf.

Before he can reply, a different blonde shows up with both of my beverages. Flirts extra hard with Sawyer because he rolls up every week in his DB9, hemorrhaging money.

"There goes your Sunday night date," I joke once she's out of earshot.

"Are you kidding?" he scoffs. "No actresses, ever. I learned my lesson."

"How's twice-divorced treating you at thirty-seven?"

He shoots me a dirty look and picks up his phone. "Fuck you. But also, check these out. They're the tour posters."

My eyes widen as he scrolls through the images. "Those are sweet. Dani did a great job."

"Rhys designed them, believe it or not."

Sawyer, hard as it must be, dredges up a look of respect. Our baby brother, Rhys, and his girlfriend, Dani, now run a design agency together. Gia bonded hard with Dani last summer and insisted they create all the promo materials for the tour. Somehow, Rhys—who seemed destined for absolutely nothing growing up—proved all of us wrong.

If *he* can transform himself, what's stopping me?

"What a turnaround, man," I finally say. "He's nailing it."

Sawyer grimaces. "And nailing the woman I wanted to."

"Six months later and you're not over her?" Sawyer claimed he was all over Dani first, and to this day harbors a beef with Rhys over it.

"I'm a Scorpio. Jealous, resentful, and I carry a grudge like it's my job." Sawyer shrugs, explaining away his personality as if the cosmos really were to blame.

Meanwhile, I digest the near impossible. Sawyer admitting flaws? Rare day indeed.

"You're coming to the tour meeting on Wednesday, right?" he continues. "I want you in the room, so we're all on the same page." Sawyer plucks his fanned napkin from the table, flicks it once, and lays the linen square at a perfect ninety degrees over his lap before dropping the warning. "Do not, under any circumstances, let Gia wrangle you into anything beyond this tour. If all this blows up like I think it will, you have a gold-plated road to a career rebirth. You don't need her."

I sink deeper into my seat by a few inches. I'm not sold on a second coming for many reasons. And the truth is, I need Gia as much as she needs me. Not for the hysteria of crowds or the pump of adrenaline when the stage lights dim. Not for the reasons anyone might think.

Certainly not for the reason Sawyer brings up next.

"And Dad's stoked to hear about your comeback. You know how rare his good moods are these days."

Fair. Being wheelchair-bound tends to suck all the enjoyment out of life. But even in his heyday as an entertainment mogul, Peter Trenton averaged one smile per month. The closest he ever came to joy was watching me on stage—living out the rock star fantasy he couldn't pull off himself.

I don't blame him for what happened to my band, but his endless pressure did play a role. Just like he shoehorned Sawyer into the family business, killing his dreams of becoming an engineer. It's hard to believe that Sawyer's too-tight sweater tells the entire tale of our messed-up family dynamics. He could've gone a size up and looked less like an MMA cage fighter, but his body is the one thing he has total control over.

Certainly not his life.

"Dad met Gia last month when we visited Mom," I reveal. "A little embarrassing, his manosphere opinions. She handled him like a pro."

"She knows what she's doing," Sawyer admits. "If she doesn't screw up, she can be the next big thing."

I frown at the plot point he's sidestepped. "Isn't she already?"

"You have street cred and legacy, bro. Don't forget it. Your star can rise again."

I fantasize for a nanosecond about bailing, if only to push back, but that ship has sailed. And Sawyer, for all his unending power-mongering, speaks the truth. I was the star once upon a time. But that's not why I said *yes* to recording the EP and Gia's tour.

I said yes because of that moment in The Troubadour last year, when everything shifted. When my soul cleared for a magical evening, and I could taste beauty once more.

To spend a minute in Gia's light is to experience a kind of magic I thought I no longer believed in.

But I agree with Sawyer, at least out loud. It's easier than confessing what I feel. Because like jamming in an 11/8 time signature, this tour will be anything but easy.

Chapter Three

GIA

Band meetings in a diner border on cliché. But I needed to get out of the house or go completely insane. Mama won't drop the chaperone thing, and between that and the upcoming meeting with Sawyer to finalize the tour details, my tolerance for being managed is officially on life support.

My bandmates sit across from me in the booth, both surprisingly lucid for a Tuesday morning. Brady Bowen, who's been drumming since he was nine, scans the menu like he doesn't order eggs over easy every single time.

"You were a hot mess the other night." He looks up at me from under his fluttery wings of false eyelashes. "That poor chick was toast if JC hadn't stepped in."

"She was harshing my vibe," I explain. "Not cool on release day."

"You sure it had nothing to do with her poaching your territory?" Tai Dominguez, Brazilian bass demon and certified ride-or-die, lifts his yellow-tinted aviators, beaming like he has me cornered.

"You're all my territory," I insist.

Tai's enormous chocolate eyes keep twinkling. "Except you don't imitate Wonder Woman when someone flirts with us."

My boys trade bratty smiles. They live together a few blocks from here, in a three-story walk-up that feels like stepping inside an opium den. Scarves hang limp over dusty lamps, and Tai's latest obsession with sitar music crackles on the Sonos. Everything's faded and frayed. And every plant they've ever owned?

Dead. Long dead.

But there's a vampy weirdness bubbling under their surfaces that caught my attention in high school and has never let up. Takes one to know one.

"I might've been a bit wasted," I admit.

Tai tilts his head. "Meaning, wildcat horny?"

"Do *not* put words into my mouth."

Brady pokes his tongue against his cheek in a lewd gesture. He's all slapstick, no subtlety or slyness. "I think she planned to have something else in her mouth."

I crumple my napkin and pelt it against Tai's precious fade. "Any chance we can enjoy breakfast without our minds in the gutter?"

Tai's gaze shifts, clocking something over my shoulder. "I think you're about to enjoy breakfast a little more."

It takes every ounce of willpower not to turn around. Besides, Brady's hyena chuckle tells me who's arrived. And, yes, anyone in my band becomes my territory—even if they happen to be rock and roll royalty with artfully styled hair and practically radioactive with sex appeal, drifting in on a cloud of expensive cologne.

"Hi, troops." JC lifts a hand, and I want to cry because why, why, why can't I remember the feel of his skin on mine? "Can you shuffle down?" he asks me politely, a reminder that perhaps he is not so smitten with my red-stained lips and slightly crooked front tooth as I am with his straight band of pearly whites. "And good morning, Fearless Leader."

He adds this as the electric shock of his warm thigh ghosts mine. I think my brain shuts down. Can't really be sure. I'm just staring at the golden ratio face that could launch a thousand ships as my mouth goes dry and my heart swells until it hurts.

JC's technically our elder statesman at the ripe old age of thirty-three, but you'd never know it. The guy's a walking ad for "rock and roll keeps you young." He has clear skin, cover model cheekbones, plus an annoyingly perfect smile that shows up, like, every other minute.

And, yeah, it does things to me.

He makes everything feel dangerous.

And not just bar-dive dangerous.

Heart-on-the-line dangerous.

Which is, honestly, way worse.

Brady claps his hands, and the booming sound pulls me out of my JC daydream. "Dude! I am *pumped* for this tour. First time outside North America. Just got my passport." I half expect him to lean across the table and kiss JC. Touring Europe was a pipe dream for him back in the down-and-out days. "And you've been there, done that," he gushes on. "Talk to me. Are the Euro kids chill and easy?"

JC sips his water, considering. Brady's a dead ringer for a young Ashton Kutcher, if Ashton were blond and proudly bi.

"No comment on the men," he says, "but in my experience, no woman is ever that combination."

Something prickles at the back of my neck. Wait—what? Is this some kind of bro bonding BS? He hasn't badmouthed women once in the past six months.

I turn to lock eyes with him. "So what are you saying?"

"Ooo." Tai rubs his hands like he's about to watch us start swinging. "Them's fighting words."

"No," I correct. "They're stupid words."

JC's eyes light on mine. "You know how the saying goes. Fast, good, or cheap. You can only pick two."

"Let me guess," I flip back. "You're fast and cheap?"

He laughs, scratching at his meticulously maintained scruff—what I call "beard lite." "I've been called worse. And Sawyer did say your personality took some getting used to."

"Oh, I bet he didn't say it quite like that."

JC's smile grows wider by the second. *I can throw all the shade I want, and he never flinches.* Plus, he seems endlessly amused at my suspicions about Sawyer. Corporate types like him can't be trusted, so I mess with Sawyer whenever I can, just because.

"Speaking of personality…" Brady elbows Tai in that way before he shares your most damning secrets. "Does JC know what the priest said when he kicked you out of Sunday School for scarfing down an entire tray of communion wafers?"

"Then washing them down with holy water," Tai adds, a bit too gleeful for my liking.

"Hey," I protest. "Not my fault they were too stingy to spring for bottled water."

JC stops laughing long enough to ask, "Did that really happen?"

"Yup," Brady crows, happy to cut me down a peg ever since I shrugged off his kiss last year. Unlike Brady, Tai actually asked before he tried to slip me some tongue.

This is what I have to work with.

"Well," JC prods, "let's hear it."

I clear my throat, shooting Brady a look. I don't mind them having a laugh at my expense, per se. Being in a band means you suck up the roasting that eventually comes your way. But how about a tale that doesn't involve me pissing off an entire religion? Something that makes me sound halfway sane to JC if he ever decides to like me.

Too late now.

I shift on the bench, plotting when I can return the favor and reveal Brady's skeletons. "He said I didn't play well with others. That my need to control wasn't healthy."

The fan above us keeps swirling a haze of burger grease into the thick silence. No one speaks. Their expressions say enough.

Like they're all wondering if Father Anderson deserves a medal for his astute observation.

JC, possibly sensing it's up to him to say something for the greater good, pipes in, "I guess you proved him wrong. Because we're all playing with you."

Seriously? That is tender enough to make me change my mind

about strangling Brady. Real-life #RelationshipGoals, sitting right next to me.

Just as my heart starts to soar, our waitress, Rebecca, saunters over wearing high-waisted jeans, her usual resting annoyed face, and a perfect blowout that must suck up all her tips.

Her eyes track all over JC. "You look familiar."

He smiles back, and what the hell? Full wattage for her? "Maybe it was that night in the dark alley?" he playfully suggests.

"You know I'd remember that," she purrs, acting all coy with her stupid hair flip.

"And yet you always forget I take my coffee with cream."

I feel everyone's eyes land on me and sit a little straighter, thinking, *Shit.* That came out exactly the wrong way. Bitchy, on edge. Vaguely murderous. Why can't I act like a normal person around JC?

"The usual?" Rebecca's eyes taper onto mine. "Toast drowning in butter with a side order of attitude?"

I hand off my menu with a tight smile. "The pancake special with extra bacon."

Rebecca finishes taking our orders, laying on the charm extra thick for JC, as I tamp down a similar flare of jealousy that swamped me before my epic stage dive last night. I know I'm too possessive. I know I can exhaust people with my endless drive. But if I don't push, people start pushing back. If I don't choose, someone else will choose for me.

Brady leers at Rebecca's departing, swinging ass, blowing out a low whistle. "Is it me, or is she suddenly hotter today?"

"Hotter because someone else captured her attention?" I point out.

He ignores me to address JC. "I'll be your European wingman every night. Take me along. I'll carry you everywhere."

JC laughs. "Not sure I have much tour game these days."

Ideally, none, I think and then realize, this is the perfect time. If revealing soul-crushing rules can ever be considered ideal.

I try for casual. "By the way, did y'all know about the no sex in the tour bus policy?"

Brady's smile fizzles. "Since when?"

"Since now."

Truth is, I concocted this ploy while stewing in bed this morning. If

JC insists on being my chaperone, fine, but no way he drags in females by the dozen and forces me to endure his endless pleasure.

"Does that include you?" Tai asks.

"Yes. This is our first time touring in something fancier than a fifteen-passenger van. I'd rather not experience a free-for-all hump space."

It's comical, their heads on a swivel at the same time. The hard vinyl bench under my butt feels more forgiving than their collective disbelief. Brady glances out the steamed-up window onto Main Street traffic, then back at Tai. Our resident slut is not happy.

"This is Europe, Gia." He taps a finger on the table as if pointing out the continent on an invisible map. "Time to taste all the international cuisine."

"Taste all you want," I say. "Just not in the bunk above me while I'm plugging my ears."

"And what happens if one of us breaks your little rule?" Tai wants to know.

I pause. Hadn't thought this far ahead. All I know is JC is like amnesia—he makes me forget everything else. Like bands are a collective.

I blurt out a number that bites, "Five hundred bucks per infraction."

"Half our weekly salary?" Brady's expression could be the next viral WTF meme.

"Call it incentive," I say.

Brady's not having it. "Uhm, I call tyrant."

JC says nothing. Maybe he feels it's not his place to chime in. Tai crosses his arms, guns on full display under the tight tank top. He earns his muscles the hard way, battling jocks on judo mats, adding a wildness to him that women cannot resist. But he moves through the world with a light touch, and usually follows my lead without pushback.

So his hard gaze, flicking between JC and me, is unsettling.

"Better get ready for The Terminator to take down all the groupies swarming you ten deep," he says.

No! screams in my head. *Not you too.* First the Sunday School story, then this? My face flushes as JC turns his head to look at me. Again with that stunning smile, this time with a cocked eyebrow in the mix.

"Tell me the story behind that nickname."

Taking a deep breath, I try to think of the fastest way to get through this conversation. Doesn't he get how hard and disorienting and intimidating it's become to be around him?

"Maybe later," I mutter.

"You didn't pull this shit with Audrie," Brady grumbles, unwilling to let this slide.

Audrie Porter, my BFF and our OG guitar player, walked away last summer. Fell for some tech millionaire we met on tour. One minute she's ripping solos next to me, the next she's barefoot and pregnant in a smart home.

Did not see that plot twist coming.

And I miss our two-and-two setup. The boy/girl balance didn't outright cancel all the dumbassery flying across the table, but it definitely slowed it down. JC in the mix means the testosterone levels are officially off the charts, but he's not like my boys.

And he continues to watch me in the same way I watched him under that thin blue studio light last October. We were at the tail end of a marathon recording session, both of us half-delirious, running on fumes, desperate for sleep. Tai and Brady had bailed earlier, and JC offered to drive me home, even though he lived a half hour in the opposite direction.

That's how it started.

Not all at once.

Little things.

He fixed Tai's busted chorus pedal without being asked. Our late-night sessions turned into one a.m. giggle fests. The meandering drives where we opened our souls, the moon roof of his Porsche 911 a window to the star-streaked sky.

At first, it felt like a blossoming friendship. But somewhere along the way, the air between us started to crackle.

Now I catch myself watching him too often, laughing a little too hard. I feel like a mangy street dog chasing after a potential premium owner. And JC dolls out crumbs of interest that keep giving me hope with nothing concrete to hang my hat on.

Well, sometimes, he looks at me like he knows. Like he's waiting for me to catch up. Or make the first move.

Something I'm too petrified to consider.

Because if my musical angel rejects me, I'll feel that sting of failure forever.

Chapter Four

JC

Breakfast ends on a high note, literally. Brady's "guy" scored some weed, and once the text comes through, he and Tai lope off to get stoned. Not that I mind alone time with Gia. The past six months, something's shifted. I feel more like my old self.

And it has everything to do with her.

"So, Terminator." I ruffle her hair, teasing a legitimate excuse to touch her.

"What?" Gia swats away my hand. "Like you haven't done anything you regret?"

A muscle around my mouth twitches. I quickly rearrange my face so she doesn't notice. But Gia has good radar, and something in my expression has blipped onto her screen.

"Sorry," she says, softer. "Kinda felt like they ganged up on me. Spilling secrets."

"You struck back hard. Didn't exactly make the upcoming tour more palatable for them."

Gia searches my face. I see her lashes flutter, quick and uncertain. "And you're cool with my request?"

If I weren't buried in deep, painful lust, then, yes, I could survive. Otherwise…

"Do I have a choice?"

She looks away, and her silence speaks volumes. Like I don't know this is her retaliation for the chaperone news.

"If I don't drive the bus," she says, "everything gets derailed. I want, *need*, this tour to be fire."

"It will be," I reassure her, stopping shy of offering to clear whatever debt she owes her parents. Not handling her own responsibilities will send Gia flying off the rails. Making it on her terms is the only way. "You've put in the work. I'm impressed."

A smile flickers on her face. "Thanks. That means a lot, coming from you."

Every so often, we land here—her bravado peeled back, letting me in. I crave these moments like the dirtiest sound screaming from my fuzz pedal. Before I can say more, our waitress swings by with the bill. I snatch it from her hand despite Gia's howl of protest.

"Not a chance," I say. "I'm paying."

Gia lunges for the bill, and my body flames, hers pressed hard against mine. My hands aren't even on her, but it doesn't matter. I feel an overwhelming need to hold the paper high above my head all afternoon.

"This was *my* treat," she insists.

I skim the bill, keeping it well out of Gia's sightline. The waitress scrawled her phone number across the top as if all her heated gazes weren't clues enough.

I crumple the bill and stuff it into my pocket. "Buy me a coffee in Europe, and we're even."

It's so not her style to let someone else run the show, as this morning proved. I'm only half-surprised when Gia practically sits on me, legs bracketing my hips. Her hair tumbles forward, grazing the swell of her breasts. I desperately need to think about something else. It's not the four cups of coffee spiraling through my system making me edgy and nervous.

Imagine crushing a Sweethearts candy, and that burst of powdery sweetness hits the back of your throat. Gia smells like that. Like a delicious possibility.

Sex and candy.

"You're not paying because of what my mother said?" she asks, an edge of accusation in her voice.

"No," I lie. "It's the gentlemanly thing to do."

Gia locks eyes with me. It feels like the moment in a song where the bridge changes key. A tonal shift, space clearing where I can ask.

I clear my throat. "What are you up to for the rest of the day?"

"Doing everything to avoid my mother. Why?"

"Wanna hang at my place for a bit? You can tour my studio. The legendary sound chamber where all the magic happens."

Those sooty lashes of hers flick up, and I see all sorts of trouble in her smile. "I asked for a tour weeks ago, so, duh… The answer is yes."

"I'm parked down the street. Let's rock."

Gia scrambles off me, and it scares me shitless how badly I wanted her to say yes. I fish out my wallet to leave five twenties on the table. The waitress attempts to catch my eye as we exit, but I've mastered the zombie walk—straight ahead, no glances. Even the slightest flicker of attention can be mistaken for interest. Admittedly, sometimes there is.

But not these days.

Not with Gia in my orbit.

It feels like I've been hard since August.

Outside, we hover beneath the awning. The rain hasn't let up, and it drenches us in the thirty-second dash for my car. Just enough time to feel the nerves in my stomach. Gia in my home isn't about bragging rights; it's something else entirely. Something that makes me unsteady because I can't unsee her sitting on my couch.

I open the passenger door so she can slide in, then join her from the driver's side. The windows immediately steam up, and I crank the engine to fire on the blowers. In my peripheral vision, I clock Gia fiddling with her lower lip, squeezing it between her scarlet-tipped fingers.

Jesus fuck.

Too many nights I've tossed and turned, hot with Gia fever.

When does it break?

Fat raindrops splatter against the windshield, falling faster and heavier. I flick on the wipers and shoulder-check before easing into traffic. Take it slow to calm my rushing mind.

"You drive like my Nonna," Gia observes. "Why own a hot car and not pin it?"

"Because every cop likes to pull over a guy in a sports car," I explain. "And I lost my license once from too many speeding tickets."

She throws me a half glance. "Once bitten, twice shy?"

I laugh, even though it feels anything but funny. Story of my life right there.

"No complaints, seriously." She traces a finger along the caramel leather dash, the whipstitching. "This beats public transit any day of the week. Not that you would know."

I give her a little smile, mock offended. "I took the bus. Once. When I was twelve."

"On the one day your chauffeur had off?"

"My childhood wasn't *that* over the top."

Of course it was. Why lie, because any Google search spits up pages of the flashy excess my parents threw around? After clawing his way to the pinnacle of the entertainment industry, damn if Dad didn't flaunt his nouveau riche status.

"Right," Gia says, heavy on the sarcasm. "Living in a castle in the ritziest part of town with hot and cold running servants. Like your entire upbringing didn't scream white privilege."

"Fair," I concede. "But that's not how I choose to live."

"You scrub your own toilets?"

"I wouldn't go that far."

She serves up a damning look. "So ... servants."

"She prefers the term *Cleaning Associate*."

A nod. Like that's all Gia needed to hear. "And does she flounce around in a French maid's outfit?"

"Is that the impression I give?"

I hold her gaze until she turns away with a soft, "Maybe."

In the spreading silence, I can feel the car interior filling with my discomfort. Now it makes sense. Her hesitation with me, us, neatly summarized in one word.

Do I blame her?

Over the past decade, every few months like clockwork, a new photograph of me pops online. Me on a date in Hollywood or Vancouver, ducking the camera flash.

But what you see isn't the whole picture.

Yes, flirting comes naturally to me. Yes, my burn rate sucks. Call it self-preservation. I end every relationship before it becomes serious. I don't allow anything more than a scratch against my armor. My personal badge of honor is keeping that shit locked up tight.

A hotshot guitarist addled with deep-rooted trauma.

Now there's a winning combination.

I reach for the stereo and flick it on. Nirvana's "Lounge Act" never sounds more timeless. A friend who makes me feel.

"This time next year," I circle back to where we left off, "when you're rolling in the dough and have a place of your own, you can flip the script. Hire a hot stud to polish your condo."

Gia shoots me a long look. "Is that the impression *I* give?"

I paddle-shift into third, opening it up to burn across the Georgia Street viaduct. Gia's question reverberates in my mind, like the anticipation that thrummed through me a year ago.

Crammed stage left at The Troubadour in LA.

Pop My Cherry was the opener, although the packed house at eight p.m. screamed headliner. The buzz on Gia had scorched through the industry like wildfire. A once-a-decade talent like Janis, Madonna, and Beyoncé, writing her own songs and delivering them with the vocal power of a cannonball.

I slipped in solo, trying for incognito with my fedora pulled low. There's a world where you can be invisible if you don't draw attention to yourself.

Gia, however, made the word "invisible" obsolete.

She stood in the beam of spotlight like a prophet conjured from earth's molten core, rattling my rib cage with sheer thrill and awe. She glowed like an ancient power I was half afraid to touch.

And now look how close we are.

Closer still, entwined with her music—music that makes me want to crawl inside of her.

"You're a giant slayer, Gia," I finally say. "That's all the impression you need."

"If everyone keeps telling me that, it might go to my head."

"Shit. And here I thought you already hit peak insufferable."

She laughs, smacking me on the arm. "For the hired help, you're pretty sassy, Jameson."

"Well, Regina, someone needs to keep you humble. We're outnumbered. Three dudes and a diva."

Gia relaxes into her seat, offering up a smile. "Now, *that's* a song title."

We're both quiet for the rest of the drive, and I like how even our silences are companionable. Half the time, my words seem to come out all wrong around her. But you try thinking straight with her pale thighs peeking out from a barely-there romper and screaming *touch me.* Hard enough to sit through breakfast with the hottest woman in the world making every forkful of scrambled eggs wobble on my fork.

I sneak a look at her profile, feeling something powerful well up in me. She must feel my stare because she snaps her eyes to mine, holding our eye contact as she asks, "Will you ever write again? Or is the itch gone forever?"

I'm too stunned to keep my face under control. I search for the wrong answer and tell the truth instead. "Actually, I came up with a decent hook a few weeks ago. Felt the flow for the first time in forever."

"Really?" Her voice curls higher. "Sounds like I need to take full credit for being your muse."

I bite back a smile. "Why does that not surprise me?"

Gia swivels in her seat to face me, eyes blazing coal black. Penetrating, brilliant, and scary. "Listen, I need to squawk twice as loud to be half heard as a woman in this business. You try being female, twenty, and barely five feet tall."

"You're preaching to the converted," I insist. "I'm on your side a hundred percent."

Her fire cools, gaze sweeping over mine. She hadn't expected me to agree with her so quickly, but I understand the shit women face in this industry more than I'd like to. And what fool can overlook the brilliance of Gia's music while it blasts them in the face?

"I wanna hear your song." She states this. Doesn't ask. Assumes in her gentle bulldozer way that the sea will part just for her. "You need to play it for me."

I turn off Georgia Street into Coal Harbour's maze of green-glassed skyscrapers. Ease down the ramp leading to many levels of underground parking beneath my building, riffling through my options. I could say no and let her beat it out of me, except that almost sounds appealing. Shit. Will the lyrics be a dead giveaway? Gia's no slouch.

"Not sure I should be sharing my best ideas with you," I joke.

"Yes, you should," she insists. "Because we're musicians. And if we can't trust each other, then we're fucked."

She holds up her fist, and I bump back. The gleam in her eyes, that pure, unbridled passion … I'd be lying if I said it wasn't an absolute turn-on. The boys might be pissed about the bus rule, but the less competition sniffing around Gia, the better. Turns out, being nominated to chaperone her is like a free pass I didn't know I needed.

Chapter Five

GIA

I'VE SEEN THE NICE AND THE CRAP PARTS OF TOWN. AND GRAND neighborhoods like Shaughnessy, where JC's parents live. We visited at Christmas after his mom kept pestering him to meet me. Their never-ending mansion made me dizzy with its scent of roses, expensive perfume, and polished floors. JC's pad in Coal Harbour is also prime-level moneybags. Fancy with many untouchable things. Sofas that look cool and uncomfortable.

But it smells like him: citrus punched with spice, clean but warm.

And holy hell, the view.

"Wow, this is dope." The view is framed by floor-to-ceiling windows, and I feel dwarfed by the craggy North Shore mountains in the distance. The vast ocean in front of them is as endless as the plush rug I'm standing on. "You have good taste," I say. "Or your designer does."

JC laughs. "I bought most of it. Fully adulting. I have an aesthetic now. And everything." He stands next to me, tall and muscled and utterly perfect, watching seagulls wage war with the wind currents. "Can I get the lady something to drink?" he asks. "I have it all."

If I knew anything about wine, I'd throw out some obscure Transylvanian vintage from the 1880s to see what his cellar is made of. Instead, I ask for a rum and Coke. You can take the girl out of Burnaby, but you can't take Burnaby out of the girl.

JC wanders into the shiny stainless-steel kitchen, where sharp knives and his chefly grace live. He loves to cook, and I bet that Sub-Zero fridge is full of fancy cheeses with names I can't pronounce.

I take a seat on his surprisingly comfy sofa. On the credenza behind me are many silver-framed photos, and one in particular catches my eye—a beautifully shot black-and-white portrait. All the Trenton men, minus Rhys, in crisp tuxes, a carpet of immaculate lawn behind them, sprawling to the cliff's edge.

"Was this taken at Sawyer's wedding?" I ask.

"That was his second wedding," JC calls back, aware of the photo I'm referring to. "Rhys keeps joking that the third time's a charm."

I study the photo. Damn, JC cleans up fine. But his father looks nothing like the shell of a man I met last month, slumped in a wheelchair, withdrawn and grouchy. He was as stunning as his sons, dark hair slicked back, arrogance in his stance. I recall how JC's body language tightened up in his presence.

"How come you're not married?"

"Haven't found my rock-and-roll bride. My mom keeps hoping, though. Right now, the pressure's on Rhys and Dani."

"They're a great couple. Inspiring."

JC returns, handing off my beverage. We cheer, my heavy crystal glass to his craft IPA bottle. Settling next to me, he drapes one arm dangerously close to my shoulder. "My family really likes you."

"Except Sawyer," I correct.

JC half-smiles, eyes sparkling. "He said you were as cuddly as barbed wire."

I give a tiny shrug of resignation. "I guess hating him is out of the question. I respect anyone who tells it like it is."

"For the record, I don't think about you that way."

My head snaps up. There's a specific tone in his voice that makes me blush.

"Because I'm paying you to like me," I say it fast, to match my heart rate.

"I'm not doing this for the money, Gia."

"I hope not." I try to pull off joke-y, while my insides turn squiggly. That look in his eyes is back. "Your allowance was probably more than what this gig is paying."

A soft laugh. His fingertips graze my shoulder in a casual rolling drumbeat. "Close."

The air stills in my lungs. For a second, it feels like he's going to kiss me. And the vague tremor in my heart tells me, once he does, things will never be the same.

"So then…" I swallow, my mouth dry as dust. "Why did you agree to this?"

In one blink, his expression shifts. I get the sense, in some unde-fined way, that I've pressed on an unexpected button. We've talked about almost everything since we met—fame, family, fuckups. But he's sidestepped any relationship chatter. And this topic.

I'd scrawl my name in blood to share the stage with him.

Did the feeling go both ways?

JC had watched our entire show at the Troubadour last March, camped at the front of the stage. When he dragged his eyes to mine, for one charged second, it felt like fire sweeping over me. It wasn't only longing in those hypnotic pupils. There was something haunted and base. Dirtier than desire.

That look seared into my heart.

After the show, I waited backstage, nerves in knots, praying he'd show up. Nothing. Not a single ping on my socials. I checked every day for weeks. Me drizzling my rum and Coke onto his hat mid-set was my lame way of saying, *I see you. Talk to me. We're the same.*

But are we?

In his eyes, am I a woman about to detonate with astonishingly debauched fantasies? He ruffled my hair in the diner like I was ten!

With my pulse racing in my throat, I shoulder-bump him. "Talk to me."

JC throws his gaze to the other side of the room before it sweeps back to me. "Because you're going to be a star. And if I can help get you there faster, I will."

My body suddenly feels heavy, like it's filled with crumbly sand. Sometimes when he looks at me, my heart feels too full for my chest, so brimming with blood that it aches.

"Wow. That's fucking extra. Thanks. Wish my mom supported me like that." My voice wavers a little. "No faith. It sucks."

"Parents are like that. Either killing your dreams, or in my case, being pushed to live out their parents' unfilled dreams."

I don't miss the way his eyes drop. Or the light tone of regret in his voice. Clouds smother the sun outside, and just like that, the room feels underlit and less welcoming.

"Is that what it felt like for you?" I ask carefully.

JC takes a long moment before he says, "According to my mom, Dad shoved anything that could make a noise into my hand as a baby. He was tone-deaf and instrument-illiterate. Brutal irony for a man in the music biz who wanted to be the next Bob Dylan." He smiles, but there's a sadness to it. "I was too young to recognize what it all meant."

"Is that why you quit? Because of him?"

I hold space for him to answer, but JC takes another swig of beer. Dammit. It felt like the right time to ask, but is there ever a right time to rip open a wound? I guess Mama does know everything. Maybe I'm full of myself, thinking this silly bout of couch talk quali-fies as a safe space where JC can unload his secrets, no questions asked.

But I'm happy to share.

"I think my mom resents me," I say into the silence, the truth quietly hurting. "My birth killed her dreams."

JC blinks. And there it is again, a shadow passing over his eyes. "Parenthood is a dream for some."

I take a slow sip of my drink. "Do you want kids?"

He drains the beer, hand over his mouth to muffle the burp. "Do you?"

"Eventually."

He spins the empty bottle in his hands. Look up the word "pensive," and his face would be there next to the definition.

A quiet settles between us.

The bottle keeps spinning.

I lean back to stare at the ceiling that goes up and up. Mom's dream for me is a life where you know what to expect, free from disappointment. She wants rules and frameworks, security, and a career ladder. Not a daughter who escaped high school with the bare minimum grades.

But sometimes you have to go for it or die trying.

"You have a lovely ceiling, Jameson."

"Thank you, Regina. It's what they call 'coffered.'"

I tip my head right to look at him. "Does that mean overpriced?"

A laugh bursts out of him, filling the room with its warm, happy sound. The perfect antidote to the weird malaise that had drifted over us.

"One hundred percent not judging," I'm quick to clarify. "My ceiling consists of ancient spackle, glow-in-the-dark stars, and squashed mosquitoes."

"Really?" His face animates. "I had those stars in my bedroom. It felt like my own private universe."

"I need to keep reaching for the stars, which is why I'm looking forward to the tour bus and change of scenery."

"Speaking of that." JC taps his knee against mine, leaving it there to scorch my bare skin. "I'm calling top bunk."

"Have at 'er. Little Miss Five Foot Nothing here can crawl into her lower bunk just fine."

"Solo," he reminds me, eyes dancing over my face. "In case you forgot your own rules. I'll be watching."

"Get that chaperone idea out of your head," I warn. "I don't need a babysitter. Especially one who…" I clamp my mouth shut, but the unspoken words hang between us like napalm.

JC's eyebrows sink. "What?"

"Nothing."

He looks skyward, a muscle around his jaw working. "I know what you were going to say."

I swallow, feeling like a crumb. "Am I wrong?"

I don't know what my face is conveying as I stare at him, heart thumping double time. An awkward beat seems to go on forever before JC clears his throat.

"Not entirely."

My gaze falls to the floor. It feels like I swallowed rocks. Well, that was special, Gia. Why not call him a player to his face while you're at it?

I'm suddenly so aware of my rainbow knee socks and leather romper. They looked oh-so-cool in my bedroom mirror.

Now I feel stupid.

This elegant space is where a man brings a woman after a civilized night on the town. A world of soft rugs and sleek, lacquered furniture. A ceiling that probably cost more than Dad's Rav4. A girl with teacup boobs and hips as straight as a ruler has no business in this manly condo.

Not when she almost accused him of the worst.

And as if I'd said those exact words, JC sits up abruptly, a whoosh of air following him as he pushes off the sofa with an uncertain smile.

"Let's check out the studio."

The tight dark confines of JC's studio are thick with the smell of warm electronics and his cologne. Framed and faded Read My Rights concert posters hang two by two, covering the far wall. And me, stapled to my chair with the lyrics he just sang to me.

"If you tell me all your secrets, I'll tell you all my dreams. And maybe we create the music in all the spaces in between."

JC touches my shoulder briefly. "Whadda ya think?"

"It's brilliant," I say, still breathless, my soul singing along, riding the melody like an ocean wave. All some women hope for is a man to say "I love you." But give me the squeak of fingers on a fretboard and a melody seared into my brain, and you might as well be possessing my soul. "I need it. I need to record it."

He chuckles, setting his Les Paul into the guitar stand. "Sorry, it's not for sale."

"Are you planning to release it?"

He gives a shrug that could mean any number of things. "Not sure yet. Early days."

I inhale deeply but can't settle. I'm in a new bubble, an out-there frontier where time and space have become meaningless. The simple G to C bridge made me feel brand-new.

"But if you don't release it…" I have to try. My voice is custom-built for A minor, my favorite key. JC knows this. And that song is a Billboard hit right outta the gate.

He pushes back and casually does a half spin in his Star Trek command chair. The backrest clangs hard against the desk. In slow motion, I watch the cold, fresh beer he brought in tumble forward, liquid sloshing all over him, narrowly missing the guitar.

'"Fuck!" JC leaps from the chair to strip off his soaked T-shirt. He chucks it into the corner, rights the still frothing bottle onto the desk, and our insulated haven suddenly feels anything but.

Oh my god.

I'm robbed of breath.

My hungry eyes scour every inch of his exposed chest, the smoothly muscled ridges rising and falling with his breath. The air stirs, and it smells like raw male. I squeeze my thighs together. There's enough adrenaline pumping in my veins to power all of Mexico. I let myself imagine reaching for the button of his jeans. I want him inside of me, to make me ache.

Our connection feels earth-shattering.

But it's too much, his gaze hunting mine, my cheeks aflame with arousal. My heart becomes a tight fist in my chest, and I wish for something, anything, to change the silence and the kind of silence it is.

Then, with his face half in the shadows and his husky voice unrecognizable, JC whispers my name.

And what do I do?

Jump to my feet, babble something about grabbing a towel, and bolt.

♫

"Excuse me, miss?"

I jerk awake from my window pillow. The bus is stopped; rain sleets sideways outside. I'm the only passenger, and I missed my stop like five minutes ago.

"End of the line." The bus driver's watery blue eyes crinkle with a kind smile. "But if you don't mind waiting, sit tight. I circle back in ten."

I sit up, disoriented. The air is heavy with steam and sweat. JC offered to drive me home (twice), but I needed time alone. And I hated how he looked like a kid with his hand caught in the cookie jar.

"Uh, thanks." I slide out of the seat. "I'll walk from here."

I stumble down the stairs and power home through the merciless storm. My Converse squelch water by the time I trudge up the driveway. Our house is dark and feels deserted. A cold wind whips the strands of my damp hair across my face. I feel nervous and queasy, my heart discovering new depths of paralyzing attraction.

The way JC stood still in the darkness, half naked, all male, the whirlwind of my thoughts fevered and wild. He looked so polished, grown-up, and experienced that my anxiety became a physical brick in my stomach, leaving no room for anything else. I wanted to kiss him and feel the pressure of the wall on my back when he returned my kiss with desperation. I've wanted that for weeks—and run when the opportunity finally lands?

What is wrong with me?

Well, I know exactly what my problem is.

I wasn't ready.

Because I'm a virgin.

I slip inside and toe off my sneakers in the foyer. Ditch the wet socks and contemplate the next month of my life. Suddenly, the idea of heading into the unknown of Europe with JC feels so overwhelming. The agony of watching him flirt, then disappear with random groupies… I can't think of a more perfect hell.

Because, of course, he'll respect my rule.

What I really want is for him to devote himself to me, and I'm not sure he can pull it off.

I head into the kitchen to make a tea. Mama texted earlier that she's at the Italian Centre, home at six. I lean against the counter, staring into space. Instead of focusing on tomorrow and the band meeting with Sawyer, my mind keeps grinding on his song.

We spent weeks in the studio together last fall, and not a peep about him writing again. So why did he sing it to me? Why today? It meant something, I'm sure of it. But replaying the song in my head, his vague, lush, poetic lyrics give me nothing.

Except for the certainty that I need to record that song. Or maybe he'd like to duet. We could Sonny-and-Cher that track all the way to the Grammys. My steel velvet howl paired with his soaring soft leather octaves? Aces.

A clap of thunder rumbles overhead. Rain falls steadily, pinging off the patio furniture Dad forgot to haul into the garage. All I can think about is how JC captured the gorgeous mess of love and yearning so perfectly, in my favorite key no less. If I'm being honest, there's an ulterior motive in wanting his song—because music means everything to him, the lifeblood coursing through his veins.

More powerful than air.

If JC gives his song to me, it's the equivalent of marriage.

But are either of us ready for that?

Chapter Six

JC

It's three p.m. on a sleepy Wednesday in downtown Vancouver. The Rock and Roll Bride Tour has turned the Trenton Talent Management boardroom into Ground Zero. It's all over Sawyer's face—he wants me to step in. Not a chance. I sat on the same side of the live-edge cedar table as Gia and the boys for a reason.

Solidarity.

For the next month, I'm one of them.

In the eternal battle between musicians and management, I know where I stand.

Gia recaps for Sawyer: "So let me get this straight. Our flat fee of a grand per show, combined with our share of the net, we're looking at a hundred grand?"

Sawyer shifts in his chair. Normally, he's in and out of these meetings within half an hour. Gia's been a force, grilling him on the finer points of profit sharing. They don't call it the music *business* for nothing.

"Demand is high in Hamburg, Madrid, and Barcelona," he says. "We're negotiating added dates; these venues can scale."

"And you get bonuses for the sold-out shows," Bettina Weber adds in her clipped German accent. Sawyer dragged his senior agent into this meeting in the hopes that another female would keep the Gia fireworks to a minimum. Ha! It takes more than Tom Brady-approved shoulder pads and severe bangs to put Gia in a corner. "We take our cut only if you make the numbers."

Gia glances at me, and I nudge her once under the table with my foot. Before the meeting, she asked me to signal her if Sawyer was taking them for a ride or playing fair. One nudge means let it slide; two means go for the jugular.

It's the least I can do after yesterday.

Gia looked shaken right before she logged every inch of my naked torso. I felt an overwhelming urge to take her against the wall. My face flamed at the images that flooded my brain. More confusion, battling with the desire ripping through my veins.

Experiencing a want so powerful, it hurt.

She's all I can think about.

"But we also need the daily socials," Bettina continues, her Botoxed brow struggling to animate. "TikTok behind the scenes, sound checks, life on the road. Engage, engage, engage. We'll monitor metrics and ticket sales."

"I got that covered," Brady chimes in. "Just hit half a mil followers."

Gia rolls her eyes. "Because you're half naked on every post."

"Dude. It works." Brady smiles like he's a Fortune 500 executive who's turned around an entire company. A CEO who wears toe rings unironically.

In all honesty, I don't miss this new iteration of the industry. It's not enough to release songs these days. You've got to feed every algorithm. And I hate social media.

One thing remains the same, though: if you have talent, everyone wants a piece of you.

Sawyer pivots to engage Shae Lincoln, the tour manager I recommended. A brawny gal with a heart of gold who loves the New Orleans Saints and owns cowboy boots in every color of the rainbow. You'd think her job would be straightforward—get the band from point A to point B—but the coordination of promoters, venues, and artists becomes exponentially harder on an international level.

But if the world were ending, she's the one I'd call to manage it. That's how good she is.

"Do you want to add anything here?" Sawyer sounds hopeful that Shae can wrap this up.

She's been munching on chips since the meeting started and brushes Dorito dust down the front of her Christmas sweater. Dachshunds and wreaths. Who would have guessed?

"This isn't my first rodeo," she drawls in a Southern accent thicker than gumbo. "Consider it locked down. We have two veterans on this ticket."

She tips her feathered electric-blue hair in my direction, prompting Gia to side-eye with suspicion.

I'm already behind the eight ball as Gia's chaperone. Double duty as tour manager assistant?

Hell no.

"This is Gia's band, and I'm along for the ride," I clarify. "The buck ends with her."

"Exactly." Gia crosses her arms. "I'm the nerve center. Daily updates, cash flow projections, the works. It all flows through me."

Brady suddenly pipes in with his one important thought. "I'm stoked for the per diem. No one's ever paid me to eat."

Tai follows up with, "How soon do we get paid? I'm like, overdue on rent."

Gia glances over at a yawning Tai. He's wearing a stained buttondown that looks like he pried it out of a dumpster. Brady's eyes have been shut behind his mirrored sunglasses for most of the meeting. I get the sense Gia expected more from her bandmates. Not rolling over to play dead and letting her handle all the tricky bits.

"We already discussed that," Gia reminds him, her voice tight with annoyance. "I'll refresh you later."

"Oh, cool." Tai stretches in his seat, muscles snapping and popping. "Any chance we can order in lunch?"

Gia sighs so quietly only I hear it. She looks heartbreakingly young, until I catch her in the sunlight streaming through the wall of windows, her petite, heart-shaped face on the cusp of ferocious womanhood. A boss babe in her tight, short dress and Converse. Screw the tour logistics. That one hole in her fishnets is driving me insane. I desperately want to finger it, widen it, ruin it.

Just to see if she'd let me.

I nudge her under the table again for no real reason other than this is my free ticket to touch her. And a not-so-subtle way of dropping hints.

The guy I've been is not the guy I will be with her.

She feels like the start of everything new for me.

The missing lifeline in my directionless life.

Gia continues to rub her foot against mine, smiling angelically at Sawyer, who never takes his eyes off us. She makes him wait a full five seconds before she says, "Okay. Cool. I think we covered it all."

And Sawyer practically leaps out of his chair to get the hell out of here, motioning me to join him.

He chatters as we walk down the hall to his office, but I'm only half-listening. Fully dialed in on the next month of my life. I know this tour will have its share of bumps; they all do. And Gia might fawn over the first cute guy with an accent… if I let him near her. But for the first time in a long time, something is growing inside me with an alarming, piercing clarity. I hadn't dared name it before, but now I know.

Hope.

And hope is a dangerous thing to feel in this business—especially when you've been burned by it once already.

♫

While Gia and the boys munch on designer pizza in the boardroom, Sawyer steers me into his office, a plush man cave devoted to platinum records and golf memorabilia. Sterile and tame compared to Dad's scotch-in-the-morning vibes when he ruled the roost.

But the personalities that now run this biz are very different than the swashbuckling moguls who came before them. Peter Trenton was swaggering and wildly charismatic. Sawyer gives new meaning to the term *bland suit*.

He settles into his overlord chair with a sweeping view of the mountains behind him. "Are you mentally prepared? The press is already circling. The hype machine is full tilt."

"We talked it through. The boys are psyched. Gia's taking it in stride." I sit on the sectional across from Sawyer and try not to think about starlets and casting couches. "Once we hit the road, it's out of our hands."

"True," he agrees, eyes briefly sliding to his monitor. "Thank Christ she's not your type. One less thing I have to worry about."

I tilt my head. "What do you mean by *your type*?"

"I mean…" Both his brows lift skyward. "She's twenty."

Interesting that he brings this up today. And knowing Sawyer, I'm doubtful this is a casual observation. He gathers intel for weeks, then ambushes you with the evidence. Once again, I'm left questioning. Every time my foot connected with Gia's under the table, it sent warm tingles through my body. What type is that other than perfect?

"Mom liked her." I hate how defensive I sound. "Said she was *refreshing*."

Sawyer pins me with a look. "A breeze every now and then is refreshing. Living year-round in a cyclone? Not so much."

"She's not a ditz," I counter. "She's got dimension. And more soul than both of us combined. Twenty going on forty."

"Yeah, whatever." Sawyer waves a dismissive hand. "I know the tour bus drill. The party scene and late-night jams. If you need to get it out of your system, do it behind closed doors. And please, don't drag it out."

Sage advice from the man whose marriages lasted six and ten months, respectively. He was less of a dick before his first girlfriend, Jasmine King, ditched him and disappeared. I've prodded him for all the reasons why, only to hear the same beleaguered response: *Don't ask.*

Still, I lose my cool. "Why are you talking to me like I'm a horny teenager?"

"Because every guy *is*, until the day we die." He leans back to stack both ankles on his desk. I don't know what's more disturbing—that he speaks the truth or his imported silk knee socks. "My point is, if her fans start shipping you two, it'll be a PR minefield. And if you get cast as the heartbreaker? Kiss your comeback goodbye." He pops open a container of Tic Tacs and crunches on a handful. "Gentle reminder: this is setting the stage for your return. We give Gia the spotlight, make her our rising star. But you stay the anchor, the legacy."

"But this is *her* tour," I remind him. "I'm temporary window dressing."

"Is that how you view yourself?" Sawyer asks, legitimately concerned, it seems. "You need to be bringing main character energy. Show up in the posts. Rock the house."

"You know how I feel about social media," I remind him. "I killed all my accounts for a reason."

Sawyer raises both hands in surrender. "Now it runs the damn world. That's why I'm saying, watch your back, because you and Gia will be filmed nonstop. And if it happens," he adds, "keep it double-wrapped. Do not derail her career."

I flinch but keep it buried. Too much history packed into that one line.

And to live with Sawyer is to live with a lifelong believer in the power of the patriarchy. Arguing will get me nowhere.

"And if you think the footsie between you two went unnoticed, guess again. Do what you need to do to keep things running smoothly, chaperone the shit out of her, but remember, your allegiance remains in these four walls."

The finger pointed at me says it all. I've forgotten many things from my inebriated teenage hellion years, but thinking Sawyer wouldn't notice every detail? Stupid.

I can't play both sides. But Gia expects me to be on hers, and Sawyer will eviscerate me if I crater his hard work. As he said, Pop My Cherry could explode like Nirvana. Scoring Gia was a coup for the company, and it all hinged on me. One messy hookup smeared across the headlines, and we could all go up in flames.

"Are you nervous?" Sawyer asks, pulling my attention back.

I hold his gaze, my stomach tightening a fraction. "I still know how to perform."

"Your last band blew up on tour in Europe—that's what I was referring to." He cracks his knuckles, a sharp, loud pop that makes my teeth clench. "Tell me this won't be Groundhog Day."

"It's cool. We have Shae." I tuck my hair behind my ears and talk through the knot forming in my throat. "This runs like clockwork."

Right now, I need Sawyer to believe in me, not look at me like I'm a washed-up idol stranded in the wilds of my thirties, living on a wing and a prayer. I can tell he's sitting on the fence, unsure if I'll blow it.

The thing is, he might be right.

And if he is? Then I lose everything.

Including her.

Chapter Seven

GIA

"Are you sure there's no vibing?" Audrie asks. "You two combusted on stage in Osoyoos. And all those weeks together in the studio, you said the energy was crackling."

We're FaceTiming, Audrie in her new Queen Anne home, a high-flier neighborhood in the heart of Seattle. She's running a bath in one of those marble standalone tubs an entire family can fit in. Rocking jewel-tipped acrylic nails and bundled in a robe at noon, she's somehow transitioned into a kept woman without even trying hard.

"Yes and no. I dunno." I rake a hand through my knotted hair, clocking her sleek, new, expensive cut. "The more time we spend together, the more I notice how he flirts with everyone. Even Brady thinks he has a chance."

"How's our favorite man-whore doing?"

"Based on his last text? Snatching up every pallet of glitter eye shadow."

Audrie chuckles. "I'm a little jealous of y'all. Remember how we

48

used to talk about our first European tour? That you'd fall in love with a tall, dark stranger, and your deflowering would be epic and sun-kissed."

My heart pinches. What didn't we talk about? Audrie knows me better than anyone. When it comes to love and romance, I'm bringing classic vibes. A big, fat Italian wedding? Yes, please. With the skirt on my wedding dress so poufy, I need to squeeze sideways through the door. I also want kids, eventually, with a loving husband who doesn't stray. And I want to lose my v-card in a way that matters. Not some one-night stand soy boy grinding me into a dumpster behind the bar.

You only get one first time, and I want to do it right.

Audrie pours purple bubble bath into an arc of water gushing from the tap, and damn, what it must be like to have decent water pressure. "All the pieces are falling into place," she adds. "At least tell him how you feel. Promise me you will?"

Little does she know I almost did. On one of those December drives back to my house, snow fell around us in big fat Hallmark-movie flakes. We were snugged in his luxury car, bathed in the light of a full moon, both of us warm and loose from Fireball shots as we finished our conversation in the driveway. JC looked at me, face in the shadows, and smiled.

And just as I worked up the courage to bust out something poetic like, "*Hey, I like you. Wanna like me back?*" he patted my shoulder (ugh!) and wished me a Merry Christmas. One chaste kiss on the cheek and away he roared. I don't know if I felt relieved that I'd escaped mortal embarrassment or devastated that I'd read the moment so totally wrong.

With that kind of luck, why step up to the plate a second time?

"The problem is," I say, "it's more than navigating my feelings for JC. I'm in bed with the entire Trenton family. Friends with Rhys and Dani. Sawyer's managing the band. I've met their parents." God, it feels like a hopeless knot that will unravel with one wrong move, and I'm scared to lose my found family. "Sometimes I think fuck my pathetic longing. Leave well enough alone."

Audrie turns off the tap. Tests the water temperature. "Which is so not your style."

"But you get it, right?" I press. "This shit can get messy fast."

One of Audrie's favorite games—classic East Van trash that defined our relationship since third grade—consisted of outlandish dares, such as the *"Would you rather?"* variety. Grade school: Would you rather have Carolyn Kramer lose her hair or Cheryl Matheson gain a hundred pounds? (Carolyn and Cheryl, the two popular mean girls.) High school: Would you rather kiss Eric Wilson or go down on him? (Eric, the unattainable heartthrob jock who spoke to me once, demanding I get out of his way.) When we were shitfaced on Amaretto stolen from my parents' liquor cabinet: Would you rather eat fried tarantula tacos or a plateful of rotten worms?

(The low point, admittedly. No right answer.)

So, no surprise, my BFF has a fresh combo primed and ready.

"Would you rather not sleep with the man of your dreams or regret not trying for the rest of your life?"

"This is more than sleeping with him, A. I've never felt this way about a guy. But I also have no interest in being number three hundred and two."

She lets out a low whistle. "Do you think he's slept with that many women?"

At his condo, JC reacted to my almost-insinuation exactly like a man who shamelessly flirts with every breathing woman would. To his credit, there's been less of it lately. But a ceasefire is just that—no guarantees.

"The thing is, I can only be number one in any man's heart. Not sure he has the capacity for that."

Audrie sighs, knowing me well enough that budging on my belief system is as likely as the sky turning brown. "We could find you a fake boyfriend. Make him jealous."

"I'm not into fake *anything*," I remind her. "In case you hadn't noticed."

Some idiot "manager" in LA suggested I invest in a pair of boobs. *Career elevation*—his exact seedy words. Those tobacco-stained horse teeth of his are probably still rattling from how hard I slammed the door shut behind me.

"Keep me posted on all the tour happenings, good or bad. My

phone is on twenty-four-seven," Audrie assures me. "Pep talks, a shoulder to cry on, painkillers FedExed. Whatever you need, I'm one text away."

My heart swells. My A-girl has my back, now and forever. "Thanks. I love you to the moon. Even though you're to blame for this situation."

Audrie pauses, mouth open like she wants to speak but isn't sure what to say. Finally, she asks, "But you forgive me, right?"

My reply comes out shaky. "Sort of."

It hurt like hell at first: Audrie whisked off into a new life seemingly overnight. My dad tried to console me, saying it's always hard when your best friend grows up and discovers life without you. The thing is, Audrie scored all the guys from day one. The quintessential ash-blonde stunner: curvy, friendly, and a totally cute drunk, giggling at every lame joke or cheesy pick-up line from the mostly starstruck dudes who flailed their way into her orbit.

Me?

I probably gave off too much power-bitch energy. The guys who dared come near me were the wannabe musicians fishing for tips on how to get signed.

Cuddly as barbed wire?

My frustration is real.

Because underneath the spikes, I'm still a woman who craves connection with someone special.

Audrie hums a syrupy "Aww, Gigi." And I don't like hearing my old, comfortable pet name laced with sympathy. "Our lives will always be connected."

I stop myself before I say it: *Yes, and no.* A baby changes everything. And with JC only a stopgap to fill our guitarist hole, the uphill battle starts soon: sourcing a new guitarist *and* a bestie while Audrie's days fill with baby talk and stretch marks and how little she sleeps. Our small, intimate world is about to split wide open, a whole chasm opening between who we were and who we're becoming.

Why does wanting it all require sacrifice?

It sucks.

"Oh, before I forget, let me read you this article I found on *Pitchfork.*"

I rub my temple and groan. "Really? Last time they called me an outlaw rock and roll shapeshifter."

"No, this one's actually not pretentious as fuck. For once."

There's a muffled sound as she pulls up the article. A tiny square of dense text pops up beside her face on the screen. I brace myself for the apex of self-important journalism.

Audrie drops into a deep, macho narrator voice: "There's something baldly brilliant about the way Gia bludgeons her way through the potent repertoire of her addictive songs, and something genius in the way JC Trenton harnesses nuclear melodies from his guitar. Credit Trenton Talent Management's CEO, Sawyer Trenton, for a vision not even an absurdist could have imagined. Pairing Gia and JC is akin to two great artists madly dragging oil pastels across a blank canvas to create a masterpiece."

"Bludgeons?" I roll my eyes. "Wow. Thanks, guys."

Audrie snickers. "They mean your raw power. No one will ever accuse you of being Britney Spears. In a good way," she's quick to add.

"I'm one shaved head and barefoot-in-a-gas-station-bathroom scandal away from her mantle."

"Nuh-uh," she counters. "You're reinventing the industry. Without being another blonde pop tart shaking her tits at the camera."

I shake my head and let out a laugh. First of all, I have no tits to shake. Second, trailblazing has its perks but also landmines. Everyone cheers on the underdog, but Pop My Cherry's rapid ascent means we now have a target on our backs. As Sawyer reminded us, we'll be under a microscope on this tour. The spotlight is hungry to catch every slip and stumble, and nothing is more unmissable than a brazen front woman eating humble pie, one humiliating bite at a time.

"You will slay, Gigi," Audrie says, lazily running her hand through the mound of frothy bubbles. "There's no other way. Ride the wave all the way to the top."

She cracks her trademark instigator smile. For one brief, white-toothed moment, she's not Audrie, engaged to the unfortunately named Paul Schlitzman and living her best life without me. We're still bandmates fighting the same battle, living the same dream. "And ride JC all the way to blissful nirvana," she adds as final slutty advice. "He is scary smoke-show."

And packing, I don't say. One of the benefits of the tight jeans JC prefers is a front-row view of Package City. Audrie swears sex hurts the first time, even with a string bean dick. Guess I should pack a muzzle just in case. Whatever hangs between JC's legs will definitely leave me howling.

If only the music snobs at *Pitchfork* could hear that noise.

♫

At midnight, I'm trying to cram a month's worth of H&M's finest into Mama's ancient suitcase. Tai said to pack light. I interpreted that as one huge-ass bag. Dad hauled the only decent piece of luggage we own to his Chicago conference, so I can't lose the battle to close the zipper on this damn thing. I flatten myself across the bag and yank with everything I've got. C'mon!

Then *zzzp,* and finally, it closes.

I sit at the end of my bed, breathing hard, sleep nowhere in sight. But I'm packed. Ready as I'll ever be for a life-changing event. And I did prepare, splurging on a lacy push-up bra and matching panties in case fate turns in my favor. (No way JC sees me in Costco cotton hip huggers.) Also scored a bikini perfect for poolside lounging once we hit Barcelona.

But our tour officially kicks off in London with two nights at the Royal Albert Hall. Holy shit. Talk about making an entrance.

We're arriving a day early to attend a swanky party for the Rose Dylan Agency, Rhys and Dani's new venture. They timed the event to kick off right as our tour starts, because of course they did. Those two have slayed the day ever since they fell in love. In the blink of an eye, they've gone from "creatives with a dream" to serious players in the media game. They designed all our tour swag and promo and asked us to attend the gala as special guests. Dani texted for my sizes last week because Rhys has designers falling all over themselves to dress us.

I wore ripped jeans and Doc Martens to grad.

Me in flowy Dolce and Gabbana?

Staggering around in diamante stilettos?

I gaze at myself in the mirror on the far wall, seeing past my reflection, mind whirling. It feels beautiful and strange, this path opening up before me. Last night, like the manifester I am, I visualized our own framed wedding picture. JC and I decked out in matching Chucks and designer finery. Miss Gia Barlow, the Eastside spitfire, fueled by Fruit Loops and pro-grade espresso, upgraded to champagne and caviar, the sky sun-filled, our families smiling.

I don't know where that thought came from.

But it felt possible.

For the first time in my life, I'm starting to understand why Audrie devours romance novels. Every queen needs a king, right?

My phone chimes on the floor, and I scoop it up. It's JC. I smile stupidly like a woman in a trance. He always makes my world better.

JC: Hey, rock star. You asleep yet?

I quickly text back:

GB: U kidding? I'll sleep when I'm dead.

JC: Not a good omen the night before a flight.

GB: TY 4 the upgrade. If we go down, at least we go down in style.

JC: Happy to splurge. It's your first trip across the pond.

No one flies business on the Trenton Talent Management dime. Premium economy, maybe, if you boost their bottom line hard enough. JC used points to score us sleeper seats in business, but honestly, I'd travel cargo for this opportunity.

JC: Get ready for your close-up. And don't forget about us little people.

My heart does a little flip. Is he serious? As if I could forget the biggest leap of my career while trapped on a tour bus trying very hard not to imagine him falling onto me by accident. Repeatedly.

GB: U still swinging by at seven to grab me?

JC: Your chariot awaits. Uber Premier.

A glow spreads across my skin. I'm floating, already imagining the European crowds losing their minds, me deep in the musical cloud where no one can touch me.

And JC…

The dizzying dream of him touching me all over, pinning me in place with those gentle hands. That look of his, melting the mental barrier I've built—the one that whispers he can't want a virgin.

My fingers fly across the screen.

GB: I'm excited. And nervous.

I stare at the typing bubbles, holding my breath, holding on so tight, it hurts. Admitting even a sliver of fear feels like cracking open the window to my soul.

The dots disappear.

Reappear.

Then—

JC: Me too. On both counts.

I stare at my screen, confused.

Me too?

What could *he* possibly be nervous about? The man has owned stadiums. He can command a crowd with a single toss of that sinful sex hair. What possibility am I not seeing?

Unless…

I feel my pulse jump. At the same time, all the air squeezes out of my lungs. I shut my eyes and center.

Slow down, Gia. Breathe.

For a second, I feel lost inside my own body. Is this the stroke of luck I need? Both of us out of our element to make it happen?

There's only one way to find out.

Chapter Eight

JC

Cars whiz past us on Hastings Street, the morning gray and lifeless as a tombstone from 1889. But in the back seat of our Prius, my world feels brilliantly bright with Gia and her energetic sparkle beside me. When we're together, time seems to stretch and bend, like we're lost in our own private dimension.

"Hey, sailor." Gia taps her knee against mine, a tiny jolt straight to my heart. "I have an idea."

I glance over, and something torrid flashes inside me. My mind refuses to release the image of her: how wild and beautiful and crazy sexy she looked in my studio.

I can't unring that bell.

"Go," I say. "I'm listening."

"It involves the song."

"My song?"

"Your song for now," she corrects.

"Uhm…" I scratch my chin. "Did I miss an entire conversation?"

"You know it's perfect for me."

I give a short laugh. "Except *I* wrote it."

Gia levels a look at me. Yes, she knows this. She's just decided it's irrelevant. As if she and her adorable crooked front tooth have the power to vanquish copyright law. Which they just might.

She smacks my arm, her stacked silver bracelets jingling like a door chime. "Do you want to hear me out or not?"

"The floor is all yours."

She blows out a breath through her berry-stained lips. "You know my tour bus policy."

"Hmmm. Very Draconian of you."

"We're going to add a little spicy layer to that."

My instincts buzz loudly in both ears. The fire in her eyes, her expression a silent flash of lightning. Nothing scares Gia, and that scares the hell out of me.

"We, as in you and me?"

"Yeah," she says. "A dare."

"Where did this come from?" Not that I put it past Gia to add a fresh twist to my already flailing inability to not obsess over her.

"Audrie always came up with these ridiculous dares," she explains. "Thought it was a worthy tradition to keep alive."

"Ah, the legendary Audrie strikes again. Do I like where this is going?"

The Prius cuts a wide turn onto Clark Drive, industrial store-fronts shuttered on either side of the empty street. Too early even for the homeless to be awake. I, on the other hand, am painfully alert.

But not expecting Gia to drop the ridiculous.

"If you tap out first," she says, "I get the song. If I tap out first, you keep the song."

Another laugh rips out of me. No one warned me of this. "So there is a world where I get to keep my own song?"

"Shut up!" she wails good-naturedly. "Are you in?"

I throw up a hand. "Hold on, cowgirl. What happens if we both tap out?"

Gia appears not to have considered the option I'm gunning for.

There's no way she taps out without tapping *me*. If push comes to shove, I'll chaperone her directly into my bunk.

"It would have to happen on the same night to be valid. Feels highly unlikely, Mr. Chaperone." Air quotes around that.

I bite back a smile. Her defiance is so misguided. And cute.

"Let's pretend you're not the only one with iron will," I propose. "Tell me what happens if we both make it through the tour without bending."

Her eyes flash. Gia is, of this I'm certain, refraining from some commentary here, something along the lines of: *Why do you have to make my life so fucking complicated?*

"Same as you tapping out," she finally says. "I keep the song."

"Nope. Not endorsing that. The only way you might get the song is if *I* tap out."

Gia's face clouds. "How do I know if you're telling me the truth?"

"That's your own personal conundrum." I shrug, kinda loving this. Based on his smirk, our Uber driver with his flashy pink turban is thoroughly enjoying our exchange. "Had we been able to shag on the bus, you'd know for sure. But..." I raise a finger to stop her protest-in-the-making. "I'm in the same boat. If you disappear, as I'm sure you're planning to, then what? All we have left is trust."

Gia slumps against the seat. That hit her like a truck. Trust, of course, is the hardest ask. Especially when I consider what she's shared about the subtle career sabotage games her mother plays, Audrie ditching the band, and what she feels is the entire universe conspiring against her age and ferocious ambition, despite the immense talent. Does she risk putting faith in me?

But here we are.

And the bigger question might be: can the great Gia Barlow, rock and roll vixen, with her mile-long line of admirers, hold out? For a song?

Except, it's not just any song. It's the perfect song.

And she knows it.

"Or we can leave it open to negotiation," I suggest.

Gia picks at a hole in her fishnets. Or should I say, makes the hole bigger, like I wanted to. "Define that, please."

"If neither of us taps out, then maybe we can talk about recording the song together."

Her eyes narrow, as if I've tried to trick her. "For real? Released as a Pop My Cherry song?"

I shrug nonchalantly. "Depends on how hard you negotiate."

Gia watches me, in no rush to fill the space. The space is the point. Does she have any clue I wrote the song for her? The lyrics practically spell out how I feel. But she said nothing after I sang them to her, other than *Holy shit, that hook is gold.*

"Maybe you and Sawyer are more alike than I thought," she speculates, very incorrectly.

Okay, yes. I launched out of bed this morning and put in some serious work styling my hair. Packed the moisturizer Sawyer insists works wonders. But he and I differ on the "second coming" he keeps mouthing off about. To step back into the insane world of rock and roll remains a giant question mark.

I walked away once already, giving up at the exact moment I should've been blowing up. Dad's prodigious musical talent flamed out, leaving a blackened rift between us. Neither he nor Sawyer tracked the real reason why I shut the band down.

Only Rhys knows the truth.

In a way, it's oddly, sadly poetic.

To punctuate my failure as a human by failing to fulfil my biggest glory.

"Hey." Gia calmly nudges me out of my head. Nudges us forward, into the unknown. "If you're cool, I'm cool. Shake on it?"

Her hand, fine-boned and pale, gets swallowed by mine. She's holding herself not calculatingly but with purpose. Very intentional. But she seems to forget there are possibilities beyond her foregone conclusion.

Nothing has hit the same since we met.

She gets my obsession over diminished chords and odd time signatures. We agree a platinum copy of Radiohead's *OK Computer* belongs next to the Mona Lisa as another example of era-defining art. We talk about everything and nothing, and now she's the person I want to call in the middle of the night.

I want to know her mystery, her unknowable depths. All the sadness and the good bits. And she seems to understand the parts of me I'm used to hiding.

Never found that in a woman. Not for a long, long time.

For me, this isn't a dare; it's an inevitability.

And the endgame is sitting right beside me.

How maddeningly inconvenient.

♫

"Excuse me." A deeply tanned flight attendant blocks Gia from entering first class. I can tell from her body language that she's going to be annoying. "Ticket, please?"

Gia shoots me a look. Our ticket details are on my phone, and I flash the screen so the attendant can verify we do not belong with the families, crying babies, and backpackers plugging both aisles behind us.

She squints at the screen and mutters, "Oh, you're together. Right this way."

She gives us just enough space to squeeze past, eyes lingering on Gia's plaid babydoll dress and battered leather jacket. A longer look at my face. One thinly plucked eyebrow rises.

Questioning our seats together, or *us* together?

Either way, I feel a flash of irritation. Yes, the hush and civility of business class is a relief. If it brands me a snob, guilty as charged. I did grow up this way. But the flip side is the same: you face judgment when you're perceived not to check all the boxes.

Gia shuffles down the aisle, taking it all in with big eyes. "This is nice."

I pause at our seats, catching a glimpse of our reflection in the bulkhead window. Me, in last season's button-down, her in plaid and leather, both of us rocking Converse. Do we really look that mismatched?

"You take the window," I say. "Enjoy the view."

After hoisting both carry-ons into the overhead bin, I walk Gia through all the bells and whistles—how the seat reclines, where to find the mattress pad, and the tucked-away dinner menu. Gia drags her eyes upward to mine. She'd deny needing reassurance, but I remember how she perched at the edge of my couch as if worried she'd leave a dent behind.

And judging from how she's monitoring her phone, she's still preoccupied and pissed. Brady and Tai raged hard last night and slept in, missing the flight. Our breakfast time in the lounge turned into a furious stream of texts and whispered curses. Shae's stepped in to get them re-booked, but Gia hasn't been the same.

"Hi. Welcome." The same attendant who almost ushered Gia into the back appears, bringing with her a haze of heavy perfume that tickles my nose.

"I'm Anita," she says, leaning in close, all smiles and claws. "Can I get you a champagne or a cocktail?" She flicks the barest glance at Gia. "And a juice for your daughter?"

My lungs strip raw. I count the passing seconds, the negative creep. I don't know what's worse, the tight, horrible silence, or Gia and her flushed cheeks. I'm too flustered to speak.

"He's my guitar player," she finally grits out, like she's explaining basic English to a recent refugee. "And bring me a double rum and Coke. Lots of ice."

Anita's smile slides off her face, and mine would too, pinned with Gia's glower. I can hear her thoughts, clear as day: *Double dog dare you to ask for my ID.*

"I'll have a vodka soda, please," I say, a strange bubble in my throat as the words come out. And I will not say anything else until I am safely drunk.

"And bring us all the snacks you have." Gia plasters on a fake smile that masks her true mission: she plans to run this woman off her feet all flight with endless asks.

Anita wisely moves on to an older couple ahead of us with a bright, forced *Hello.* I clear my throat, praying this moment shrinks into a story we tell ourselves later and laugh. Not even five minutes in, and I feel like trash that someone forgot to take out. So much for the high life.

"Don't go too crazy with the booze," I warn her. "It dehydrates you."

Gia holds my gaze for a long five seconds. I watch her breathe, the rise and fall of her chest. The sad realization suddenly smacks me in the face —I sounded like a father.

Can I ever catch a break?

"I'll drink however much I want." She flips her hair, chin high and proud. "Even if it takes ten drinks to forget I'm not supposed to be here."

Crossing one leg over the other, she angles herself toward the window. Fuck. She's retreating behind her armor, the electricity from our dare fizzing out hard. First, the boys screw up, then Mr. Chaperone kills the buzz.

That's what I get for trying to protect her.

What she heard was control. What I meant was care.

But maybe with Gia, those things can't coexist.

Chapter Nine

GIA

Wow. Wow. Wow.

My head spins in every direction from the back seat of our town car. Life before felt small. This feels huge. And I am just a speck compared to the sheer size and oldness of London. The steady drizzle of rain while the driver loaded our bags smelled centuries old. All the dark stone buildings look like they've been plucked from a fairy tale.

It makes Vancouver feel like a backwoods Legoland.

JC, texting nonstop with Rhys since we landed, glances over. "All good?"

"Yeah," I breathe. "This is wild."

And intimidating, I don't say.

I thought I was ready for this, but now I'm wondering if I even belong on a stage this big. I'm still catching my breath after the razzle-dazzle of Heathrow. Crowds on a mad dash, ten different languages echoing in my ears. JC rested his hand on the small of my back, steering me through the chaos. The heat lingered far longer than the brief touch.

"Wait until we get to the hotel." JC's knee bumps mine, and he doesn't move it. "The Rose Dylan Agency has pulled out all the stops."

And then there's that.

The Savoy Hotel. Our glitzy home for the next twenty-four hours. Dani booked us suites, and the gala introducing their agency takes place in the River Room, a sophisticated venue where no woman in fishnets has ever set foot, guaranteed. She also wrangled up a beauty SWAT team to make us red carpet ready. Not saying I'll transform into a princess, but at least the crowd won't wonder if I recently escaped from jail.

"Are they meeting us there?" I ask.

"Around noon," JC says, thumbing through texts on his phone. "That gives us time to clean up and relax. Oh, and Rhys and I plan to grab a drink before the event. A director he wants me to meet is in town. Could be another film to score."

My heart pinches. A reminder that before this tour even starts, JC walks when it's over. Back to his life before me. And, quite possibly, without me.

"And it sounds like Dani has your afternoon dialed in," he adds. "You two will be doing the diva thing."

"Hardly," I mutter under my breath. I didn't sleep a wink on the flight. And I'm still a little drunk, judging by the blur around my edges.

JC bumps me with his shoulder. "Hey, chin up, rockstar. This is how you leap. Every media bigwig in Europe will be in the room tonight. All eyes on you."

I take a breath. Right. Like I can just *choose* when to be a flawless socialite, floating around an alien landscape of martinis and million-aires. Will they see through my pumped-up smile to the world of crushed beer cans and stained jeans I normally inhabit?

"No pressure, right?"

"You will kill it, Gia. I have no doubt."

JC leans over and ruffles my hair. Again, with the fucking hair ruffle? He has *no idea* how close I am to biting that hand. And I want to believe, a little too much, that the glimmer in his eyes is more than faith that I won't shoot myself in the foot.

Honestly? If he keeps looking at me like that, I might start believing in fairy tales.

♫

I'm flipping through endless beaded, bedazzled gowns stacked on a wardrobe rack, when JC and Rhys pop into Dani's suite to say hello before they take off for JC's meeting.

"Looks like the beauty brigade is in full swing," Rhys quips.

It's more like Sephora exploded in here, leaving behind a landslide of high-end cosmetics. The makeup artist arranges her brushes like flowers in a vase, and next to a table full of fancy shoes, our stylist and hairdresser are deep in conversation over tonight's vibe.

JC admires a red satin stiletto, the thin ankle strap adorned with a glittery band of diamonds. His arm brushes mine, turning my insides into a pile of crumbs.

"I think you'd look great in these."

"Not sure I can even walk in a heel that high," I admit.

"Heels take getting used to." Dani grins at me. "We'll practice your strut in the hall."

Rhys laces an arm around Dani's waist and whispers in her ear, making her giggle. Blond and sunny to JC's dark mystery, Rhys's face is, like, weirdly perfect. He makes every head turn, mostly to figure out if he's human or an AI creation. But he's got serious depth, is thoughtful and down-to-earth, and trails after Dani like the happiest golden retriever.

Dani's a few years ahead of me in life and love, but I want to be like her—poised, stylish, successful, and have my own Trenton look at me the way Rhys looks at her.

"We'll be back by seven," he says to Dani. "Is that cool?"

"No later than seven thirty, please," she warns. "Formal intros start then."

JC gives me an easy wink. He looks like he'd be cool hanging out with the glam squad. "Can't wait to see what you two come up with."

Dani shoos them out. "Go have fun. Rhys has been dying to hang with you all week."

"Love you, babe." Rhys drops a lusty kiss on her mouth that makes my heart stutter. "I'm psyched for tonight."

Once they're gone, Dani elbows me with a sparkle in her eye. "Now the fun starts." She wanders into the adjoining lounge—apparently nothing in this hotel comes in one room—and rolls out a trolley stacked with cheese, grapes, chips, cans of Coke, and a sleek bottle of Equiano rum way beyond my pay grade.

I swing her a grateful smile.

We bonded from the minute we met last summer. Soul sisters, if a rough-and-tumble musician and a polished princess could ever be related. Her skin looks airbrushed in real life. I've got toothpaste drying on a zit. She makes it all look effortless while I'm kicking and screaming my way through life like the class act I am.

Gotta say though, I could get used to this pampered world damn quick.

♫

An hour later, I'm feeling lightheaded from lack of sleep, top-shelf rum, and hairspray. Marta, the hairstylist, is busy transforming my hair into a complicated updo. Dani looks like a million bucks in her emerald velvet gown, and we're both tipsy enough to slip back into easy conversation. She's just finished telling stories about JC and Rhys as kids—powder kegs of trouble—and it makes me curious.

"Can I ask you a question? About JC?"

Her hushed voice drips with scandal. "Don't tell me ... are you two...?

"No," I blurt out. "Nothing like that."

She hums her disappointment. "Rhys and I were hoping it might happen. After your gig in Osoyoos, everyone was talking."

It wasn't my intention, but I set myself up for failure that night. Debut with JC on a star-filled evening in wine country and practically have musical sex on stage in front of the Hollywood elite? Who lives down that hype?

I glance at Josephine, the intense Portuguese stylist who is hemming the metallic slip dress I chose and lower my voice. "Did Rhys ever tell you why JC walked away from it all?"

Dani pauses, dabbing smoky perfume on her wrists. She sees it on my face: the legit desire to understand the human Rubik's Cube JC is. "Rhys said burnout. That he needed to go quiet for a while." She leans closer to whisper, "Between us, I don't think that's the full story. Has he said anything to you?"

I relax a notch. I'm not the only one with questions. "No. I just want to make sure we do whatever it takes to make him feel comfortable."

Her face lights up. "I know he feels very comfortable around you already."

"He said that?" God, could I sound more hopeful?

"Not in so many words." Dani meets my eyes in the mirror. "When he joined us on Corfu for New Year's Eve, all he talked about was how inspiring it was to be in the studio with you. He called you his sonic soulmate. It sounded like he missed you."

The room shrinks around me, dark and whispering. JC had invited me to Greece, and I bailed. Spent an hour recovering from a heart attack after seeing the flight price. I told him I had a family thing I couldn't get out of. He'd shrugged it off with a casual, "Too bad. Would've been fun."

Hearing this news, doubt floods my chest. Did he really want me there? Why didn't he say more?

I flip the conversation back to Dani. "You and Rhys seem super happy together."

She sighs, a sound of pure contentment. "We are. It's been great. We're helping each other grow into who we need to be."

"Thanks for the discount on all the tour designs." I roll my eyes. "Sawyer, the tightwad."

That launches a ten-minute roast of the infamous elder Trenton, who once macked hard on Dani. Thank god she chose the right brother.

When our dissing peters out, she asks, "Anyone special in your life right now?"

"Playing the field," I lie, for protection. Dani's my girl, but she's also deep in the Trenton family. And Marilyn, JC's mother, was on me like white on rice at Christmas, fussing over JC like he wasn't a full-grown man.

"As you should." Dani leans back in the director's chair, eyeing me with an approving nod. "You're glowing, girl. Not just from the hair and makeup. Don't waste that on the wrong person."

I chew on my thumbnail. "How did you know Rhys was the one for you?"

She laughs. "It sounds so lame, but it's true: When you know, you know."

"Did Rhys feel the same way? Has he ever told you?"

"He knew," Dani says with the warm glow of nostalgia. "Almost right away. But sometimes knowing scares the hell out of them."

My body reacts in a way it shouldn't. Could JC be scared to make a move? Hard to believe a man with his reputation would hesitate if he really wanted me.

Dani rests her hand on my shoulder. "Can I ask a favor?"

"Of course. Anything."

"Keep an eye on JC. He hides it well, but I get the sense there's a sadness in him. That one extra layer he keeps hidden, even from Rhys."

What feels like a spear passes through my lungs. My thoughts exactly, that he's carrying around something. "But they're so close."

"I know." Her look says I'm not alone in this. "Rhys said JC can talk his way out of, or around, anything. It's a skill and his deflection method."

Ain't that the truth? Every time our conversation veers into personal territory, he steers us back to something neutral. It's a relief in some ways to hear this, if only to confirm I'm not insane.

Marta pauses her assault on my hair. "Are you talking about the handsome, dark-haired chap?"

"He's my guitarist," I say with pride. "She's dating his brother. The blond hottie."

"He kept stealing looks at you while you sifted through the dresses." Marta winks at me in the mirror. "Blokes like him don't have couture on their minds."

Dani grins and squeezes my hand. "See? I think you need to lean into that."

My heart does a funny flip in my chest. I take a breath then ask The Question. "You don't think I'm too young for him?"

"I think you're the right amount of kick-ass he needs," Dani insists. "Everyone wants a piece of him, and you've flipped the script. He's in awe of *you*."

Marta engulfs me in one more haze of hairspray. "And tonight, the entire room will be in awe of you two fierce dames."

For a second, I don't recognize the woman in the mirror smiling back at me. I picture JC seeing me like this, and my breath catches. What happened in his studio felt like a preview of something deeper— that maybe he sees more than just Gia the bad-ass rocker. But what happened on the plane shredded my hope. It felt like he was embarrassed to be with me.

I adjust the neckline of my dress and smooth my hands down the shimmery fabric. Throw my shoulders back.

I belong in this world, his world.

Tonight, at this gala, surrounded by all those people watching us … maybe it's time to throw caution to the wind.

Give them something real to see.

Chapter Ten

JC

GEORGE ALTMAN IS LIKE SOMEONE ORDERED OUT OF A KEN CATALOG— Hamptons tan, rare Ferrari, Keto evangelist, and a supermodel girl-friend named Starr who paints his toenails while he reads *Variety* pool-side. Someone I dislike immediately, on principle. And he spends the better part of an hour walking me through every gritty beat of his noir film. The one he's desperate for me to score.

I nod when I'm supposed to and massage his ego.

"Love the atmosphere."

"Lots of potential."

I don't know how much time we've wasted here, but weirdly, it's Rhys who saves the day. Rhys, of all people. Mr. Whatever Works, the proud owner of a snazzy vintage Rolex, cuts the meeting short.

"We need to head out." He taps the bezel. "It's six thirty."

I clap George on the back with a fake and hearty "I'll be in touch," because that's generic enough to pretend I truly care. The reality is, I don't give a flying fuck about George and his passion project. I'm only halfway in the room, the other half already at The Savoy, scanning the crowd for one person.

Rhys waits for George to leave before he gives me a look. "Alright. Spill. The film is funded and ready to go. What's the deal? His man bun? It was kinda lame."

Ah, sarcasm. Rhys, the master. He knows it's the fastest way to cut to the chase with me. But how do I articulate that life in the LA hustle holds zero appeal if Gia's not at my side? The thought of wandering the streets and bars again, chasing whatever it is I can never find, depresses me. And after spending the past six months in Canada with the Gia opportunity, I'm not missing the US political chaos in the slightest.

"It's a few things," I admit. "Not in the proper headspace right now."

After sliding his phone back into his pocket, Rhys asks, "Is it her, the tour, or both?"

Concern pinches his forehead in the middle. I could lie, but he'd call me out before I finished the sentence. We've always had twin energy, even though I'm three years older. He knows me like he knows his own shadow.

"Mostly her," I admit.

"Does she know you're into her?"

"No." I scratch the back of my neck. "Maybe. Fuck, I dunno. It's complicated." Meaning, how can Gia look at me—thirteen years older, arguably washed up—and feel any kind of blind, mindless desire? After the incident in my studio, she practically sprinted out the door, refused my offers to drive her home, and took the bus in a monsoon.

Rhys nods with a thoughtful expression. "Will you be alright?"

"Yeah, yeah." I wave off diving deeper into the topic he's hinting at. "No need to worry about *that*."

He frowns, not buying it. "Have you told Gia?"

"Fuck, no." I reach for a handful of complimentary peanuts, crunch nervously, and ask, "Have you said anything to Dani?"

Rhys makes a gesture of zippering his mouth shut. "Anything you've told me dies with me. But c'mon. No bullshit between us. What is it about Gia? Why now? Why *her* band?"

The lights dim, and some shoegazey guitar drone starts moping in the background. Meanwhile, my mind churns into overdrive. Every music publication swarmed like piranhas when I killed Read My Rights—*What happened? Will you return? How does the rest of your band feel?* I filtered out the real reasons, and the buzz died down fast when I blamed exhaustion. Who in their right mind questions a musician over that? That's practically page one in the handbook, right after sex, drugs, and rock and roll.

So why Gia?

Question of the day.

And anyone else but Rhys would get a partial answer.

In the long pause, I draw tight circles with my highball glass on the bar. Rhys waits patiently for me to share, and that, frankly, is more disarming. I hate being vulnerable, the powerlessness of it.

Like a bug on its back, belly exposed.

Finally, I say, "I feel like life is passing me by. Every day I lose another chance, you know? Cooped up in a room with directors breathing down my neck. Other musicians telling me what to play. My success feels safe, like I'm phoning it in." I work down a swallow and pause. That's the most honest I've been in months, even to myself. "It's a slow death for me."

Rhys considers that for a moment. "Why didn't you tell me this before?"

"It's always been there." I look at him with a bare open expression. "I just buried it."

"But how can you be in a band and tour after what happened?"

I meet his steady gaze and realize the lightheadedness I feel is me holding my breath. Rhys always brings a level of care to his words, and this question gently pokes at my doubts and fears. And the answer isn't cut-and-dried. I love being in a band and the magic of playing live, but the tour grind is where the ghosts live.

It's a dilemma with no simple answer.

And I know Gia wants me to stick around as her permanent guitarist. Her hints haven't gone unnoticed. God, Gia. She's made me come alive, made me feel like I have a purpose. There's so much I want to share with her, but how does this ever work?

I shrug my blazer on. "Should we blast? Dani will read us the riot act if we're late."

Rhys handles my usual smooth evasiveness the way he propped up the backstory I constructed about the band falling apart: by playing along.

"Might be nice for *you* to get in trouble for once." He elbows me in the ribs, not entirely lovingly. Fair. I was the one who could sweet-talk my way out when our youthful antics landed us deep in shit. Rhys, painfully shy, took the brunt of the blame. And Dad harassed him endlessly for being unfocused and lazy.

One day, he'd had enough. He flipped us all the finger, ditched Canada for Europe, and stayed there for sixteen years.

I never want to feel that abandoned again.

Rhys finishes his drink and signals the bartender for the bill. George dragged us into a trendy hotspot filled with bankers and bureaucrats. Six drinks and Rhys is out two hundred pounds.

But at least he pays for shit.

We head out, brothers in arms, literally, arms slung across each other's shoulders. A spring in my step, one step closer to Gia.

♫

At first glance, the River Room is everything I expected it to be: tastefully decorated and packed with well-heeled guests, the kind who run companies and invest in Bitcoin. Dani's manning the front lines and frantically waves Rhys over. It's a big night for both.

"Catch you in a bit, bro," he says, huge grin as he strides away.

I hang back, cataloging the room. There are two open bars, pouring the good stuff. Waiters weave through the sea of glittering gowns and tuxedos, offering canapes and smiles. Photographers track the room, trying hard to blend in when their cheap shoes and cheaper blazers are a dead giveaway.

I crane my head for any sight of Gia. The real one—not the babe with a wedding veil pinned into her hair and holding a posy of blood-red roses, grinning at me from various banners peppered around the room. She looks foxy as hell dressed in white fishnets and a babydoll dress, bracketed by her groomsmen, Brady and Tai.

She was a bag of nerves over that photo shoot. But I loved the concept. Told her you need a bride image for *The Rock and Roll Bride Tour*.

Now, where is my frontwoman?

I shoulder my way through the crowd, and like magic, the throng parts, revealing a woman poured into a column of molten silver that kisses the floor. Her pale back faces me as she chats with a burly, bearded man in a kilt.

Whatever standard operating procedure exists for me stalls out.

That's not just a dress. That's a problem.

It throws my breathing off.

And sparks of guilt flicker around my brain. I need to find Gia. Forget the hot clench of my heart and my eyes burning a path up that dress. But I can't stop staring at this tall, slender creature. Her raven hair is piled high in an elaborate updo, secured with what might be an antique letter opener.

Then she turns, and the whole evening tilts.

The layers in the room become sharper, sweeter.

I've seen Gia a hundred ways—onstage, in the studio, barefoot in ripped jeans—but never like this. Her neckline plunges in a V that stops just shy of indecent, dark eyes made more enormous with a fringe of thick fake lashes. She's wearing the shoes I liked, ones I like even more because they turn the sway of her walk into slow, deliberate sin.

And because the curve of her lips is so much closer when she stops in front of me.

"Hey," she spreads her arms out, "what do you think?"

I don't know what to do with myself. Speech, apparently, is a lost art. But I want to blow up every bastard tracking her with bald-faced hunger.

Which would, unfortunately, include me.

"I don't know if a single word exists to describe you in that dress."

She smiles shyly. Then she leans in to whisper, "It's all good until I have to pee. So much fabric to deal with." When I don't smile back, Gia reaches for my hand, tugging it. "You look stressed. How did your meeting go?"

"Fine," I say distractedly. "Just another film."

Her expression turns quizzical. "That's a prize-winning response."

What can I say? It used to mean something, my life in Hollywood. But with Dad's stroke, Rhys and Dani settling part-time in Vancouver, and now Gia, sticking close to home is the new black.

I'm struggling to frame this in a way that might make sense to her when a photographer ambushes us from behind a pillar. He aims his camera and snaps away, the bright flashes momentarily blinding me.

The fuck!

I raise my hand and blurt out aggressively, "Hey, buddy. Ask first, please."

"You're JC and Gia, right?" the guy asks, his British accent bright and cutting. Eyes alight with paparazzi payout. "How about a kiss?"

My guard immediately goes up.

Sawyer warned me of this.

To keep us under cover.

Without another thought, I grab Gia around the waist, half-dragging her through doors that spill onto a deserted outdoor patio. She struggles to keep up in her heels and a dress not built for sprinting.

"I figured we'd be safe from the pap in here," she says, a little short-winded from how I rushed us out.

I lead her further into a dark corner where the muddy, mineral smell of the nearby Thames wafts over us. "Not in the UK. They're intrusive and predatory. One thing you'll quickly learn is to protect your privacy."

It sounds like Gia's about to say something when she slips on the pavers, slick from recent rain. She wobbles, off-balance, and a soft cry of surprise tears from her throat before I catch her. Both my arms wrap tight around her frame, and the heat of her body radiates like a furnace through the slippery silk of that dress.

Our gazes collide in the heavy, dark evening.

We breathe in tandem, plumes of our breath co-mingling in the cool air.

Gia laughs, but it sounds tinny and small. "You think I need to be protected?"

My fingers map the shape of her back, acutely aware of how the sensation sends a tiny thrill shooting up my spine. The move here is to say *yes*. I volunteer to be her superhero, all day and every day. George and his film natter left my soul charred and lifeless. The big-dick energy in the River Room, eager to have their way with Gia, fills me with territorial rage. I can't think about a film.

I can't think of anything but her.

I slip my hand into her updo and tilt her chin higher. "Yes, I do," I say, my voice wavering.

Gia breathes against my mouth, and I feel her in every nerve ending in my body. We've veered into dangerous territory, the crackle between us just the right amount of intense. If we were a couple on a TV show, this is where viewers on the couch scream, *"Kiss each other!"*

And then it finally—*finally*—happens.

She kisses me, not tentatively, but all in. Deeply, madly, letting out a moan so suggestive, my brain goes haywire at the sound. I kiss her back, harder, more desperate. Her tongue slides into my parted lips, and all my thoughts detonate into nothingness. Boom, I'm done. Lost in wonderland. A surge of adrenaline rockets through me, and I stumble like a drunk into the stone divider separating us from the garden.

Gia rocks tight against me, like she's dying for it.

Join the club.

Our kiss has unlocked something in my soul, releasing me from my paralysis. I devour her with so many different kisses, savage and sweet, the most intense yearning consuming me. I want to possess every inch of her. Throw her onto the damp grass and lose all my patience. Ravage her until she screams.

"You taste like gin and sin," she says with a trembling release of breath. Her hand gropes for mine, sliding it up onto her tit, the ready rise of her nipple.

I mutter, "Holy shit," and squeeze my eyes shut, burning the memory of her aroused flesh into my mind. It feels like my heart is about to fly out of my chest.

This is insane.

She feels so much better than I imagined, and that makes it so much worse.

Not a single prayer exists that I can stop myself.

Mouth hot against hers and wildly turned on by her rising moans, suddenly a voice jingles in the quiet. Gia's name posed as a question.

Shit!

I pull back sharply, square my shoulders and squint at the backlit figure. My vision swims, and I can't make out anything in the dark. Our kiss obliterated all my senses.

Gia speaks first, a breathless "Dani?"

"I hope I'm not interrupting," Dani says. "Or we can move the photo op out here."

The thundering roar in my ears dies, but the devastating effect of Gia pulses like a rocket between my legs. To compensate, I move away from her.

"No," I say in a too-bright voice, "we were just…"

"Discussing the set list," Gia finishes, smoothing the front of her mangled dress.

My eyes slowly adjust in the dark, just in time to clock the smile that touches Dani's lips. She knows exactly what kind of set list we were working out. Inside, the party guests schmooze on, unaware.

"I bet it'll be a rager," she says.

Chapter Eleven

GIA

How is this fair?

Only in my world do I wake up alone on a bed bigger than Noah's Ark, my scarred heart forever tainted by last night. Staring at the ceiling, it's like I exist in some weird fog. I feel trapped in my head, unable to think about anything but him.

I kissed JC first, but he had taken me, with insane hunger, against the wall. His mouth was a gin-soaked dreamland I kept falling and falling into, and some sober, tomorrow part of my mind screamed *no, not here,* while my body vibrated with the thrill of *dear fucking god,* yes!

How I made it through the gala without crawling over JC like an out-of-control vine is a miracle. Dani kept shooting me *I know what happened* looks, while every cell in me felt delicious, hot, and transformed.

I roll over to push the button above the nightstand. Velvet purple drapes slide open to reveal a heavy gray January sky. Rain falls in a steady drizzle, and the mist swirling along the Thames reminds me of how I floated after our kiss, my skin dusted with giddiness on the taxi ride back to the hotel. How JC smiled at me in the back seat, his eyes lit up; the seductive curl of his lips carried what felt like a promise. My heart felt full for the first time in weeks.

Then, poof—the dream night ended like a slap in the face.

Tai and Brady lounged like wharf rats in the hotel lobby, waiting. They'd flown over with Shae on a later flight, dumped bags in the tour bus, and beelined to the hotel. After some next-level begging, JC agreed to booze it up with them, giving me a helpless shrug of *it's the bro thing to do.*

I pretended not to give a shit. Easy to yawn along with Dani and Rhys and claim to need a good night's sleep more than Guinness-fueled fuckery orchestrated by Tweedle Dum and Tweedle Dee.

But I gave plenty of shits.

And still do, judging from how I'm struggling to contain the flutter inside my chest.

Holy hell, he's got a banging body. I felt him, hard and hot, pressing into me like last night's heavy, humid air. And the sensual possession of his tongue set off tiny fireworks in my heart. He tasted so good.

I was a slave, a goner.

I let myself surrender for two minutes of incredible electric urgency.

And now, it's back to normal.

I feel like Cinderella the morning after the ball. My borrowed dress and shoes lie on the tufted bench at the foot of the bed, to be packed up this morning for delivery to someone who can actually afford them. The minibar I intended to trash with JC still intact, unlike my heart. All because my prince got sidetracked by my infernal step-brothers.

I reach for my phone and power it on. In a moment of warmth and silence, my heart skips a beat. JC sent me a text at two a.m.

JT: Wish you were here.

I'm grinning before I realize it. He knew exactly how to kiss me, and rolled his hips to meet mine with devastating precision when my fingers tangled in his hair. Night and day from high school dances and boys with sour beer breath grinding hopeful boners in all the wrong places.

I text him back *Good Morning*. After a beat, I send a peace sign emoji. I hope he's awake. It's ten, and we're meeting Dani and Rhys for breakfast at eleven. Then off to the tour bus for bag drop before sound check. How am I supposed to get through it? Every nerve is frayed at the thought of JC and me naked and touching.

His lips were so soft.

What will they feel like down there?

I can't help smiling at that.

But it's time to say goodbye to silk sheets and a bedroom larger than my front yard. I kick off the duvet and stumble into the bathroom, a glittering palace of subway tiles and too many shower nozzles to count. I shower for twenty minutes—no one yelling at me to conserve water—then swan around in a robe, stuffing every complimentary amenity into my bag. And I'm going to order steak at breakfast, because why not?

Well, here's why.

The danger of tasting the high life this early in the game is like JC kissing me.

I want more. Lots more.

I want us.

♫

Okay, now it hits me.

Gia Barlow in the Royal Albert Hall. I'm actually here, standing on the same stage musical legends have graced. This is crazy! And what will it feel like to have five thousand fans singing along to my lyrics? Next time I talk to Sawyer, maybe I won't throw shade. He's getting it done.

Shae clomps around in her Old Gringo boots and faded sundress, even though it's eight degrees outside, barking orders on her walkie to the roadies loading in all our gear. Totally oblivious to the magic glow of the crimson velvet seats and gold-flocked wallpaper because she's been here before.

JC, too.

I glance over at him, crouched down to adjust his pedal board, a sweet custom purple sunburst Les Paul slung across his shoulder. He's been quietly drifting in his own world ever since Brady asked him on the taxi ride over how it felt to lay down such an epic show.

Almost thirteen years ago to the day, Read My Rights played a sold-out show here. I've seen the grainy YouTube clip enough times to know the crowd went full bananas when they encored with "A Day in the Life." Leave it to JC to slay an almost untouchable song, whipping the Brits into Beatlemania frenzy.

JC didn't offer a reply to Brady, only a brief, indeterminate nod, eyes hidden behind aviators.

I'm not the hoping-wishing-praying type, but is he giving any thought to our kiss? JC staggered in late for breakfast, bleary-eyed and apologetic. Sat across from me, next to Rhys. Smiled and said hello. Dani side-eyed me, questioning, like me. Did he regret what happened? Or was he downplaying things in front of Rhys? They went off in their own world, reminiscing and joking. To see JC so loose fascinated me. I could totally see those two as shit disturbers.

While they gabbed, Dani excused herself to take a call, and I ate my steak and fries in silence, trying to think of something super-brilliant to say that was not *Take me now, you glorious, hot manifestation of everything I desire in a man.*

I wanted to have a minute of peace with JC, but then the boys showed up, we all piled into a taxi, and here we are.

So far, no alone time to talk in private.

"How's the vocal fury holding up?" Brady calls out from somewhere behind me, snapping my attention back. He crosses the stage to join me at the front. Shirtless, as usual. "Or did you go all soft after your bougie swankfest?"

"Nice try." I point to the rafters. "Any pigeon sitting outside will feel it."

"Sweet." Brady nods and keeps on nodding. "You had us worried."

My eyes slide to his. "About what?"

He pauses, maybe thinking about what he's going to say for a change. "The past few months. Audrie walking. The Magician joining us." He tips his head toward JC. "All your new fucking rules. The shift is real."

"Nothing's changed," I insist.

Brady laughs. "Says the chick who strutted into The Savoy dripping in bling and attitude."

"Attitude is my trademark, in case you forgot."

"How can we forget, when you remind us every day?"

I absorb that, and yet the words catch me by surprise. Is he throwing down bitterness for real? His unblinking eyes tell me nothing, other than he never met a stare-down he didn't like. Maybe he's wiped from last night. JC shared at breakfast that their merry band of musketeers wobbled home at three in the morning.

"Someone has to keep this ride rolling along. It's not easy." A twinge of irritation leaks into my voice. "I have good days and bad. I'm human."

"Then don't forget we are too." Brady's gaze drifts off to a duo of roadies squabbling over cable and who needs more of it. "And last I heard, humans make mistakes. Sorry we missed the flight and the gala. But it would've been nice for us all to party together after the fact. A band is a team effort."

Shae interrupts us—the sound mixer is ready in ten. True to her management skills, our sound check hums along right on schedule.

When she's out of earshot, I whisper-talk to Brady. "Get it out of your thick skull that we're not in this together, alright? Tonight, we bleed for it. Let's turn the floor as red as those seats. Capiche?"

"Cool, cool." Brady shrugs it off like he's shrugged off his gold star hangover. "We rock and roll. Business as usual. Fucking going to hammer this joint tonight. Right, buddy?" he shouts at Tai, deep in conversation on his phone.

Tai flashes the peace sign and strolls offstage. He doesn't even look at me. Tai's more sensitive than Brady, and I shit on them hard yesterday for missing the flight. But it's more than that. Tai picked up on my disappointment upon finding them in the hotel lobby last night. The thing is, I wasn't mad at them. It wasn't personal. Just me not knowing what the hell to do with the person who literally consumed my tongue and soul and then left me hanging in my own swirl of feels.

Business as usual? Not exactly.

I swing my gaze stage right, where JC continues to futz with his pedals. He's not a fan of digital modelers to fake the right sounds; he says pedals are more intuitive than fiddling with buttons and knobs. It's how he plays too. No shortcuts. No faking it.

Just raw, instinctive, and heartbreakingly real.

His two albums didn't go platinum by accident.

But is it an accident that JC said nothing about his last show here? He's frustratingly tight-lipped about anything deep in his past. Just as a strange feeling is carving out a space in my gut, JC looks up and smiles, eyes crinkling with that easy charm.

And all I can feel is him.

♫

The door to our dressing room bangs open, and Shae hollers, "T-minus five, friends. Everyone on deck. It's showtime."

Brady launches into his pre-show routine of tuck jumps and Tarzan-like whoops. (Impressive, considering his painted-on bell-bottoms.) Tai stretches out his back, channeling Carlos D's lookbook of stovepipe pants, dress shirt, and leather suspenders. JC? In his predictable uniform of T-shirt, Diesel jeans, and Converse, he's calm as a yogi master.

Or pretending to be.

We've spent enough time together for me to read the signs. He fidgets with the subtle gold hoops in both ears and tucks his hair back repeatedly when he's preoccupied. But he's rested. After sound check, he crashed hard in the dressing room, jet lag, and his late night catching up to him.

I spent the last five minutes doing laps up and down the hall to shake off the butterflies. You cannot be unaffected before a show. It's total system override. Heart slamming. Brain goes fritz. This is the edge of everything.

Why we do what we do.

"You ready, champ?" JC approaches me with his slow, beautiful smile.

I blink up, meeting those piercing eyes gone past gray into storm-black, pupils blown wide. Just like last night, when our tongues tangled, and he breathed hard and fast.

"Hell yeah," I say. "And thank you. For being here. For everything."

My gush of gratitude earns me a stifled laugh from Brady. Out of the corner of my eye, I notice Tai's posture shift, the smallest hitch in his shoulders that makes me feel like I've just said something wrong.

Whatever.

My heart is tripping all over itself, hands tingling with nerves.

As we make our way to the stage, the house lights drop, and the roar of the crowd crests into one giant sustained note of expectation. That sound. God, that sound! I can feel it in my chest, that bass-heavy rumble of anticipation. Everything feels heightened and bright around the edges. It's impossible to contain the rush right before you go on stage. It's more profound than any other life experience.

I've waited months for this night, and now it's here.

Before we walk out, I raise my fist and wait for the solidarity bumps from my boys. The Pop My Cherry call to arms.

One last breath to force my lungs open. Ready to blow them apart.

Here we go.

Hello, London.

Chapter Twelve

JC

It's midnight. First show in the can. What a performance. Gia had the fans eating out of her hand, and we staggered off the stage, arms looped together, glowing with exhilaration. If the reviews land right tomorrow, this tour really kicks off.

My skin still burns with leftover adrenaline, and the buzz takes forever to wear off, which is why we're here: outside some dance club in South Kensington, ready to blow off some steam. Punks and goths, cigarette tips glowing orange in the dark, wait in a line that snakes around the block.

Brady flags the muscled bouncer with his usual panache. "Yo! We're on the VIP list. Team Cherry."

The bouncer—young, Black, and profoundly unimpressed—shoots him a look and talks into his earpiece, blocking us from sneaking past his mighty clipboard. Dude is cranky, and we're getting sour looks from the crowd. When he finally unclips the red velvet rope to wave us inside, wails erupt behind us.

"Take us!" "Fuck you, wankers!" "We've been waiting for hours!"

I slide my arm around Gia's shoulder as a shield, ushering her past the anger. Sorry, not sorry. The rock star life does have its perks. Inside, a hostess in a sparkly jumpsuit guides us to a private booth Shae wrangled on the fly. It sits high above a dance floor throbbing with sweaty bodies. A spotlight shines on a spinning disco ball, throwing rainbow shards around the low-ceilinged bunker.

A Duran Duran remix thunders in my ears.

"Should we divide and conquer?" Tai yells at us.

Brady thumbs at me. "I'm sticking close to this groupie magnet. How many chicks swarmed us last night at the bar? Must've been at least a dozen." He peels my arm off Gia with a seductive smile. "You and me, bro. Team Cherry."

Tai grooves to the beat, ready to rock. "A few shooters, then dance floor?"

The boys crowd the hostess guarding a table stacked with enough booze to guarantee my body will feel like a biohazard disaster tomorrow.

Meanwhile, I can feel Gia's stare burning into me.

"You want to dance?" I shout.

Something flickers behind her eyes. She makes some space between us. "Don't let me cramp your style."

Her words land like a gut punch. I've been waiting all day to be alone with her. "That's not what I asked."

"I'll be fine on my own, Mr. Chaperone." Her gaze skims the crowd in a way that feels like she's purposefully avoiding mine. "Sounds like you can handle flying solo."

Ah, now I understand. And a flash of irritation ripples through me because why did Brady dump that news? I specifically chose a table away from the crowds last night. *He* waved all the women over who kept flashing us looks.

And I asked Gia to join us at the pub yesterday, but she brushed us off, said we should have our guys' night. She knows band dynamics matter and that sometimes you need to play the long game to keep them in balance. And with our kiss pinging between us like a ricochet, I'm still off-balance.

We have things to talk about.

I lean in, my mouth brushing the warm curl of her ear. "I'd like to sit with you and chill. Kick back and people-watch. That cool?"

With impeccable timing, Brady cuts in, shoving whipped cream-topped shooters at us. "Down the hatch, bitches!"

We toss them back, the sweet bite of crème de cassis and vodka going down smooth. I take Gia's shot glass and set mine down with hers, making it clear the two of us are hanging back.

"We'll catch up in a bit," I shout.

Brady rolls his eyes, muttering something lost in the pounding music, and drags Tai out onto the dance floor. Gia watches them go, arms crossed tight. The curves of her body and the sounds she made when our tongues dueled last night find their way to the front of my mind. I'm ready to climb the walls or rip all her clothes off and take her right here.

Boldy, I take a step closer and nudge her with my elbow. "Rum and Coke?"

Her gaze flicks to mine for a nanosecond, just long enough for me to understand that the social dynamic of her band has changed, and she's not sure what to do about it. But then her mouth curls up with a smile.

And the intense fluttering in my stomach dies down when she says, "Yes, please."

♫

An hour later, the club is going off. Strobe lights flashing, partiers sway in a blissed-out trance, the music a thudding drum and bass that feels like steel screws drilled into my brain.

But Gia? She feels incredible.

We're thigh to thigh on the couch, looser, louder, much drunker. I'm conscious of our position, the contact point of our legs warm to the point of distraction. Her cheeks are flushed, lips wet with spiced rum. Every time she leans in to shout-talk, her breast crushing against my shoulder destabilizes me.

"Sorry," I yell back. "I can't hear you."

"You wanna walk around outside?" she tries again. "My brain's getting scrambled."

Yes. Please.

I get up and stretch out my legs, palming our hostess a tip. She asks if we want shots for the road, but we both decline. Gia does one last sweep for Tai and Brady, but no luck. They vanished in the crowd ages ago and have been MIA since.

"I'll text them," she says as we shoulder past vapeheads and arguing couples crammed in the exit corridor. The hall reeks like leather and pot, a bad mix of cheap perfumes. Outside, the cool night air is a heavenly relief. So is the ability to think straight.

"Where to?" I ask, breath fogging in the cold.

Gia burrows into her hoodie and stomps her sneakered feet. It's almost one thirty a.m. "Might as well make our way back to the bus. Unless you wanna rage harder."

I smile at her. That would be a *no*. "Let me find us an Uber."

I'm nine-tenths hammered, my drunk heart soaked with whatever mix of drinks I inhaled at the club. But by the time our driver and his strange-smelling Kia drop us at the designated lot for the touring vehicles, I've sobered right up. Enough that I can open the tour bus door without groping around like a wasted fool.

I flick the lights on, dimming them to soften the glare. Gia chews on a nail, surveying the unglam space. All buses, it seems, are designed to strip joy from any soul unfortunate enough to enter one.

"It ain't The Savoy," I joke.

"It's cool." Gia shrugs. "Cozy."

We'd dropped our bags earlier, and our luggage sits clustered together in the middle of the lounge like a long-lost family reunion. Stacked in the narrow space that funnels into the rear kitchen are four bunks, two on either side. Gia opens a lower bunk curtain, shrugs off her hoodie, and tosses it onto the mattress. Shakes out her hair.

A sinuous little dance move follows, sending a cold shot of nerves up my spine. Gia uses her body on stage like an athlete, all flow and poetry in motion. Her crawl across the stage during "Feel Me" made me flush hot. Was I the only one imagining her without clothes on?

Doubt it.

Suddenly, I'm very aware that it's just her and me.

"Will you sleep on top of me?" she asks.

Three seconds pass before she realizes what she said. By then, I'm laughing my face off.

Gia groans, scrubbing both hands over her face. "What I mean is—"

"I'd be honored," I finish.

"Jesus," she says, a smile lifting her voice. "That was super awkward."

"If you want to shower or change, I can wait outside."

She slides her gaze to mine with a curious, widening smile. "Are you nervous?"

"No," I lie. "Just being polite."

She keeps studying me as the first fat drops of rain *ping* against the roof. I swear her dark eyes get bigger every time I look into their depths. "You weren't polite last night. I like *that* version of you."

Gia steps closer. In a weird reactionary do-si-do, I step backward, stumbling right into her giant suitcase. For a frozen moment, my arms flail for balance. Then I crash hard on my tailbone, not drunk enough to numb the jolt of pain.

A half groan spills from my lips. Fuck. I'm going to feel that tomorrow.

Gia sidles closer still, peering down at me like a kid fascinated by an upturned beetle. "Too much to drink, Chaperone?"

I wince through a laugh. "Probably."

She offers her hand. "On the count of three?"

My motor skills feel too toasted to pull this off. Sure enough, I grab her hand, she pulls hard, I wobble, and suddenly we're collapsing together in a tangle of limbs and laughter. I manage to sit up against the couch, head spinning from the booze. Gia scrambles upright, but instead of moving away, swings a leg over me and settles in my lap, bold as anything.

"Hi," I breathe.

Gia captures my chin between her thumb and forefinger, her eyes searching mine. Lord knows the depravity she'll find. "Good memories tonight? Back in the saddle?"

"Yeah. No sweat."

She laughs softly, leans in, and flicks her tongue along my jaw. "But you're sweaty. And you taste good."

She wriggles her body closer, the contact sending tiny shocks through my already shredded nervous system. My erection swells, warm and thick against the inside of my thigh. There are only so many ways two bodies can meet, but I'm thinking of at least ten right now.

"Gia." My voice sounds far away. "What are you doing to me?"

Her brows tilt in an expression of mocking threat. "The same thing you're doing to me."

She starts rocking back and forth, every stroke pulling another groan from me as my denim stretches tighter. She doesn't rush, doesn't do anything other than torture me with perfect pressure. I'm not sure if I'm calming down or getting more excited, but I'm positive I don't want it to stop.

She buries her face into my neck, her breath falling hot onto my skin. Overwhelmed by the sensations—the alcohol, her scent—all of them hitting in one giant wave, I drive my hips into her hot center.

And she feels me, hardening into steel.

"Is this good?" she whispers. Her hands slide under my boxers to grab handfuls of ass, sending a ripple of pleasure cascading down my spine.

I groan, "Too good," and nip her neck, leaving a trail of gentle bite marks down her throat.

She keeps grinding, using my ass as leverage, little moans spilling from her mouth, both of us working the groove of our dirty synchronized rhythm. She's controlling the shots, but I'm throwing every hundred at her.

Rob the fucking bank.

"Jesus, Gia." My breath is clipped, coming out in tight hisses.

Her mouth crashes onto mine, and I gasp into that kiss, each breath sparking out of me like smoke. I can feel my orgasm building hard, and I want her to come with me, but my own release hijacks me.

I peak, suddenly and sharply.

Wave after wave, violent and bright.

Blood roaring in my ears.

I'm still lost in a rollicking sea of white-hot pleasure when the sudden sound of Brady's howling, drunken laughter echoes from outside.

Gia stiffens, her eyes blown wide as she scrambles off me. I'm willing my heart to stop beating so fast when the bus door flies open, and Brady and his vintage Air Jordans mount the stairs. I panic, diving face-first onto the carpet.

He sees us in the dim, mutters, "What the hell?" and stops cold.

Tai, hot on his heels, crashes into him. "Dude," he slurs. "Keep going."

Brady smashes the lights on full blast. I squint into the searing brightness and want to speak, say something, anything, but I'm in another dimension, my whole world reduced to this: warmth spreading in my jeans and trembling thighs.

Behind me, Gia tries to contain her panting. "Hey."

Tai squeezes past Brady to get an eyeful. His nose wrinkles like he's about to sneeze. "It smells like the sex tent at Burning Man in here."

I can feel my face flush redder than it already is as my mind races for any viable excuse. I start to pry carpet fibers apart like I'm living the *Law and Order* dream.

"Bro, you alright?" Brady asks.

"My contact fell out," I say the first thing that pops into my head. "Dry eyes from the show."

The boys exchange suspicious glances. Both of us have epic, mussed hair, clothes half-pawed off. Brady scratches his head, the full extent of his investigative instincts, apparently. "You wear contacts?"

It's raining harder now, and the boys are soaked. The air feels humid and heavy, like a weighted blanket on my skin. The wetness in my boxers starts spreading, sticky and uncomfortable. Fuck. The longer I'm stationary, the more obvious it will be.

I exaggerate plucking an invisible contact from the carpet, cradling it in my palm. "Got it! I'll be right back."

I shuffle to the bathroom like the hunchback of Notre Dame and can hear the conversation turn heated through the thin walls.

"Is this why you ditched us at the club?" Brady demands. "For a banger session?"

Gia: "I texted you both to say we were leaving."

Then Tai: "Are you two like an item now?"

Gia, vehemently: "No. We were talking about the show. Ways to fine-tune."

Brady, unimpressed: "Did you think of asking *us*?"

Gia: "You were a little busy blowing the night up."

I splash my face with water, my breath still coming in short bursts. Euphoria rushes through every vein, my afterglow backed up with no place to go. I let the water run, then soak a washcloth to deal with the mess in my boxers. After a thorough rinse, I hang it back on the hook Shae labeled with my name on masking tape. Thank god each of us has our own towel bar.

I lean onto the sink and close my eyes. My muscles feel tight and achy from the show. All my thoughts are spinning wildly out of control. If the boys dragged me out for another interrogation, I don't know what I'd say.

All I want is Gia.

And they better get used to it.

Chapter Thirteen

GIA

MY EYES POP OPEN AND SLOWLY ADJUST TO THE LIGHT CUTTING IN through the bunk curtain. I slept like the dead, forgot about food entirely, and now I'm wicked hungry. But food means leaving the bunk, and I'm not ready to face JC. Or the boys. I can hear them all coming to life in the lounge, the smell of freshly brewed coffee making my stomach growl.

Just another day on tour.

Except nothing is the same.

It never will be.

Maybe I should've thought of that, but not a whole lot of thinking went on last night. With JC's mouth on my neck and my legs wrapped around him, nothing else existed. It felt good to let go. To stop being in control for five goddamn minutes and just *feel* something. And damn, I felt his erection pressing into me, like it could pin all my sharp edges down.

That's the thing they don't tell you—sometimes the scariest part isn't crossing the line.

It's how much you liked it.

I grope for my phone, more than a little married to it. Powering it on, I prepare for the usual flood: messages, fan edits, and a few low blows from the old guard who do not get me. Instead, headline after headline smacks me in the face.

JC Trenton Steals the Spotlight in London Comeback

Is Pop's Lost Prodigy Ready for a Full Revival?

Gia Barlow's Band Brilliantly Powered by Former Teen Idol

My stomach twists. I scroll faster, hoping to find balance. A sentence. A line. Something. But the narrative is already rolling downhill. Article after article with his name in the headline and mine in the subtitle. I'm barely a footnote in my own tour.

I blink fast, trying to absorb it all.

Maybe I should be happy because the buzz is real, the show was insane. But all I feel is this dull thud behind my ribs, like I handed the mic to someone else, and they started singing my songs.

Tai's roaring warrior laughter bursts out from the lounge. Then Brady chimes in, too loud, too Brady:

"Bro, JC, you *broke* the internet. And Shae said our merch was picked clean! New orders flying in. Ka-ching! We be rollin' in it now, thanks to you."

A flame of despair burns a trail into my heart. I chuck the phone against the wall and sink deeper into the bunk, willing the foam mattress to swallow me whole. For sure, they're all reading what I'm reading. The sting of tears hits, and I swipe at them, angry with myself. I hate being this affected. But I've worked too hard to become invisible now. I clawed my way here. This is *my* moment.

And, as if I needed to feel worse, it suddenly occurs to me that the photographer at the gala had asked if we were *JC and Gia.*

The photo of us that blew up online—of course, they picked *that* one—was JC, head turned, eyes downcast, like he was about to dive head-first into my plunging neckline.

Caption: JC Trenton Steals the Spotlight—and the View.

My fingers fold in and tighten, nails gouging into both palms.

This is the shit I have to deal with for the next month?

It's like an entire alien force of Sawyers has infiltrated my planet, where men rule without question, and everyone accepts it.

But you don't have to, Gia.

I crawl out of bed in my PJs. I can't stomach putting on my dirty stage clothes again for the dart into the bathroom. I lock the door behind me, crank on the shower, and run water until it's blistering hot. Crouching in the tiny acrylic stall, I make myself small in the only private space available to have a proper breakdown. Showers are supposed to be short to conserve water, but I will stay here until my skin turns blue from the cold. Until my tears wash away the humiliation of the day.

♫

"There she is." JC's smile warms as he takes in the cleaned-up version of me. He's holding a novelty mug that says GIVE ME TEQUILA OR GIVE ME DEATH. "Coffee's on. Can I grab you one?"

A fresh ache quakes beneath my ribs. Why does he have to be considerate *and* the same wild man who actually bit my fucking neck, moaning like I was a life-altering experience? Why does he have to be more talented?

"I'm good." I cut my gaze to the door. "Heading out for breakfast."

JC glances down at my laced Chucks. His smile falters. "Want company?"

Tai and Brady, locked in a heated battle to kill each other on the dual video game, barely clocked my entrance. Without looking away from the TV, Brady mutters, "Pretty sure the queen wants to hang with the new king."

My chest puffs with indignation. "What does that mean?"

"It means," Tai says, "that maybe this band is about to break through to the next level faster than we ever imagined. We found the missing link."

"You mean our *temporary* guitar player?"

It comes out with bite, more than I anticipated. JC looks at the other wall, a faint flush coloring his cheeks. I see it in his face: the flicker of uncertainty. We had no privacy last night after Brady and Tai interrupted our explosive roll on the floor, leaving us buried in unfinished business.

Brady levels a look at me over his shoulder. "Why don't you take JC out for breakfast instead of being a solo bitch? Show some gratitude."

"Hey!" JC's voice cuts hot and sharp. "Chill, dude."

I hike a stubborn chin. Now he's coming to my rescue? I can't handle this morning. "I can stick up for myself, thank you very much." JC blinks, surprised into a whole new line of confusion. "And thank *you* for nothing." I stick my tongue out at Brady, who rolls his eyes in that perfectly annoying Brady way.

"Maybe you two should have fucked last night," he mutters. "You'd be in a way better mood."

I swallow down a string of razored insults, spin around, and storm to the bunk to collect my phone and purse. JC follows me, cornering me into the kitchen at the rear of the bus.

"Hey," he starts, reaching for my arm. "Listen…"

I shove his hand away. "No. I'm not listening. Not to you."

The sharp edge in my voice hits him like a physical thing, pushing him a step back. "Is this about last night?"

"That was a big mistake."

JC recoils. I see the hurt flash across his face before he reins it in. "If I crossed the line, I'm sorry. I thought…"

He trails off so mournfully, I want to scream *Are you that clueless? Last night was everything! Can't you see past my level of petty?*

"Don't overthink it."

I try to shoulder past him, but he grabs my arm. "Gia. Stop. Look at me."

A long silence, while things move behind his stormy pools of blue-gray. Something comes over me, but I will *not* break.

"What? I'm looking at you."

I'm channeling a full-Italian diva: legs planted apart, fists parked at my waist. Wet hair, no makeup, eyes still puffy from crying in the shower. This is pathetic. I'm better than this. And JC counters my brittle behavior with a low, intimate tone that sends my insides sloshing.

"Fine if you want to eat on your own, but can we step outside and finish this conversation?"

"There is no conversation. We were both wasted. Shit happens on tour, right?"

I shrug, daring him to argue, and JC's bewildered expression is like he's expecting me to say this is all a joke. My face flashes hot, and I'm already demoralized on reflex—I am that bitch.

Before he notices the glimmer of unshed tears, I hurl past the boys and shoulder the bus door open to escape into the tart morning air. All of London is back to drab and barren, the brilliant high of last night only a faded memory.

Fuck!

It feels like a rock has formed in my stomach. My body pulls in on itself, the thin, sour rain smelling like wet disaster. I have no idea where I'm heading. The roads are stuffed with bumper-to-bumper traffic, and car horns bleat at yet another tourist who forgets to look the other way at every crosswalk. I pass a Tesco, a McDonald's, a hole-in-the-wall curry joint, but the idea of food sliding down my throat, the mere act of chewing, is a useless farce.

I want to shrivel up and die.

JC looked at me last night like I was the only person in the Royal Albert Hall, even while the crowd screamed his name. But it isn't particularly useful to fall for a guy whose bright sun of accomplishments eclipses the moon.

In other words: myself.

♫

Instead of scrawling my thoughts into the pages of a diary with pink ink, I sort the fucked-up pieces of me into lyrics and music. Walk miles every day and usually feel better by the end, armed with a workable tune to tinker on. But after an aimless morning that starts with bangers and beans and dissolves into walking in circles, I've got nothing.

Only nervous expectation.

I treated JC like a right twat, as the Brits say.

Too chickenshit to travel with my band to sound check, I hop a taxi and find JC on stage, dialing in his favorite VOX amp. An apology is the deeply meaningful thing to bust out, but for whatever unimaginable reason, I start with a punch in the face.

"So, about your song."

He glances at me, eyes guarded. "Hi. And what about it?"

"Since you tapped out, it's mine."

I'm in no shape to process the storm that dances in his eyes. Or his curt reply. "Is *that* what last night was all about?"

"I'm just sayin.' We laid out the terms of our dare in advance, and you–"

JC cuts me off with a firm grab of my elbow, steering me offstage into the wings. I feel more trouble brewing instead of resolution as he blazes a look at me. "What the hell is going on, Gia? This morning, you told me it was all a mistake. Now you're hitting me with this? Forget it. And do I really need to clarify what tapping out means? Penetration. Insertion. Real, actual sex."

My chest pinches. "Are you saying what happened wasn't real?"

He stares at me like I've sprouted two heads. "That was as real as it gets. For me, anyway."

"Because you had an orgasm. I didn't."

His mouth parts in surprise, and why shouldn't it? Now I'm throwing some A-class idiocy into his face.

"You sat on me like I was your favorite armchair," he reminds me, "and, yeah, things got crazy fast. That wasn't my intention. Is that what's bothering you?" His eyes are dark now, wounded and searching mine like he's trying to find the version of me from last night —the one who let him touch her like that, who let him in. "Because why are you doing this?" He doesn't wait for my answer. "It's all the shit online, right? That's the real issue. Nothing to do with *me*."

I lift my chin, all righteous indignation. "They're writing glowing stuff about you, so, yes, it has everything to do with you."

There it is—the truth.

The reason for my full complement of neurotic girl shit.

JC breathes in deep, weariness creeping into his voice. "I don't control the media, Gia. And *you* asked *me* to play in your band because, apparently, I have skills. You want some hack instead? You want to read *those* reviews?" He's moved past frustration into anger, but he claws it back just as quickly. "I did what I could to hang back last night. Made sure the spotlight stays on you. If I need to play from backstage tonight, I will. Tell me what you want."

He punctuates that by throwing up his hands. Waits for me to step up to the plate. His directive was an unmissable slow pitch even the most useless rookie could clobber.

"Not *that*," I finally say, an overflowing fountain of contrition he immediately challenges.

"Then what? Offer up a solution. Don't mindfuck me." The stubborn fold of his arms is the equivalent of a slap in the face. I feel the floor fall away and the horizon spin. I can see the moment he clocks the regret on my face, and when he calculates how rarely I look regretful about anything.

He clears his throat and says, more gently, "I'm all in, Gia, on every level, in case that wasn't obvious to you."

I think about his crumpled face last night and how he let himself moan. That I did straddle him and ride him like a cowgirl, pressing my lips to his neck to taste the show in an entirely different way. JC isn't a threat. He's Jameson Chevalier Trenton, one of my all-time inspirations. The man who left me blinded by stars, then kissed an unkissable carpet to save my bacon.

In the deepest hours of sleep, he was the vision my mind circled back to.

"Yo! Sid and Nancy," Brady barks at us from the stage. "Can we get the party started?"

JC stifles a laugh, and I think, *screw it, Gia. Laugh with him*. The tension seeps away, and for a suspended moment—only a few seconds in real time—I feel closed in and protected by his gaze.

Until he impressively shatters any shred of my false victory. "For the record," he adds, "the song is still mine. And you just blew up all your negotiation credits."

I heave a sigh. Maybe this time, I'm the one backing down. "Fuck me. Truce?"

His lips quirk into a smile I absolutely do not deserve. Then he dips his head, lips nuzzling my earlobe. I suck in a breath and squish both eyes shut as his warm, wet tongue glides over my triple skull piercings. Shameless as I am in emotional manipulation.

When he murmurs, "I'd like to fuck your dirty little mouth," it's the next best thing to music I've ever heard.

♫

The crowd tonight doesn't notice when I fumble the lyrics to "Bite into the Chaos," too busy losing their minds over JC's shredding solo. But I noticed her. Not in a red flag way. Not at first.

Just … curious.

She's older, maybe forty, with styled honey-blonde hair and sad eyes. Someone I'd expect to see in a fancy bar with a glass of chilled wine in hand. Totally out of place here, crushed in with the fans, high on every consumable, punching the air with their fists. While half the loveable freaks scream their intention to marry me during "Rock and Roll Bride," this woman—this stranger—she isn't screaming or filming or moshing in a haze of ecstasy.

She's there … *watching*.

Watching JC, cloaked in shadows.

She looks like she knows things she shouldn't. Like, maybe she knows him. Is that why JC entrenches himself close to the amps, borderline offstage? I'm in no position to demand anything of him or my boys tonight and refuse to ask them a single question to deepen their uncertainty about me. And that lady? I'd like to will her into negative space, but she's there all night until we break for the encore.

Then she's gone.

I tell myself to forget her.

Types like her show up occasionally, wearing expensive blouses and real diamonds, paying top dollar for a StubHub rip-off. Maybe she was a lawyer or accountant reliving her youth in the stiffest, most joyless way. Or another wayward groupie radiating sad girl starter pack vibes.

I've seen plenty of those so far.

With more on the way, no doubt.

Post-show, we cram into a bar on the edge of collapse to party with the local blokes and lasses. The yellow light from ancient fixtures makes everyone look jaundiced, while a rickety sound system blares Oasis so loudly that it bleeds my ears. The boys bask in attention, but I fight back anxiety whenever another swarm of women circles JC. They coo and fangirl, hands lingering on his arm or shoulder, and he flirts back with that damn sexy smile.

Sitting at the bar, I watch the scene unfold as the grip on my rocks glass tightens. He should be saving that smile for me.

But he wasn't the difficult one today.

I shit all over my fantasy man and have only myself to blame.

Mama always says that my drive for success could alienate me from my closest friends. My baby-brained attack on JC now feels fully idiotic. Angry at him for being that good, instead of raging at myself for not being good enough to keep the spotlight where it belongs. Of all the badly timed meltdowns, this is the one that could have turned him off me for good.

I feel faintly nauseated.

In need of support.

I find a dark corner to hide in, toss back my rum and Coke, and whip out my phone to ping Audrie. We text, on average, twenty times a day. Now, in less than seventy-two hours, my oldest friend, who said she had my back twenty-four-seven, has gone radio silent.

GB: Hey. We wrapped London.

GB: Miss u.

GB: What's up?

It's only what, five p.m. in Seattle? But it might as well be midnight. Because she doesn't text back.

Chapter Fourteen

JC

The next morning, my body and mind slowly and painfully recover from last night. I'm sitting in the lounge, nursing a cup of coffee. We cleared the darkness of the Chunnel, and our bus motors through the rugged beauty of the French countryside. Empty roads and shifting morning light, treetops skimmed by birds, Paris only three hours away. Gotta love Europe. In Canada, you drive for hours, and there's still more Canada.

"Hey, stranger." Gia appears, trailing steam from her shower. She plunks down next to me and fires up her phone. "You look so serious."

I laugh, even though it hurts to. Better this than yesterday, clenched with the intensity of our scrap. Order restored, if organizing the chaos in my heart is humanly possible. My eyes travel over her legs and her messy, wet hair. She smells warm and dangerously sexy.

"I think you're confusing hungover for my resting professor look," I joke.

Gia grins. "You'd make a hot prof. Convince an entire generation of TikTokers of the merits of higher education."

"That's setting the bar high."

"You'd slay at anything," she insists. "One of those people who try anything and, boom, master of the craft."

"For that to be true, I'd have to try my hand at something other than music."

"Which is not happening, ever. The world needs your brand of magic. Clearly."

Gia elbows me in the ribs, her form of apology. She knows she overreacted. There are some wrongs you can never right, but I'm not holding Gia entirely responsible for her blow-up yesterday. Blindsided by emotions she didn't have the vocabulary to process properly, she'd blamed me, irrationally. I read it right, in the end. If she thinks she's cornered the market where uncertainty masks genuine feelings, guess again.

Because what went down between us is the kind of real that drives you batshit crazy. The kind you don't recover from.

Her kisses make me want things I shouldn't want.

"If you wanted…" Gia seemingly plucks the word out of my brain, "there could be a permanent towel rack for JC in Pop My Cherry's bathroom."

"Are you two pretending to flirt or real flirting?" Brady grumbles from his bunk, his voice deep and croaky. "Either way, it makes me want to puke."

"You already puked twice last night," Gia reminds him. "Do you even chew your food?"

Brady erupts in a fit of phlegmy coughing. Both he and Tai have been dead to the world since passing out last night. Can't say I've missed the military-level testosterone blast while they virtually kill each other. Or the feet in dirty socks on the coffee table.

After clearing his lungs of grit and vape tar, he says, "Gia, fuck off, from the bottom of my heart. And JC. Bro, if you join our band permanently, I will crawl over and kiss your feet right now."

"Thanks for the offer," I answer. "Not sure my liver can hold up with the under-twenty-five patrol."

Gia's gaze narrows in on me, but she says nothing. We both did our thing last night, pretending not to clock every move the other made. The crowd at the pub went apeshit when we arrived, and I didn't entirely mind the flock of females flapping around me, because Gia, with her murderous glare and flared nostrils, told me everything I needed to know.

Sometimes the best medicine is humble pie.

"Practice makes perfect," Brady, the prince of sound advice, chimes in. Then, "Later, dudes. I'm going back to sleep."

Within a minute, he's snoring loudly. The humming grind of the bus engine sounds operatic in comparison.

Gia flashes me a look. "You make it sound like you're old. Old is, like, eighty."

A hollowness carves out in my chest, a flash of her in that dress at the gala. It made me think of her at my age, a gorgeous sylph of a woman, the world at her feet. And me, pushing fifty.

Everything I've told myself about me and her, the logic, the anti-logic, hums helplessly in my heart. I used to think love was the leap. Now I know it's the landing that ruins you. I'm on the wrong side of thirty to be setting things in motion without having some idea how they'll work out, but Gia makes me forget how endings work.

Which is why I'm tied in knots over a woman whose story has yet to start.

"Jameson," Gia whispers, obviously not wanting any other ears listening in.

"Yes, Regina?"

"The other night." She pokes my foot with a fishnet toe. Her eyes are all sparkly. "I liked it."

I scratch my head in mock confusion. "Remind me again what happened?"

She slants her head to one side with a look that means she knows perfectly well I know what happened. "Apparently, you wear contacts."

"Apparently, I saved you five hundred bucks."

She smiles. A different smile. We're having an entire conversation with our eyes.

"My knight in shining Converse."

"At your service, my rock and roll queen."

She's trying hard not to laugh as she says, "As long as we're clear. About everything." Gia rearranges herself on the couch, resting her stockinged feet on my lap. She drops her head to the phone, taking her loaded gaze with her. "Now, excuse me while I light up social media."

I force myself to breathe evenly. Her feet are inches away from ruining me. I kept my hands off the morning-long ache between my legs, my dick so hard it hurt, our fully clothed sex on an endless loop in my mind. I feel myself drifting back to that, because, god, it was beyond amazing. I can't explain to myself how good it was, that it was all I wanted with all my heart. To fuck the woman I considered a good friend, maybe even a best friend, with desire so deep and true, it scared me.

I steal a look at her, all fire and tiny everything. She blew every circuit I had, taking control, searing straight through all the dark layers wrapped tight around my mind.

The aching explosion left me cross-eyed and reeling.

I wanted more. I wanted her to touch me all over. I wanted to make *her* explode.

She gave me what I needed, and I left her unsatisfied.

That guilt burns hot.

There's a lot of that going around.

My heart's beating fast, mind spinning backward as I stare out the window. I saw her last night, in front of the stage. Took many steps backward until I ran out of space.

Neither Gia nor the boys said a word—not even an offhand *Didn't that woman look familiar?* Not that they would've placed her as Amber Devlin, the drummer from my old band, Read My Rights. It took a few songs and her steady stare before *I* connected the dots. My nose-ringed ex-lover, who liked to whistle showtunes, eat an alarming amount of poutine, and crawl into my bunk to indulge every fantasy a nineteen-year-old could conjure up, was near unrecognizable as a polished corporate blonde in a blazer.

The last time we spoke, she said I was dead to her.

Last I heard, she'd moved to Spain.

Her disappearing act benefited me in that the messy destruction of us was neatly packed away like forgotten summer clothes. Maybe she'd relocated to London. Maybe her appearance was a one-off, morbid curiosity; time passing, wounds healing.

Or maybe it was something else.

"Hey." Gia's voice snaps me out of the fog.

I find her eyes reluctantly. "Yeah?"

"You look sad."

"Nah, just a little tired." I wiggle her big toe as Gia studies my too quick, too fake smile, weighing it against whatever truth she sees behind my eyes. My mind keeps racing, trying to fill in the blanks, the vague, unfinished outline of me and Amber.

Not something I want to think about at this moment.

But if she shows up in Paris, I'll have to rethink a lot of things.

Like I said, there are some wrongs you can never right.

Chapter Fifteen

GIA

Also cliché: the band photo op in front of the Eiffel Tower.

But holy shit! *The* Eiffel Tower.

You only see it for the first time once, and it makes you appreciate what architecture can do. And thank you to whoever controls the weather in France, because the clouds finally broke just as all four of us hit center frame on the grass for our first official European photo shoot.

I'm working the stylish Parisian angle in cherry-red capris and black flats. The humidity wrecked my Amy Winehouse updo into a full-blown 80s hair band casualty, but you can't wipe the smile off my face if you tried.

Because JC is like Paris in man form.

Sexy and romantic and lit up with a certain glow.

And he's radiating dream-man vibes, one arm slung across my shoulder. Magic-hour glow kisses his stubbled jaw, those mercurial eyes somehow the same slate-gray as the iconic landmark we're standing in front of. I'm physically incapable of not looking at him when he's close.

And I'm not the only one.

A swell of tourists surrounds us, phones raised, everyone trying to capture the circus that is my band lighting up the Paris afternoon.

Pick your crazy. We just doubled it.

"Space, people. Merci." Shae shoulders through the semi-circle of fans, her cowboy boots and ten-gallon hat commanding instant respect. That look takes guts in Paris.

Click. Click. Click.

JC leans close, murmuring, "You look amazing. Cover of *The Rolling Stone*."

Wow. This feels like a living dream. It's like I'm walking in on a scene from my own life and realizing the details aren't anything like what I remember—JC, not Audrie, beside me, posing for photos in Paris and not some hick Manitoba town. My favorite guitarist ever in *my* band.

"Oh my god!" a twenty-something woman in a poncho gasps, her attention bouncing between JC and me. "Wait—are you two, like, together-together?"

The breath in my lungs stills. This is one of those moments you can't prepare for. Some fast talking is required, and cue Brady, half-drunk and draped in a ridiculous pink feather boa.

"We have money riding on that answer," he hollers back.

JC laughs, his eyes bright, hair loose and flowing. "Strictly musical, I promise."

The woman and her curly-haired friend giggle, asking JC to pose in their selfie, which he too happily obliges. A stab of jealousy pierces my heart. He *knows* what he does to the opposite sex. Didn't our conversation this morning set the record straight?

What is this?

I'm drowning in feelings, like, right over here.

Click. Click. Click.

"And I've got better taste than that," I blurt out, sharper than intended.

JC throws me a surprised look. Curly Hair scoffs, her brown eyes mean slits. "Right," she says, voice dripping with condescension. "Where have you been eating?"

There are several good reasons to shut up and not ramble the combative response that comes as naturally to me as breathing. But if I can be counted on for anything, it's disruption.

"If you—"

Tai's fingers slip through mine, stopping the words cold. His grip on my hand means business, although his voice is soft when he whispers, "Down girl."

With heroic determination, I swallow my pride. He's right, as usual. Tai's got a sixth sense for when to defuse a situation—my savior, dressed in camo pants, wife-beater, and black puffa.

"Thank you," I mutter.

"Over here!" the photographer calls, snapping our focus back to her lens.

I slide to Tai's left so he can deal with JC's perfect cocktail of pheromones.

Smile for the camera.

Click, click, click.

Ignore the distractions, Gia.

But JC has awakened something wild and dangerous in me. When I pinned myself against his erection on the bus, every part of me came alive. The heat curling up my spine, the blood rushing to my head.

But will I regret giving myself to a guy programmed to melt every female heart?

Click, click, click.

Suddenly, I feel a hand on the small of my back. Tight, warm circles drawn repeatedly with JC's palm.

Jesus. Really?

Paris, you're killing me.

♫

After the shoot, we ride to the top of the tower. JC wants to treat us all to a glass of champagne at the bar. But first, we scatter like dice to

109

admire the 360-degree view. The whole city glows pink and gold, light spilling over rooftops like honey.

I wander to the handrail to take it in. That's where Tai finds me. He parks himself beside me, blocking out a couple talking loudly in German.

"This is unreal," he says. "Beats Burnaby by a long shot, huh?"

I nod toward the crowds below. "I overheard some loser down there say Paris is old, shitty, and overpriced."

"Philistines!" he declares in a fake French accent. "History screams at you from every corner. Makes me feel sad for the Main Street hipsters who think vintage means buying jeans from the eighties."

"Do they even sell jeans here? The Parisians are so put together."

He eyes my capris. "You look super cute in those."

I bump his hip. "Thanks. You're looking mighty fine too. If those hoes weren't slobbering all over JC, you might've had a chance."

Tai leans against the railing, hands clasping together. He's quiet for a beat, jaw grinding in that thinking way. Then: "Remember how I stepped into your girl fight in ninth grade? Saved you from suspension?"

I shoot him a look. "Is this your way of saying I haven't changed?"

"Au contraire, mademoiselle. I knew then you were a force. Had no clue you'd end up crashing through everything in your path."

Something tics in my jaw. "That makes me sound destructive."

"Damage can be of the nonphysical variety." His tone leaves that open to interpretation.

"So you're saying…"

"I'm *asking* if this JC thing is a crush, the real deal, or a power play?"

"You really think I can make JC Trenton do anything?" I conveniently skirt a real answer. "C'mon. Huge bands have begged him to join. He turned them all down."

"But not us."

"I told you; he came to The Troubadour gig. Liked what he heard. Our band is on the verge. He gets to claim he was part of it."

"That's my other point," he says. "If I wanted a comeback, I'd do the same. Ride the wave of the next big thing. You see what I'm saying?" Tai studies me. Even in the bleak Vancouver winters, he looks tanned and healthy with his bronzed Brazilian skin.

"I'm not going to let him ruin what we have."

His eyebrows knit together. "You sure about that? 'Cause, right now, it feels like our tour is happening in a fucked-up season of *The Bachelor*. You two are bringing the drama, and we're stuck in the middle."

"I highly doubt—"

"Gia," he interrupts. "You just dissed him during the photoshoot, in public. Hate to say it, but you sounded like a jealous bitch. That kind of shit gets captured on camera, and we go viral for all the wrong reasons." He pauses. Sighs. Looks off into the distance. "I'm here to play music. Not to be a bit player in a soap opera."

A Japanese man wedges closer to us, angling for a selfie. We shuffle down to give him space, giving me precious seconds to cool my head. Brady and Tai have come to rely on me and have slacked off because I do it all. They show up when they need to, and so far, that's been enough. But with JC in the mix, I sense a strange rift.

The smallest thread is beginning to unravel.

My next words come out tight. "I take it you're speaking on behalf of you and Brady."

Cue Brady's loud cackle echoing across the observation deck. Tai and I glance over at Brady and JC. Side by side and laughing. Shoulders touching.

After a beat, Tai says dryly, "I think he wants to sleep with JC as bad as you do."

Something like a frown tugs the corner of my mouth. "I do *not* come across that desperate."

He shrugs, and I groan inwardly. I haven't said a thing to either of my bandmates about my feelings for JC, but I fritz out like bad electronics whenever JC even talks to another woman. It's like he knows how badly I want him and finds joy in torturing me.

Touché, Barlow. I see your move from miles away and will drive you crazy with temptation because I'm JC Trenton, and every woman wants me.

I look at the ground, hair tumbling forward so Tai can't see the expression on my face. "If you were in my shoes, what would you do?"

There is a long beat of silence before he replies. "This is the beginning. A million lifetimes ahead. Places to go. People to meet. Guys to shag."

My throat tightens. "But I like him. A lot."

Tai reaches over to tuck my hair behind my ear. His eyes are kind. "I'm glad it's him and not me. When you focus on something, no pitbull alive can stop you. But you can't look at a guy as a goal. He's not a conquest. If you treat him like one, how do you think he deals with that?"

I feel strange sparks shoot up my spine.

I'd like to pretend I thought about that.

Because, yeah, I chase what I want. Always have. Winning is the way I keep score. And no man before JC made my insides clench when they walked into a room, or made my heart explode, serenading me with a song. He's never played fair from the start, the second he looked at me like I mattered. Like we were equals.

Like we were inevitable.

"Bubble time!" Brady yells. "The Magician's paying. Let's toast the sunset with the good shit. Très magnifique, oui?"

Tai and I exchange eye rolls. Classic Brady—loudest man in Europe—no care in the world with a hundred glances from offended tourists.

Seconds before we rejoin them, I squeeze Tai's hand. He's right. I need to dial back my emotions. Forget trying to orchestrate and let things between me and JC unfold in real time. If I walk outta this with a mangled heart, fine. Let me weep in a corner until all my tears dry up.

But no universe exists where I can douse what JC's ignited in me.

Quietly, with all the belief I have left, I tell Tai, "I will not fuck this up. I promise."

Chapter Sixteen

JC

I slosh more red wine into my glass, a full-on vacation pour. Try to drown out the noise of the damn question that's been doing laps in my head since the photo shoot.

What is my problem?

Plant any random woman in front of me, and I can reach the end goal without even trying hard. And who cares if I fail, because none of them matter.

None of them, Gia.

"Yo, bro." Brady swaggers up to me in a tight pair of lime-green shorts. Every detail on display. "You have a sec?"

I, we, have fifteen minutes. Possibly less if our opening act, a humorless trio from Belgium called The Shoppe Girls, continues to mutilate the crowd into submission with ear-splitting basslines and toneless singing. Nothing better than having to warm up a catatonic audience.

"Sure," I say. "What's up?"

He bites into a celery stick, chewing with his mouth open. "Nothing. A one-on-one."

We're backstage at the Zénith, a concert hall famous for sitting smack in the middle of a forest, in the heart of Paris. Tai's lurking near the craft service table, stuffing his face with artisan crackers. Gia took off for the bathroom. Brady steers us to the sectional in the corner and I take a seat, like I'm expected to. He pours his tanned, long limbs across the scuffed burgundy leather and waits, not pushing an agenda despite clearly having one.

When he finally says, "This stays between us, K?" it's with all the verve of a kid at spy school practicing clandestine delivery.

I arch a brow. "Depends on what *this* is."

He flicks a glance at Tai. I get the sense that they flipped a coin to decide who would handle this discussion. "You know we're super grateful you stepped in, right?"

"Glad it's all worked out."

"What are your plans after?"

"More films. Session work." Jesus, not even an ounce of interest in my voice. Might as well have a vacation in hell waiting for me. "Why?"

Brady finishes his celery, all humor leaving his eyes when they skate across mine. "Just hear me out."

I take a long pull of wine. Here it comes, epic lecture about to drop.

"You know Tai and I go way back with Gia?" Brady waits for my dutiful nod before continuing. "We've never seen her tied in knots like this over someone."

I smile politely. "And you're... worried?"

"Thing is, there's no middle ground for her. It's either superstardom or living in a cardboard box under a bridge. And she will burn both ends of every candle to achieve her dreams."

"Admirable quality," I say. "And rare."

"I know, dude. She's bona fide. A ripper. And this is her life. *Our* life," he stresses, in case the context has gone over my head. "And your life, as you said, you slide right back into whatever you were doing before."

My brows shoot up. "Are you saying I have no skin in the game?"

He squirms, as if he'd rather be celibate than answer. "More like, we're worried about the JC effect on Gia. All this…" His hand sweeps left to right, indicating our dressing room packed with Bordeaux wine and real cheese, because it's France. And because it's not a dive bar with a bowl of Cheetos and warm cans of Pepsi. "It's because of you. And until we work up to that level of success on our own, it will disappear just as quickly."

Patience wearing thin, I cut to the chase. "What are you saying?"

"What I'm saying is…" He glances over his shoulder, tracking if Gia has returned. In the clear, he swivels back to face me, voice dropping low. "I get it. She's hot. Every guy wants a piece. I tried, and no dice. Props to you."

He flashes a congenial grin. Not a jealous bone in his player body, while I'd contemplate violence if any guy made a move on Gia. Because something more than a friendship has shimmered between us from day one—a specific tension of two people destined for each other.

I take another sip of wine, bracing for the *but* I know is coming.

"But if her heart gets dragged through the gutter," he says, "we have to live with Devastation City."

"You think I'd play her like that? Cut and run?"

"Not on *purpose*." Full dramatic pause. "I think she's in over her head and clueless to a world without you in it."

I give him a long, evaluating stare. My falling hard was a gravitational inevitability I didn't see coming. But Gia clueless? Like *gently failing* is how she'll be remembered.

"Flattered you think her place in the world has anything to do with me," I say. "She did fine before I came along."

"And Europe did fine until the Black Plague hit," he flips back.

Ouch. Gia's storming through my blood, and Brady just made it clear I'm a walking virus. Hell of a pep talk before a gig. No point trying to hide my exasperation when it's written all over my face.

"What do you want? Give it to me straight."

We eye each other with clear mutual discomfort. There is very rarely an occasion when a woman's male friends sit you down for a talk and it's a good thing.

"I don't want her to get hurt, okay? I don't want her to get so wrapped up in you that she forgets us. I don't want her to land in Vancouver, dark and crazy. She's all claws when she wants something bad." He rubs his face, leaving glitter streaks across one cheek. "And you, my friend, are either faking it that you don't see how far gone she is, or hand you the trophy right now for Best Actor in an Unaware Performance."

I fight the temptation to laugh. Brady, with so many layers of realization. In less time than it takes to scramble an egg, he exposes my six months of comprehensive Gia pining for the C-level shitty performance it was.

"And if you think you're fooling anyone, bro, guess again. Freaking obvs-city on the bus the other night." Brady rubs his thumb and index finger together. "You both owe us scratch."

He scans my pupils, I'm certain, to call out my nonexistent contacts. Let him stare all he wants. I've learned over thirty-three years that life is a never-ending series of compromises. They want me to behave in a certain way. And I won't act in the way they want.

Brady and Tai don't understand that I can't go backwards.

The door crashes open, and Gia struts in with so much skin on display in her excuse of a dress that my mouth goes dry. Her hot stare steadies on Brady before it flips to me. Not even three seconds, and she's picked up that our man-huddle involves her.

So why not throw it in our faces?

"Is Brady your new boyfriend?" Gia slides next to me, plucks the wine glass out of my hand, and guzzles the remains.

"Turns out, JC's more of a three-way guy," Brady says with a wide grin.

Gia laughs. "You wish." She sets down the empty glass, then says, "Dibs," and hooks an arm around my neck, tugging tight and tilting my mouth higher. Her lips crash against mine in a kiss of electric fire, her tongue, hot and slick, sliding into my open mouth.

It singes every nerve in my body.

She kisses and teases until my huffs of surprise melt into sighs. The scream in my head urges me to cup her ass and grind us together, but as her possessive kiss turns devastating, I can barely hold on to anything other than the desire to be inside her.

"Alright, alright. Time out," Brady says. "Point made. I'm getting a boner."

Gia tears her mouth off mine. My anticipation is already showing, more than a little aching.

"Uhm..." It's the one word my mouth can shape. Not a single coherent sentence to add to this conversation.

Brady stands. Something in his expression tells me I'm being pitied. "Bro, you are going bankrupt on this tour. Better write us a blank check and call it a day."

He ambles to join Tai at the craft table, while Gia curls into my warmth, like she's a cat and I'm her favorite sleep pad.

"You ready to light Paris on fire?"

"They know." I aim that husky warning directly at her sly smile.

"Duh." She twirls a lock of my hair around her finger, unraveling me with every slow, delicate coil. "I just kissed you."

"Is that cool?"

"I want everyone to know what we've both known all along."

Gia's gaze sharpens, holding mine like a challenge. I scan her face, searching for any sign of weakness, but her confidence is diamond-cut, sealed with heated determination. It finally hits me. I've been too casual and careful, leaving Gia no choice but to take the lead. It's time to kick things up a notch. Easier said than done, though, all this thinking and action, when I'm still trying to remember how to breathe. Gia strokes my earlobe, the tiny gold hoop studded within it, and her touch creates this urgency that radiates a hot tingle.

I want to take care.

Touch her how she deserves to be touched.

Not some random tour bus takedown.

I suppose that and the audience roaring their delight when we walk out into the spotlights minutes later distract me. Then I feel it. A disturbance in the air. That instinctive pull to scan the front row for her familiar face.

Boom. Biggest fear realized.

Panic presses hard against my chest. I make my way stage left to grab my Les Paul from our guitar tech. Slinging the guitar over my shoulder, my hands tremble, unable, unwilling to make eye contact with space beyond my immediate periphery.

I draw a breath and then release it.

Strum the opening chords of "Blackest Nights."

When I look up, Gia's gaze is locked on the front row.

On Amber.

My entire body feels encased in stone, trapped in some surreal world where I can pretend everything is fine when it isn't. A reminder that nothing is ever over. It sits in the dark, like a box at the foot of the stairs, ready to take you down when you least expect it.

My old bandmates, Heath and Ari, warned me—*Don't shit where you eat.*

Brilliant advice, in retrospect. Emphatically ignored. About to bite me in the ass for the second time, I'm certain.

Gia greets the audience with a hearty, "Bon Soir, Paris!" and the place goes nuts. A shoutout in the local language, guaranteed to spike the energy. Meanwhile, I'm tracking the darkest place on stage to hide out.

Because Amber is looking right at me.

Right through me.

My fingers fumble the B chord I've played a million times, and I don't feel ridiculously nervous for no reason.

Because right after that…

Gia tracks her gaze all the way to me.

Chapter Seventeen

No way this is a fluke. Front and center, second show in a row, in two different cities? That either catapults you into superfan status or *maybe I need a bodyguard* vibe.

But that woman ... she didn't give off extreme energy.

Other than being extremely interested in JC.

The final notes of our encore dull just a fraction as I stalk offstage. My heart feels red and raw, like crushed cranberries. JC stood deeper in the shadows tonight in what felt like a direct response to my suspicious stare before we kicked off the night.

He noticed me notice her following his every move.

I weave between the roadies hanging out in the wings, desperate for a drink.

Do I ask?

I need to.

This requires unpacking.

Shae greets me in the dressing room with a hug and shoves a frosty bottle of Evian into my hand. "Nice work, nice work. What a song to send them home on. Unforgettable!"

Props to Brady and his idea to encore with Daft Punk's "Get Lucky." We gave it a grungy, dirtier edge, and the Parisians lapped it up like crème fraîche. The cherry on top was the magic of my voice twining with JC's, spiraling high into the rafters. We sounded perfect together, better than my usual vocalists, who pile into the dressing room seconds later.

"Did I call it? Huh? Huh?" Brady throws up a hand for a high five. "Full iconic. Tell me that did not go off."

I slap him back. "Where's JC?"

"I dunno. Taking a piss? Slap a GPS on him, you'll sleep better."

He slides past me to the craft table, popping a slab of brie into his mouth, unaware of my turmoil. That all I can think about is how JC's face went dark when I busted his little stare-a-thon.

"This is your window to get cleaned up," Shae reminds us all. "Thirty minutes until the fan zone."

Tai strips his shirt off, wincing as he sniffs his pits. Funny that his six-pack does nothing for me, while a glimpse of JC's ripped abs sends me outta my mind.

"I need a shower," he announces to no one in particular.

Brady elbows Tai, his smile a devious glint. "A meet and greet is like grocery shopping. I'll take that, and one of those, and that entire aisle. Please and thank you."

Tai's gaze jumps from mine back to Brady. "I hope you have a room booked for all your conquests."

"Aww, fuck, Gia," Brady moans. "Can we get off this stupid path?"

Before I tell him *no* for the tenth time, JC strolls in. Instead of his closed-off body language from the show, he seems far more relaxed. I search his face for something, anything to tip me off. But all I see are his sparkling eyes sweeping over me.

"Great show, Boss," he says. "I never knew you could speak French. What other tricks do you have up your sleeve?"

Mama, fluent in English, Italian, and French, insisted I learn all her languages. Helpful on a European tour. In Burnaby, not so much.

"Plenty. If you think I have zero command of anything outside of music, guess again."

JC helps himself to a chilled Evian, raising it in a gesture of *cheers*. "You command every space that dares surround you."

His easy smile. Is it for real? Or is this his way of buttering me up so I forget what I saw? We stand there for a long moment, the rush of the show still humming between us. My eyes flit from his face to the floor, and back to that wondrous mouth that does wicked and wonderful things to mine.

Listen, I'm not a fool. You don't invite a hot guitarist into your band and not expect others to notice the same qualities. Just as I'm going to ask about that woman, JC rocks the world I thought I had under my control.

"May I have a word with you, Miss Barlow?"

"What's up?"

He walks us into a dark corner piled with coils of cable and crew jackets. My combat boot taps the floor in double time. I'm aware of every nerve, every current rippling between us.

"We have two nights in Zurich," he says.

"And?"

JC tilts his head, like I should pick up on something other than the tour schedule I know by heart. When I don't, he says, "I'd like to treat the queen to a royal stay at one of the finest hotels. If she'll have me."

I feel my lungs squeeze. My mouth definitely drops open. JC's intention is broadcast all over his face. I'm so not ready for this plot twist. "You're springing this on me now?"

"You wanted us to be clear. About everything." JC steps closer, only an inch between his heart and mine as his voice dips low and dangerously sexy. "Yes or no?"

Wow. One simple loaded question. This is JC in full force: a wall of potent charm, endlessly provocative eyebrow raises, and the most damning detail of all, that he treats me with an almost courtly formality. Asking, not demanding. Leaving me a living, breathing symphony of dirty-ass thoughts.

A vulnerable blush spills across both cheeks. I still feel the crush of those biceps against my rib cage when he howled my name the other night. And he felt so huge, straining against his jeans. Will he even fit inside of me?

Hello, Gia? Time to answer!

Sweet Jesus. This man could quite possibly ruin my life, has already put a massive dent in it, and my thighs are fucking liquid.

What else am I going to say aside from, "Yes."

♫

Fans come out in good weather, in bad weather. They drive for hours to experience a band they could enjoy on Spotify in their living room while eating bad Chinese. I'm grateful they spend their money to buy things I've created and care enough to connect. And honestly? I'll sign anything—your divorce papers, body parts, a baby—just get me out of here and into Zurich already.

But I smile and live through the meet and greet, because that's what you do when fans swarm, gushing over your music. You give them your best. Even when your brain is doing donuts over the man who just invited you to a hotel suite like he was asking you to prom.

A tiny brunette with two nose rings and a glitter shawl passes over a worn vinyl of our first album, *Tasty Like You.* "This record saved me," she raves. "It got me through tough times. Especially 'Blackest Nights.' Sorry if this sounds lame, but you are literally my hero."

I feel a gathering in my throat. To touch someone's soul, to have it mean something. There are no words. My fangirls relate to that tune because, somewhere along the line, a man has blown up their self-worth. My first boyfriend, Alec the A-hole, dumped me after I refused to put out. He called me a prude, and other things too ugly to mention. Then he spread a pack of lies, telling anyone who would listen that I was useless in bed.

I cried for an entire week, all the black winter nights tumbling into one another. But my revenge tasted sweet. A petty little sore like Alec deserved a loud, public, and in-your-face declaration that my virginity remained intact.

And so, Pop My Cherry was born.

"Thank you." I sign across the cover with my Sharpie. "I came out of hell with that album. That was the first song I ever wrote."

She walks off, clutching it like a gold bar. I feel that high again, that strange electric rush that comes from being seen, even if it's by a stranger. And Brady is making the most of every stranger. He's on his second bottle of wine, fully holding court with two fans laughing and one slipping him her business card with a wink.

Tai leans forward so the young Asian fan with sharp, razor-cut bangs worshipping him can snap a selfie. She pulls back and squeals, "Oh my god, you smell so good."

"Pretty sure you're smelling tour bus and despair," I joke.

"Just keeping the band brand honest," Tai flips back.

The fan cracks up at that, then barges the line to fawn over Brady. I smile, loving how he interacts so genuinely. This may come as a shock, but I like that not all the attention is on me. We are a band, in the end. Half the time, the boys act like barnyard animals and slack off more than I like, but they are in deep. I do miss Audrie, though. She's still not responded to my texts.

And where the hell is JC? He left for the bathroom and is still MIA.

He is hot.

He is talented.

He is *very* good at misdirection.

Did he sense my paranoia about that woman and sweep me off my feet to shut me up? Whatever the case, I'm scanning the corners of the room and keeping watch on the door. Maybe my imagination needs a Xanax. Maybe this other woman isn't a loose end from JC's past? Still, I'm keeping my boots on and edges sharp, just in case.

Because if she shows up again, I'll need more than a killer encore to hold it together.

A rush of fresh air cuts into the hot, stale room. Shae, running a tight clipboard game, steps aside, and a familiar silhouette of heartbreak approaches. JC slides into the empty chair beside me, hair freshly combed, a whisper of cologne trailing off his skin. He glances at me, his expression open. Tender. I feel gravity pulling me, sinking me straight into the gates of erotic hell.

But then I think, *why, or for whom, did he freshen up?*

The next fan in line, a heavy-set Middle Eastern dude, leans in and whispers with bad-breathed earnestness, "Magnifique. Vous êtes beaux tous les deux ensemble."

JC throws me a quizzical look, but I leave him in the dark. Mr. One Language Only can stay on a need-to-know basis. I already know we look beautiful together. And I bet we'll look even better in Zurich.

Preferably horizontal. In a five-star suite, where all I can do is hang on and feel.

Oh, ouais! Apportez-le.

Bring it on.

Chapter Eighteen

JC

A CASTLE IN THE CLOUDS FOR MY QUEEN? SOLD.

I sip my coffee, scrolling through one jaw-dropping photo after another of The Dolder Grand hotel on my phone. Perched atop a forested hill, it commands a serious view of Zurich, and the only available suite is at a "fuck you, peasants" price, but whatever. At a certain point in life, all you do is swap what you own for better, pricier things. And I have money to burn, courtesy of Dad's trust fund pumping five figures a month into my account.

I can splurge on the things that matter.

After booking the room, I kick my feet onto the coffee table, savoring the quiet. Gia and the boys prowl Zurich, leaving me alone in the bus to catch up on emails: George Altman—all hot and bothered to work with me—and two indie bands with an ungodly number of generic songs pleading for me to spice them up. Sawyer lands late tonight, and he's angling for brunch with Gia and me tomorrow. The

Paris reviews are on fire, and he's already planning to spin her trajectory straight into the heavens.

It's coming, only a matter of time.

Gia's charisma lands true. She's authentic, someone you immediately want to watch win. Fans love that big, creative energy bubbling beneath her skinny jeans, her full-volume charm making her too easy to fall in love with.

And because chemistry is an alchemic thing, for reasons I don't completely understand, this is where I find myself: captivated by a fireball almost half my age who's blazed her way into my heart. I recognize the danger; I've spent months guarding myself from her pull. But Gia is where fantasy meets every day with a hefty dose of senseless obsession.

The formula tonight? Get my passion under control. Shake off the apprehension of making love to pure white-hot zeal. Not that Gia's a maneater (okay, maybe she is, if I believe Tai and Brady's wild stories), but every guy has trade secrets and signature moves. Classified shit that makes us, us. No one's complained so far, and I'd like to keep the bar high.

Hence, the over-the-top hotel.

No way we're slumming it on our first night together. She needs to understand that she's not some backstage fling. What I'm feeling is fucking real.

As real as the text notification that pops up on the screen.

Holy crap.

It's Heath Lorrie, my old bassist.

We've kept in touch, do the LA lunch scene every now and then, but it's eleven in the morning here and two a.m. LA time. He swapped the grind of music life for the classic three-pack of mortgage, wife, and kids, and is asleep before midnight seven days a week.

Or so I thought.

HL: Hey, bud! Looking good on the tour. Royal Albert Hall. Fuck, man, did that bring back memories!!!

JC: Why are you awake?

HL: Caitlyn swallowed a LEGO piece. Just got back from emergency. Four hours of hell.

JC: Shit. Is she alright?

HL: Already asleep. Fucking four-year-olds. Hate them. LOL.

I crack a smile. Heath loves being a father. It must beat his thankless job as manager of Pasadena's fine dining haven, The Olive Garden.

JC: What's up?

HL: Amber pinged me on Facebook. She asked for your number.

An icy chill runs down my back. Exes don't just show up out of nowhere, but what the hell does Amber want to talk about after thirteen years?

HL: Is it cool to share? I know things didn't end well with you two.

That's an understatement. I sent our relationship to the great smashed hearts graveyard in the sky.

JC: What else did she say?

HL: The usual surface shit. Hi. Hope life is good.

HL: Haven't replied to her yet. I can say we've lost touch. Whatever you want.

I take a long swallow of coffee. As much as I dreamed of us reconnecting during that one painful year, I've moved on. So why was I on pins and needles during the meet and greet, gritting my teeth every time Shae opened the door for a new batch of fans to descend? Even this text chain floods my chest with guilt.

More of it.

Before Gia took off with the boys this morning, she casually threw out—*Hey, did you notice the older lady in the front row last night? She's been tracking the tour.*

It was a vague question directed at no one specific, although I knew it was one hundred percent aimed at me.

And I tried to sound just as casual. *"The next Gia Barlow superfan."*

And she said cuttingly, *"More like a JC superfan."*

Then Tai saved my ass with, *"Maybe one day, Tai and Brady get a single fucking fan."*

I hightailed it into the shower to let the trio duke it out.

Classic middle child: I avoid conflict like shit on the sidewalk. But I can't dodge Amber forever. Whatever she wants, I need to nip it in the bud. I can't have her hanging over my head when Gia and I are this close to happening. And what's next? Ambushing me outside after a show? Hello fucking awkward.

My fingers fly across the phone to respond.

JT: I'm sure she just wants to catch up. Pass it on.

HL: Consider it done.

I pause, something else flickering in the recesses of my brain.

JT: What's her Facebook handle?

Heath sends the link, and my stomach drops. Like every other creeper, my Facebook account uses an alias name. Why didn't I think to look for Sally Marshall, the fake name Amber used whenever we checked into hotels? There it is: a private account with fifty-four followers. The profile picture is her old Ludwig kit.

My phone pings again.

HL: What's the scoop? U in Gia's band permanently?

Welcome to my existential crisis. Forget Sawyer's Italian loafer on my ass, shoving me into the spotlight. Or that my interest in touring long-term is essentially nil. But the idea of Gia on the road without me triggers a black hole of jealousy in my heart.

JT: Not sure.

HL: You still have it, bud. We could've been huge. But no regrets. Ping me when you're back!

I set down the phone, my hand trembling. Suddenly, I'm thrust into this: scouring through ancient news and raking over the sedimentary layers of shared wounds. Not high on my list of priorities.

Not tonight.

Our night.

But Dad always drilled into me: *Be prepared for everything.*

Like it or not, the ball's in motion.

Unfortunately, defense was never my strong suit.

I track Gia down at noon in a funky bar on the Limmatquai, a trendy shopping street not swarming with stuffed-shirt bankers. For noon on a weekday, the Swiss are remarkably alcohol-friendly. The place is packed. And Gia looks like fine art reimagined by rock and roll—one of those untamed beauties of the Renaissance with a tumble of hair and secrets in her eyes, drinking rum and Coke.

I slide onto the barstool next to her and do a once-over of my surroundings. Chrome fixtures, heavy on the crisp white paint. A lone waitress juggling drinks and trendy hipsters.

"How did you find this place?" I ask.

"Google," she says. "So far, worth the hype." She tips her highball glass in my direction. "Better catch up; you're two drinks behind me."

I laugh. As if anyone could keep up with the rocket named Gia. "Better slow down, champ. Day drinking creeps up on you."

"Did you get your nap on?" she asks, biting back a smirk. "Wouldn't want you yawning during the show."

"Is this where the old jokes start?"

"You're not old; you're classic."

"That really helps."

A bartender with over-sized sideburns shuffles over, checking out Gia while I order a Pilsner and another rum and Coke. Generic Euro pop warbles softly through speakers.

"Did the boys ping you?" she asks. "It sounded like they had debauchery on the brain."

"Yeah, Brady tried to corral me. They're checking out the red-light district."

Gia tilts her head. "You passed that up?"

Read My Rights tore up this town, once upon a time. We tagged every hash bar and peeler joint, like any pack of teenagers cut loose in Europe would. Great memories, and not even one I plan to share at this juncture.

I shrug and spin a coaster on the marble-topped bar. "Been there, done that."

"Even the live sex joints?"

I shoot her a look. "I have zero interest in watching strangers get it on."

Gia props an elbow on the bar, resting her head in the upturned hand. I get the distinct feeling she doesn't believe me.

"What?" I ask. "Are you surprised to hear that?" It slips out more aggressively than intended, all the Amber crap brewing in my mind. I tuck my hair behind my ears, a nervous tic that crops up whenever I feel pressure muscling around me.

"It's a revelation," she says. "You never talk about what's going on in your heart. And I know you have one. I felt it pound hard the other night."

The memory makes me a bit dizzy. The world felt like it was crashing around us in the bus. I was hers—fully, completely. I drop my gaze, but I am very aware of her watching as heat seeps onto my cheeks.

"Speaking of personal stuff…" I redirect the conversation back to her. "You haven't told me where the *Terminator* nickname came from."

Gia lifts a brow. "Is this a tit for tat? I share first, then you?"

"Most of my life is splashed across the internet. You have an unfair advantage."

Her velvety red lips curl into a smile. "Just the way I like it."

"So, then, Miss Schwarzenegger…" I face her straight on. She's not getting out of this.

The bartender sets our drinks down, and Gia waits for him to leave before she starts in a low, measured voice. "Our high school had this talent show every year. I applied in eighth grade. Mama wanted me to sing one of her original songs. Insisted I learn how to collaborate." She sips her drink before continuing. "I rehearsed it, got feedback from my music teacher. She said the song was dated, not right for my voice. Said I was good enough to win, but not with Mama's song."

Her eyes slide to mine. I think I know what's coming.

"I swapped it with one of mine. Terminated her song without asking permission. And I won. Standing ovation."

"How did that go over?" I ask.

She smiles cryptically. "Mama was in the audience. Her rage was biblical."

"Ouch. Real-time termination."

"She grounded me for a month. Called me The Terminator instead of Regina the entire time."

"For real?"

Off my genuine shock, she says, "I'm telling ya, she's a piece of work."

We both drink and stare silently into our glasses. Can't say I'm surprised. Brady and Tai have made overtures to Gia, the steamroller, collaboration a four-letter word. In the case of the talent show, was she protecting herself from her mother's sabotage, or is she incapable of partnership? I've seen the controlling side of her.

Plan to turn the tables on that dynamic tonight.

But first…

"Have you considered that she might be jealous of you?"

She shoots me a sharp look, her face slowly reddening as she realizes that I've steered us straight into the truth. "Of course she is," she finally says. "That's what makes it so hard. I bet the idea of my success scares the shit out of her."

I think for a minute while she trains that expectant gaze on me. "Knowing that, maybe you don't battle so hard. Show her how much music means to you. That's your common ground. Lean into it."

A dude in faded overalls appears out of nowhere, interrupting our flow. He slides onto the stool next to Gia to order a drink, tossing his wavy hair as a signal that he's got moves. I flash him a look. Easy, tiger.

"Anyhow, there's the story." Gia nudges her knee against mine, asking, with heartbreaking sincerity, "Do you still like me?"

I slide my gaze off Mr. Overalls to look at her. She's crashed my world of normal, and something beyond her sheer physical appeal makes me turn to jelly inside.

How can she be asking that question?

"I liked you from the moment I saw you in The Troubadour. That hasn't changed." I drink down a healthy chug of beer as if I can drown out the vivid memory of her that's haunted me ever since. "But tell me, what did you learn from the talent show?"

Gia picks at the hole in her ripped jeans. Takes her time before replying. "That I need to be a team player. I was struggling, doing everything on my own. Then I connected with Brady and Tai, and Audrie stepped in. The momentum shifted."

She looks back up at me, and there's something raw in her eyes. "But I'm still scared of letting go. Of trusting someone else to care as much as I do. Because what if they don't? What if they let me down?"

I feel that truth land in my chest. She's just described my exact fear —the reason my band fell apart, the reason I've been holding back with her.

"Yeah," I say quietly. "I know that feeling."

Gia studies me. Somehow, I know the question she plans to ask before it slips out. "So what happened with Read My Rights?"

I become aware once more of the dryness in my throat and take another swill of beer, but it's suddenly harder to swallow. Every night I say nothing, the lie grows a little larger. I can't be with her without her knowing the truth. But I've waited this long, and one more night won't matter.

I hope.

"Remember what I told you at my condo? My Dad took every opportunity to shine the spotlight on me. He dragged me out to play at the office Christmas party and corporate events. Don't get me wrong," I'm quick to add, "music turned out to be my thing. If he'd put a tennis racket into my hand instead, maybe I'd be chasing a different dream. Who knows? Luck of the draw, I suppose."

The disco beats suddenly fade out, and I lower my voice to match the quiet. "He lived vicariously through me, and it was in his nature to keep pushing. Eventually, I snapped. Walked away from everything he wanted for me. Or, truthfully, for himself." I pause, the rest of it, the whole truth, lodged in my throat. "That's the short version, anyway."

Gia waits, letting silence do its slow, surgical work. Her brows settle into a flat line as she thinks. "Are you here because of me, or him?"

In my peripheral vision, the bartender clocks us, calculating his chances.

Take a number, buddy.

"You, obviously."

Something in her expression shifts. "How come you didn't hit me up after The Troubadour? It felt like we had a connection."

I feel my cheeks catch fire, redness betraying me. I look away. "The usual. Fear."

"Of what?"

She sets her hand on mine and stays silent, waiting for me to go on. But I don't.

To chase her meant to chase all my forgotten dreams, to be branded a hanger-on, a starfucker, a desperate wannabe.

Or something worse.

I squirm on the stool before I slide off. "I need to use the bathroom."

Scanning the far end of the bar, I feel floaty and disconnected, like I'm having an out-of-body experience.

"You're acting mighty defensive," Gia observes.

My own laugh catches me by surprise. It's perfect, really, exactly the comment I deserve. I'm guilty of stepping closer, only to retreat, all the growing layers between us getting denser and more complicated.

"This from a woman doing everything in her power to tear my defenses down."

Gia smiles and tugs on my jacket, caging me between her spread legs. She covers my heart with her hand. I hold my breath, and the only sound in my ears is white noise. When she touches me, nothing else matters.

"See what I mean?" Her voice is the barest sound. "You have a heart. And it beats loud and true." She searches my eyes, like there's an unintended answer buried in them. "Tonight, no holding back. We get real with each other, K?"

The bar suddenly smells different, like when the top note of a perfume fades into a smokier, more mysterious secondary layer. I'm already in a weakened state from earlier, when Gia strutted around the bus half-naked, and my breath slowed until my lungs practically stopped working.

Oh, I like you, Gia. Too much, in fact.

Thing is, I haven't been upfront about Amber, the song, or my intentions for it. Gia hasn't brought it up in the context of tonight, and I'd feel less wary if we didn't agree to make it a warped deal point for intimacy. I don't want to be the incidental sitting between her and the song.

I want her to like me for me.

I need to be enough.

Because I wasn't once before, and it almost killed me.

Chapter Nineteen

Do not come home pregnant.

Mama's famous last words, fired like a warning shot, the morning I left for Europe. But I'm not stupid about risk. When I float through the doors of the hotel tonight, birth control will be locked and loaded. For thirty francs, I bought the world's tiniest box of condoms.

Nothing's cheap in Switzerland, including peace of mind.

I shake off a shiver, waiting for the tram on Bahnhofstrasse. It's cold but sunny, the perfect weather for a wander around the lake before sound check. I close my eyes for a moment, anticipation running riot through my veins.

JC didn't mind when I cut out early from the bar, saying I had some personal shopping to do. He seemed rattled, and I felt a near-blinding relief when he said he couldn't wait for tonight. I was worried I poked too hard, pressing for details. But JC opened up more than he ever has. He put himself back together almost immediately, shutting our conversation down abruptly, his eyes doing a careful circuit of my face.

It almost felt like he didn't trust me to know his truths.

Oh, JC. I want to sink my teeth into you and never let go. Tell me all your secrets. Burn me into your soul.

I'm so lost in my thoughts about tonight that I almost miss my tram. I scramble on board, the doors nipping closed behind me. Two women my age sit on the bench next to me, laughing at some private joke. My heart turns heavy. Not a word from Audrie, and where is my BFF when I need her?

I look at my phone, cold and silent. Just as I lie to myself, saying it doesn't matter, the screen lights up with a FaceTime request. My silly high-pitched laugh is the sound of all the stress leaving my body. Some other petty Gia might ghost Audrie to prove a point, but this Gia needs advice to guide me through the biggest event of my life.

I barely get out a "Hey, girl," before she unloads, words tumbling out on top of each other.

"Oh my god, Gigi! I'm so, so sorry. Long story, but Paul surprised me with this trip. We took a float plane, a helicopter, and then a boat to this remote lodge. I lost my phone and just got it back from the float plane people. But holy fuck, fuck, fuck, you guys are lighting it up. Talk to me!!!"

Like a little girl handed the biggest gift at her birthday party, I can't stop grinning. Why did I ever think she'd bail on me?

I dish every juicy tidbit in glorious, graphic detail—the cities, the crowds, JC, and me. She laughs until she snorts at the story of JC diving onto the floor for a fake contact hunt.

"You two are *dirty*. He sounds fun." Audrie sighs, a little wistfully, if I'm not mistaken.

"Paul isn't fun?"

"Of course," she quickly says, "but it's millionaire fun. Those people."

"Do you feel like you don't belong?"

She clears her throat before answering, "Sometimes. I'm younger than all his friends, and most of them are married with kids. I mean, they're cool. We're having fun." She plasters on a smile, but I can read between the lines.

The Seattle tech dudes speak a different language; they're a different breed. Paul and his hedge fund buddies drunkenly stumbled into our gig at The Showbox in downtown Seattle on a lark. He practically drooled on Audrie, all starry-eyed with lust. Got her number and made his move. Not saying what they have together isn't real, but if you fall in love with a guitar player, and a year later, music is nowhere in her life…

Audrie flashes a smile. "Enough about me. When are you two making it official?"

I suddenly feel all sparkly. "JC got us a hotel room tonight."

"What? Are you shitting me?"

"I'm sending you a link to the hotel. It's insane. Like James Bond would stay there."

The tram stops at Bürkliplatz, a quaint lakeside park. I exit and hurry across the street, drinking in the majestic mountains, the lake at my feet. Will it all look and feel different tomorrow? I feel that tug of inevitability. A profound sense that my life is changing, like hers.

"Gigi!" Audrie screeches. The eagle has landed. "This is a castle!"

"Right? Fully prepared that they frisk us at the front door."

"Are you ready?" she asks, the intonation clear.

I take a deep breath. She can read me like a book. "I think so."

"He knows, right?"

"I'm not saying anything until it's too late. When he can't back out."

She peers at me from the screen with that mothering look she's perfected over the years. "Cashing in a v-card is a big deal. And from everything you've told me, JC strikes me as the kind of guy who wants to know in advance."

She's right, and it deflates my bubble of confidence. But it's taken us six months to get here, and I'd hate to be completely undone by a little thing like virginity. More importantly, how does *that* conversation start organically?

Audrie pulls me back with a sharp, "Hello?"

"Yeah, you're right," I say distractedly. "I'll bring it up."

Meaning, I'll drift through the moment slightly drunk. I can't lose this night to fear.

"What about supplies?" she presses.

I pull a face. It's like she's ticking off boxes on her Virgin Checklist. "I'm not showing up with a suitcase full of dildos and lube, if that's what you mean."

"No, silly." Her voice quiets. "You might bleed after."

I plunk myself onto a bench, rubbing my forehead. Great. Now there's that to worry about. Stains on hotel bedsheets come with the territory; bright red ones, however, scream very unsexy.

And alarming if you don't expect it.

Just my luck. My plan to lie naked in JC's arms as a beautifully deflowered princess now involves worrying about leakage. I wonder if all the new-age feminists who claim god is a woman thought their arguments through.

"If you don't hear from me until tomorrow," I say, "it's all good."

Audrie chuckles. I texted her once at ten in the morning, asking how her date the night before went, and the little slut texted back, *"I'm still on it."*

"If it's all good," she says with a wink, "your phone is the last thing you'll be thinking about."

♫

Three hours later, we finish sound check, and I'm ready for some hot tea with lemon to soothe my throat. Maybe a hot shower, because the one in our dressing room is twice the size of the one on our tour bus.

On the way into the bathroom, I bump into Brady, literally, as he exits a stall.

"Hey. How was your red light special?"

"Okay." He shrugs, nonchalant. "You've seen one pair of tits, you've seen them all."

I laugh. "Am I talking to the real Brady?"

He fluffs his hair in the mirror and says flatly, "Do you even care?"

I try to find his eyes in the mirror, but he evades mine. Barely said a word to me during sound check. "Anything you want to talk about?"

Brady spins around, lighting up a spliff he'd tucked behind his ear. After a monster inhale, he blows a long stream of smoke and offers me a hit. Not sure why—drugs aren't my thing.

I decline, and he says, "Kayla pinged me again. She'd be fire for the band."

Kayla is Kayla Sloane, one of the guitarists we auditioned before JC committed. She's a shredder and seems like a good egg. But still…

"I said we wait until after the tour," I remind him. "I don't have the bandwidth to think about it."

His eyes narrow. "Is there some side deal you and JC are cooking up? Sawyer coming to town feels awfully convenient."

We all crammed into a taxi to get here, JC mentioning our brunch with Sawyer tomorrow. I don't remember much of the conversation, in all honesty. Not with my leg touching his. How is he so warm?

And how many times do I need to defend myself to Tai and Brady? "Sawyer's coming to schmooze promoters," I inform him. "There are no secret deals, no side bullshit. No one is making moves on my band."

Brady flicks ash onto the floor. "You mean *our* band."

"Yes," I say tightly. "Our band."

We engage in another weird round of eye contact wrestling. I'm in no mood to pick a fight, and Brady's in a mood I can't figure out. Feels like a big, dramatic *Love Island* moment is about to hit.

"JC told Tai about tonight," he finally says. "Hotel lovebirds. You too embarrassed to tell me?"

My cheeks go hot. I didn't broadcast that for a reason. Now it feels like another black mark against me.

"Look on the bright side," I say. "The world is your shag oyster. Just stay out of my bunk."

Brady takes another hit of the joint, talking through his exhale. "Oh, so the rules fly out the window when you're getting it on?"

"Seriously?"

"Be careful, Gia."

I find his eyes, dark and stormy. "Why are you saying it like that?"

"Because JC doesn't need you or us. And you know the biz. A million Sawyers looking you in the eye while lying through their teeth. Ruthless. Scheming. Grabbing what they can."

"JC isn't like that," I insist.

He shuffles closer, smelling like stale beer and attitude. "What makes you so sure?" he asks. "A guy like him doesn't need to slum it with a newbie band unless he sees leverage." His mouth twitches. "I'm not saying I don't like him…"

"I don't have time for this," I cut in, all my happiness from earlier suddenly evaporated. "You and Tai better stop trying to poison me against JC. Just because he's more talented than both of you doesn't mean he has ulterior motives."

Brady looks at me for a long moment, joint dangling comically from his lips. Just me and his gold glitter vest, moccasins, and miles of tanned torso.

"Makes sense you'd cozy up to the guy who's fast-tracking you to where you want to be," he scoffs. "Can't credibly claim to be surprised, can I?"

The strange light in his eyes gives me a shivery little charge of trepidation. I think of his sloppy kiss last year—I assumed it was nothing but a drunk fumble. Lines get crossed all the time between band members.

Half the time, it means nothing.

But the way he's looking at me means everything.

"Hey," my voice hitches, "listen—"

"Guess I'm SOL, huh?" he interrupts. "No trust fund or bougie Porsche. No mysterious legacy to get you all wet?"

He butts out the joint in the sink with vicious stabs. I rein in my anger because I realize Brady's bile is coming from a jealous place. But I need to alter the path this rock is rolling down.

"I like JC for who he is, not for his money or what he owns. And your sex life is more ADHD than you. You know I'm a commitment girl."

"Committed to a guy who's almost twice your age?" He rolls his eyes. "Jesus, Gia. Major daddy vibes."

My mind's a sudden whirlwind, with no anchor for all my spinning thoughts. The vibration in my gut says *don't bring it up*, but the words spill out before I can stop them.

"You don't know the full story."

He leans against the counter, crossing one ankle over the other. "Lay it on me, sister."

I hesitate, swallowing down the tangle in my throat. Can't come up with a lie to save my life. "He wrote this song. A killer single. Perfect for us. And we have this dare going…"

Brady erupts into laughter. "A dare? You serious? Let me guess… transactional fucking?" He sees me blush and howls again, louder. "Wow. You're more of a cold-hearted bitch than I thought."

Somewhere in the hall, I can hear Shae barking at the roadies, but she's not loud enough to drown out the words that sting like acid.

"Brady!" I shove him hard. "That is a shit thing to say. Why are you being such an ass?"

He shoves back harder. Meaner. "Because you deserve it."

I stagger backward, a flurry of emotions rushing through me at warp speed. Brady, violent with me?

"You write songs in your sleep, Gia," he spits out. "You don't need his. And I hate to break this news, but no musician worth their salt gives up their music for pussy. Especially not a Trenton who lives in the back end of the industry." He smiles, an evil grin that spreads across his entire face like a nasty oil slick. "But I would pay money to see his face when his finger's knuckle-deep in your ass and you whip out a contract and pen."

"Fuck you." I'm shaking. Reviled. I feel so small and helpless.

But he keeps on going, crushing salt into the wound. "That chick in the front row you were talking about earlier? The older one? There's something between them, one hundred percent. If I could pick it up from behind the kit, I'm pretty sure you did. JC's no saint. Watch your back. And fuck you too."

He kicks the door open and storms out.

I feel all the blood drain from my face. Brady and I go back to high school, before he slept with every gender and pronoun. I had no clue he liked me *that* way. But the black pain gripping my heart isn't about him.

It's about JC.

He is a mania of mine, and I can never get enough, but he isn't *plotting*, is he? And if he knows that woman, why didn't he cop to it? I looked right at him this morning, asking the question. But he dodged a direct answer, devastatingly hot with his bedhead and sleepy eyes.

Maybe Brady's messing with me just because he can, because he's twenty-three, jealous, and not above *Asshole 101*.

Besides, JC has no reason to lie to me.

Or does he?

Chapter Twenty

JC

Gia wanders down from the second floor of our suite with careful steps on the polished travertine stairs. The shock on her face hasn't worn off.

"The closet up there is bigger than my parents' living room. How much did this place cost?"

I shrug and smile. "A mere pittance."

"You're such a liar. Look at this foyer!" She throws her arms out, gesturing at the vaulted ceiling where a crystal chandelier the size of a Honda Civic hangs. "And I peeked at the room service menu. Who pays a hundred francs for a sandwich?"

If Gia knew what I shelled out for this hotel, she'd spin us out of here and demand a refund from the front desk lady who was as gray and friendly as a photocopier.

"Do you like it?"

She makes a funny sound, spinning the thin silver band on her thumb repeatedly. "I've never been in a place this fancy."

"It looks good on you. C'mere." I open my arms and bundle her in a hug. A muffled "thank you" thrums against my chest, and when she lifts her head, I see the chaos engine that will drive us into the night and all its possibilities.

"Hi," she says.

"Hi."

"Come here often?"

A laugh bubbles in my throat. "Only with you."

Her palm slides under my shirt around my lower back, and when I run a slow hand up her rib cage under her top, she shivers. More nervous than me? Possibly.

"Is this okay?" I ask.

"Mmm, yeah. You smell good. And your eyes are crazy. I can never tell what color they are."

"Pantone's color of the year: Infatuated blue-gray."

Her voice dips low and flirty. "I like the sound of *that*."

She's so warm, rubbing the whole front of her body against mine. My body feels electric. I can barely breathe.

I feather the next words. "I have a surprise for you."

"You need to kiss me first," she says, smiling and rolling her hips against me.

My grip tightens on her waist. Gia's kisses are like physical chemistry distilled to warm lips and reckless tongues. I want her like I crave minor key songs. How my entire body lights up with both is just fucking delicious.

I part her lips, and her tongue plunges against mine. She feels so good, but good isn't the right word—it's too weak, too average. Her mouth on mine is a sweet, slow assault, and every single thing that mattered in my life slips away as our kiss deepens. We moan in unison and Gia trembles in my arms. It feels like I'm holding on to a shooting star desperate to blaze.

When we finally come up for air, she breathes, "Wow. You really know how to kiss."

"Are we done?" I tease. "Time to watch TV?"

"The only thing you're watching tonight is me."

She grins as her hand slips between us to stroke my erection. Every nerve in my body erupts in a cloud of flames. Through gritted teeth, I mutter, "Careful. And yes, to you being the main attraction. But first, surprise time."

I tug Gia and her protest of *No more surprises* into the living room, spreading my arms ta-da style at a silver trolley delivered earlier. Stocked with enough highball glasses to last us a week, frosty cans of Coke, and enough rum to black out on.

"Wow. Spiced. Kraken. Good old Bacardi." Gia's finger drifts across the top of every bottle. "You're spoiling me."

"Actually, I'm just trying to get you drunk."

Gia laughs, then cracks the Captain Morgan, swigging straight from the bottle before she offers it to me. I take a decent pull. It's the good kind of burn.

"No need," she says. "I'm guaranteed putting out."

"Because of the hotel?"

She weaves her hands into my hair, pulling me closer. "Because of you."

I set the rum down and melt into her kiss, our tongues slippery and rum-soaked, Gia demanding more, like she wants me to brand her where no one can see.

Crazy feelings flood my entire body.

The night started in a bit of a funk—Gia's mood was pitch-black. Judging from how scarce Brady made himself pre-show, something went down.

But a ripper performance does wonders for morale.

Without Amber forcing me into the shadows, I played freely. Roused the crowd at the front of the stage, side by side with Gia, guitar behind my head, peeling off notes to match her iconic howl. We veered off the stage arm in arm, easing backstage on cloud nine.

I'd missed that sense of floating away from myself, everything so easy.

Never thought I'd experience it again.

I press Gia against the wall and kiss her deeply, palming her nipple at the same time, coaxing it into a tight bud with slow, devastating circles. She grips my ass, and I can feel it bubbling to the surface, the need to shred her jeans, press her thighs wide, and lick and suck and torment her until the tang of her center on my lips is all I can taste. Watch her thrash and cry out, experiencing it all: the seizing muscles and curled toes, the full body shudder.

"Gia," I scratch out. "Put your arms around me."

Her slender wrists circle my neck, and she's practically weightless when I scoop her up. She burrows her head into my chest with a fluttery sigh.

"This is so romantic."

Keeping track of all the things I want to do with her has been a highly unnecessary drain on my time and energy. Putting one foot in front of the other to climb the stairs is all I can focus on.

I feel her pulse in so many places.

In the bedroom, I lower Gia gently onto the sateen sheets, her dark halo of hair fanning across the pillow. Lace sheers suspended from a circular track on the ceiling whisper to me to ditch the velvet tiebacks and close us in.

Which I do.

When we're cocooned, I kiss her softly. "I want you to remember this night forever."

She blinks up at me. "I will."

I trace a finger across the swell of her lips, down her throat to the V of her T-shirt. A warmth spreads through my chest all the way to my toes. I'm so ready for her, but I wish this bed had a built-in camera so I could snap a memento of her framed in the picture window. The lights of Zurich glitter like fireflies across the still, calm darkness of the lake, and I've never seen anything more perfect.

"Can I undress you?"

She laughs into her palms, failing to hide the nervous grin spreading across her face. "Yes, please."

Both hands work their way under her Joan Jett t-shirt, my fingertips splaying the width of her rib cage, taking the fabric up and peeling it over her hair. I fumble with the clasp of her bra, and the reveal of her breasts sends a tidal wave of sensation over me.

Gia is beautiful; I knew that from day one at The Troubadour. But to take in the specifics of her pink peaks and creamy skin surrounding them is to believe in a black kind of magic.

"That's all you get," she murmurs. "Sorry."

I kiss the crown of her head with a sound of disagreement. "You're all I need. And don't apologize for being you."

For a dreamy stretch of time, I love her breasts with my mouth. Suckle until she moans. I feel a different kind of hunger, a new kind of need. The idea of us, here and now, all the magic dust she's sprinkled on me, and not the six million other guys who would take out my eyes for this chance.

In my peripheral vision, I see the red digital glow of an alarm clock.

So much time and hardly enough.

I press a gentle kiss on the rise of her stomach, and Gia rocks her hips higher with a deliciously dirty moan. When I rest my palm against her low-slung jeans, there's a microsecond of stillness—a last moment of looking at each other. I'm trying not to let my face show what I feel, the enormity of it.

"Are you ready?" I ask.

"What does that mean?" Her question comes out a little rough around the edges.

"We go at your pace is what I mean."

She nods, exhaling a long breath. "Just go slow, okay?"

I unbutton her jeans, tugging the zipper lower. She wriggles free of them with my help, and my mouth goes dry at the sight of her pale, slender body and scrap of scarlet thong. One final layer until she's fully exposed.

"You need to take your clothes off."

I laugh, the directive so genuine, so Gia. "I'm glad someone here is thinking straight."

I peel off my t-shirt and chuck it across the room. Her eyes burn over my torso as they did in my studio.

"You have so many muscles," she says, her voice throatier. "But not the big, stupid kind."

"I have other, bigger stupid things if you're interested."

I wink, and she makes a strange, tight sound, like she wanted to laugh, but it wasn't funny.

"Sure."

I slide my finger past the satin fabric onto her warm, wet center.

Gia shudders, and the air shifts, alive with something unexplainable. When I look at her, there's tension in the corners of her mouth.

"Can I touch you there?" I ask.

"Yes," she says, tight and determined. "Just … keep going."

I sit back, bearing my weight on both heels. Her breathing is shallow, tiny fists bunched in the duvet.

Bracing herself.

I'm trying to figure out what all this means, because it means something. All the dangerous things she did to my body the other night do not add up to this.

"We don't have to do this tonight if it's too soon."

"Of course we do," she insists. "You spent all this money."

"That's beside the point."

"It's fine; I'm fine." She tries to shake it off, but her voice is unsteady. It's like someone telling you it's fine with a tear-streaked face.

A thought crashes in, piercing the dark corners of my mind, and I almost dismiss the impossibility of it.

Until I don't.

"Jesus fuck, Gia." My swallow snags in my throat. "Please tell me you've done this before."

Her vulnerability becomes tangible, something I can feel in the space between us. I search her face, all the uncertainty on it. The longest five seconds of my life pass before she finally imperceptibly shakes her head.

My throat closes off, my chest tightening as I slowly twist myself to sit on the edge of the bed. A thousand different emotions crash through me. I push the heels of my hands into both eye sockets to center myself.

"Why didn't you say anything?" I choke out.

She scrambles up to sit beside me and peels my hands away so she can look me in the eyes. "Because it had to happen one day. And I want it to be with you."

It suddenly feels hot in here, way too fucking hot. Sweat beads in the hollow of my throat. The universe keeps spinning, me unable to stop it.

"Brady and Tai kept telling me you had all these boyfriends."

"I lied," she says, her voice small. "I got close once, but I couldn't do it. Not with him."

I search her face to make sure she understands what I'm about to say. "This is once in a lifetime, Gia. It needs to be special."

"Was your first time special?"

"Not particularly," I admit. "And I kind of regret it."

Losing my virginity had nothing to do with bragging rights. All I cared about was getting my rocks off. Because what fifteen-year-old guy wishes for a real moment instead of a dirty in-and-out in the basement of a girl I didn't really care for. Whoever said youth was wasted on the young nailed it.

Gia kisses my cheek, which must be as white as the sheets. "I won't regret this. I'm ready. I've waited so long. I care about you. More than I fucking should."

Something twists deep in my chest. Her sitting there, lit by the moon, sends a crushing tenderness through me. Full one eighty on all my debauched plans. That ship has sailed. Now we're alone in the harbor, and I'm actually kind of freaked out.

Edgeless and floating.

I swallow hard, trying to keep the waver out of my voice. "I've never taken a woman's virginity."

"Then it'll be a first time for both of us."

She tucks a lock of hair behind my ear, and the fragile clench of my heart feels a little like an exposed nerve. I stare straight ahead, eyes swimming in the dark. All the mindless sex, and not once was I faced with this. I'd like to believe my reaction would've been the same.

"If we do this," I say, "there's no taking it back."

"That's kind of the point."

Climbing onto my lap like I'm her personal beanbag, she scoops my hands in hers, placing both sets onto the warm rise of her breasts. Her dusky eyes lift to mine. "If we keep talking about it, it will only get weirder. I want this," she says, her voice firm, mind made up. "I want you. We're both adults. You have my consent, a thousand percent. Isn't that enough?"

An overflowing amount of enough is what she is. And she's

waited, now offering herself to me, the broken-down guitarist she's breathed new life into. I want to feel the heat of her skin, the fire that courses beneath, the salt of sweat and tears. I want to dip myself into her core and come fucking undone. She has no idea the power she has over me.

"I don't want to hurt you," I whisper.

Suspended in a delicate and meaningful silence, her eyes skim mine. Cradling my face in the heat of her palms, she kills me softly with seven words.

"It'll only hurt if it isn't you."

Chapter Twenty-One

GIA

There. I said it. Six months of fantasies, wants, and wishes blurted out. Desires laid bare, strewn like seeds desperate to blossom. JC slips his hands over mine, and my stomach twists with anxiety. Did I kill the mood? Does he see me now as naive and inexperienced? I have no idea what's coming or how to stop it if it's all wrong.

"Are you sure?" he asks, his voice the barest scrap of sound.

I catch something in his expression, a hot flame of need, and push through the nerves. "As sure as I won't be the next Sabrina Carpenter."

A lightning-quick flash of emotions dances over his face, and suddenly, he's laughing. Laughing! I feel boneless, relief flooding out of me. I didn't realize, not until now, how much angst I've been holding on to. I'm ready to laugh it off if needed, but he meets me here, in the space between serious and playful, pressing a featherlight kiss on my forehead.

"You're sexy when you're funny. And when you're not."

"So, all the time?" I say in my best smoldering voice.

JC wordlessly scans my face. I feel more like myself again, free of the crushing weight but lost in his eyes, each its own cloud of swirling blue-gray smoke.

"Okay then," he says. "We're doing this."

My reply is a tight tremble. "Hell yes."

I love listening to how his breathing changes when his hands roam up and down both arms. The thrill of it beams light into the darkest part of my soul. We're finally here. No JC flirting or come-hither Gia BS. Nothing coded. There is nowhere else to go, and nowhere else I'd rather be.

I lose my next breath with how he kisses me, sensual and soft, tongue sweet and unhurried. Just thinking about what's coming makes me crave his touch. He's older and more experienced. That comes with some advantages.

He kisses along the arc of my throat, lower and lower until his head dips between my breasts. His tongue travels against my hot skin to curl around a swollen nipple, sucking it deep into his mouth.

I can only moan and dig my nails into his scalp.

"You're such a turn on," he murmurs, his breath warm against my aching, tender flesh. "I've never felt like this before."

I blush, feeling wanted and vulnerable and stupidly in need of reassurance. My boobs are beestings, and his lust for them is as true as sunshine in July. "Really?"

"Gia, you're impossible to forget."

The dirty-white light through the lamp shade brightens the hunger in his eyes. It dawns on me in a slow wave. All this time, I've just been trying to keep his attention. Figured he liked prettier and softer women, and a lot less mouthy. Why else didn't he try to contact me after The Troubadour?

Because maybe you poured a drink on his head?

I feel my stomach twist again, gentler this time.

JC finds my eyes. "What's so funny?"

"Nothing," I say quietly. "Everything. What you just said. It's how I feel about you."

He touches my hair, and the broken smile on his lips almost pulls my heart out of my chest. "What the fuck have we been doing all this time?"

I shrug, smiling back. "Being idiots."

He laughs and sits back on his knees. Two gentle hands pull my hips forward, and he lunges on top of me, kissing me hard enough that our teeth clash. I know the hot curve of his ass from the other night, and my hands spread open wide to clutch that fine flesh. And I'm kissing him back with everything I've got.

Possessive and powerful.

When he finally breaks our kiss, he's flushed and breathing hard. Everything's hard.

"Don't move," he says.

JC rolls off the bed and unbuttons his jeans. Flashes of us together in the bus blitz through my mind. I rolled with the punches, too thirsty for him to think straight. But when his jeans fall to the floor, my stomach surges with an ache so specific to him.

We look at each other for a long moment.

Damn, he's beautiful.

Then he strips the boxers off, and I'm suddenly so unsure what to do. The whole big hands, big everything logic is distressingly accurate.

I drag my eyes up to his face. "Wow," is the clever thing I say.

He smiles, crawling onto the bed. He kisses me, slow and dirty, as his fingers hook into the side of my special bought-on-sale panties. So much for those being any highlight. They're yanked off without a second glance.

"Fuck, Gia," he whispers. "Look at you."

I feel so exposed under his hot gaze. Anxious he's measuring me against some invisible standard. I want to please him so bad, and I'm worried I won't. The desire hasn't left—it's still there, warmth low in my belly, awareness of him as a physical presence. Now tangled with anticipation of a different kind. Wondering if it will hurt and what it will feel like.

I watch him drop between my legs. He presses his warm palms flush on my skin, like he's searing bar chords into trembling flesh. Pushing my legs wide, wider, widest. Everything that makes me a woman suddenly bared and there for the taking.

I look down at his face between my thighs, eyes shining, hair falling forward. He's watching me so intently, his skin lit up by the moon.

"If it gets too crazy, let me know, okay?"

Oh, god. This is it.

I bite my lip and tell him I'm ready.

His warm breath gusts against me before his tongue gently licks my seam. I fist his hair, gasping in shock.

"Is that good?" JC murmurs.

It feels like … where are the words? Where do I even begin?

"Amazing," I whisper back. "Keep going."

With my approval, he dips his mouth into the wild, screaming jungle of chaos waiting for him. He sucks my ready little clit into a throbbing bundle of anticipation and stokes the burning desire into a near-fatal level of ache. He ignores my cries from the whiplash of my body brought to the edge of an impending explosion before he backs off. Then he starts tongue-fucking me with deep, wicked strokes.

I moan, my stomach tightening in response. His halo of stubble and the rub of it burns exactly as I imagined.

"JC," I pant.

His mouth suddenly moves off me. "Too much?"

"No!" I clarify, a little too frantically.

He sits up with a lazy twitch of a smile, completely aware of how desperate I sound. I shiver as he gropes through his jeans on the floor, pulling out a condom.

Those eyes are heavy and low when he says, "We're not done. Not by a long shot."

He rips the package open with his teeth, and I'm mesmerized by how a tiny piece of latex engulfs his fullness. He positions himself, and the warmth of him pressing up against me feels huge. I jerk my hips higher, but he grips them and forces me to be still.

"I'll go slow," he says, his voice rough with a deeper edge to it.

He starts to penetrate me with a careful, testing thrust of his hips. I shut my eyes. My whole body begins to shake.

"Gia, are you okay?"

I stare up at the concern etched across his brow. My breath is coming out of my mouth in tiny gasps. "It's fine. It's fine. Are you in? All the way?" I glance down. Fuck. Still miles to go. "What are you, like nine, ten inches?"

He lets out a hazy laugh. "I'll take that, but more like seven. Point two."

"Jameson," I breathe. "Tell me you did not slap a ruler against that thing."

"Of course not, Regina," he says, the tiniest bit amused. "I used the tape measure from my tool kit. Like a real man."

No, no, no!

But yes to our laughter. It keeps me tethered to the moment instead of spinning out into anxiety. This is just beyond.

"I think you need to go deep and get it over with it," I say. "Bottom out."

He nuzzles my jawline with the coarse scratch of his whiskers. "Always so demanding."

"Do not—"

Whatever remains of that sentence dissolves into a juddering gasp as JC sinks to the hilt, the pain sharp and biting. I jerk my hips back involuntarily to relieve the shock of him filling me.

"Gia," he says, his voice sounding far away. "I'm here. I'm with you. Tell me what you need."

A raw ache grips my throat, and I suck in air, panting like a dog in heat. "Shh. Shh. Shh. Just hold me for a minute. I want to feel close to you."

He shifts his hips slightly to ease the pressure. His entire body is trembling with the effort to control himself. "This is crazy," he breathes. "I'm about to explode."

His eyes have wild white rings around them, like a cornered animal, and his nostrils flare as he takes short, erratic breaths. I can smell his male musk, spiked with exertion and that familiar citrus scent.

"Just tell me when," he says with a barely-there whisper. "I'm going to make love to you while I touch you. Is that cool?"

I nod, heat creeping up my neck. I'm having trouble breathing. He pushes up on one arm and pulses, slow and steady, stretching me, pain dulled by the thrill of him throbbing deep inside me. Darkness swirls around us, my blood half adrenaline.

"Fucking hell," I mutter.

"Gia." He swallows hard. "You feel incredible."

His free hand dips to my clit, and he draws precise, maddening circles with his finger pad. My walls squeeze tight around him, a sparkling kind of awareness funneling lower until both of my feet start to burn, toes curling into a tight pinch.

"JC." My voice is thin and weak. "I think it's happening."

"Already?" he rasps. "Fuck. Hold on."

He starts moving in and out of me with less control, heavy burning strokes, the sensation of him spiraling my own desire faster and higher. It feels like he's lit a match to a whole warehouse of fireworks inside me, and the orgasm shimmers on the fringes of my peripheral vision before it slams through me.

A split second of wild muscle-clenching, and I howl at the sky, the pleasure like nothing I've ever known. The room feels like it's cracking wide open, the walls flowering with colors I've never seen before. And I thought I'd heard every sound that could come out of JC, but as he surges against me, as deep as he can go, my name mangled in his cry is a raw melody stripped of all polish.

Then another beautiful chain of explosions rips my heart and mind apart. I'm crying out like a wild thing, and the last of his release trembles out of him, his face twisted with the pleasure rocking his body.

When I go lax, he does too, collapsing on my chest. His fingers, those beautiful things that coax the heart-dropping notes from any guitar, curl in my hair. Stillness surrounds us, as delicate as the French lace curtains and the slow retreat of his heartbeat against mine.

I hear his faint, "Goddamn," but I don't know what to say.

So many things in life exist on a spectrum.

Good, bad. Hot, cold. Up, down.

Positives, and the chances of me recovering from this are deep in the negatives.

Chapter Twenty-Two

JC

Everything feels more vivid and fragile at the same time. Hazy details sharpen into hyper-real focus: crumpled sheets, our mingled scents, liquid fire rippling through my veins. I'm still hard, buried inside Gia, paralyzed from the chaos of release.

A million emotions ball in my throat.

"Hey," I manage with great difficulty. "You okay?" I brush hair from her forehead, scanning her face for signals. "Nothing hurts?"

Gia blinks up at me, eyes deep-sea dark. Swallowing air in deep, earthy gulps. Her entire body, all the precious inches of her skin connected with mine, trembles. "Everything hurts. But in a good way." Then, in a tentative voice, she asks, "Was it okay for you?"

My abs feel shredded. A slow, burning coil of an orgasm snaked through every muscle as I clawed back my instinct to plunder and fuck her. Despite my need, I rode her steadily but also carefully, until her intense arousal caught me off guard. Whimpers funneling into wide-eyed gasps of her own building pleasure. How wildly she came.

No wonder my entire body is a mass of tingling sensations.

I feel this quiet amazement, to be her first.

My heart brims with so many things.

I brush a kiss onto her forehead. "You were perfect." And because Gia seems to be cataloging every micro-expression with a look I can't decode, I ask, "Did you like it?"

A laugh spills from her lips. "It was so fast. But it felt good. *You* feel good."

She molds her hands over my backside, and I shiver, my body a live wire of sensitivity. Her touch feels different now, more tender, more significant. Suddenly nothing feels simple.

And Gia would surely deny needing the surge of protectiveness that rumbles through me, but she has to realize continuing forward now carries completely different stakes.

I should say something. Anything that marks this as a significant moment. But words feel too small, and my throat is tight with things I don't know how to name. I don't want to move yet, but I can feel her ribs expanding beneath me, working for each breath beneath my weight.

I slowly pull out and roll off her, dropping onto my back beside her. I feel slow and delirious, like medication slowly fizzing through my bloodstream, all the unknown emotions I fought free to roam.

"I need to use the bathroom."

Gia's soft voice has an undercurrent that sounds a little soul-baring. Her lashes flicker self-consciously, and my gaze follows hers south, onto the condom streaked with red.

The weight of the silence shifts.

I'm now part of her story in a way that can't be undone. I don't want to make a big deal out of it, but it kind of is. Despite the intense desire to keep her close, a little privacy goes a long way.

"Take your time." My voice is low and thick. "I'll be here if you need anything."

Not one sound in particular makes my heart surge—it's the combination of the soft rustle of the sheets as Gia untangles herself, the patter of her feet across the floor, water running in the shower. My worldview before narrowed to one possibility: living every day as the guy who takes her to wild, dirty heights.

How catastrophically short-sighted.

Because that wasn't just sex; it was ceremonial. Bigger than the act itself. Nothing in my life has ever compared to this moment. Sated and deliciously at peace, my body still trembles with little aftershocks.

Of course, this bliss couldn't last.

My phone pings, and I stare up at the lace curtains, giving my head a little shake.

Really?

Now, of all times?

I debate not answering, but it might be Sawyer or one of the boys. I roll over, reach for my jeans, and tug my phone out of the front pocket. A cold shot of panic zips through me as I stare at the message from Amber glowing in the dark. Is this some cosmic joke?

AD: Can you meet tomorrow night after the show?

The silence stretches, spreading out until it covers the entire room. I squeeze my eyes shut, but the roller coaster in my stomach keeps churning. Part of me is relieved to face this, to put to bed what's been running amok in my mind for years.

The other part is pure resentment.

For an entire year, I waited for Amber to come back to me. To call, email, or send one lousy text to ease my anxiety. I got sweet fuck all. Now she shows up, intruding at the worst possible time. Cold resolve settles over me, and I power off the phone, dropping it on the floor. Amber can wait, wonder, and worry—experience the same shit I did on all those sleepless nights.

I yank the sheet across my torso and try to relax. My thoughts race and scatter. It's a lie to say I genuinely have no idea why she wants to get together. We both made mistakes—painful, misinformed ones. Yes, I'd like to take back everything I said or didn't say, but I've spent too many years excusing her. And now, what I thought might never be with Gia suddenly feels possible.

And Amber's not stealing that from me.

To regain my bearings before Gia returns, I dispose of the condom, tidy myself up with Kleenex from the box on the nightstand, and double-check my phone is off. By the time she emerges from the bathroom, my breathing has steadied. The sky outside glows from the light of the moon, and she's like a shadow crossing the room, quietly crawling into bed to snuggle up to me.

"That was so good," she whispers. "Thank you."

I stroke her still-damp hair, no longer loose-limbed because Amber robbed me of this moment. "I..." Air, breathing—somehow, it's all eluding me. "I booked you a massage tomorrow after lunch."

She shifts to meet my eyes, smiling at me in a way that hurts because she's where I want to be: lost in the high of us. "Really? You make me feel like a queen. Next time will be even better. I promise."

I barely hear her words, my mind spinning to tomorrow night. Seconds tick by before I find my voice, trying to joke my way out of self-preservation mode. "I might need some time."

Gia murmurs, "I'm in no rush," and then we're kissing—deep ones and soft ones, reckless tongue-probing ones. I'm not sure I've ever experienced anything so chaotically powerful. But it's also confusing. I see Amber in my head but feel Gia.

I pull back, lost in a hundred jumbled memories, leaving Gia staring up at me, expectantly waiting for me to say something.

When I don't, she asks, "Are you okay?"

Jesus. This can't be happening.

"Yeah, sorry. I just ... it's all a little overwhelming."

With the softest of touches, Gia palms my cheek. I desperately want to fess up and not be that person skulking behind her back with secrets and drama. Safety and comfort are within my reach, but I'm not sure I can reach for them.

"That's so sweet," she says. "You handled it perfectly. Handled me in all the right ways."

"Good." I mean it with all my heart. "C'mere." I shift slightly so her head rests on my chest then kiss the crown of her hair. Breathe slow and deep to quiet my thumping heart. She snugs closer, spooning her warm body against mine.

For a long minute, we're quiet, two lovers in the dark.

"Hey." She traces the length of my arm with her finger.

"Hi. All good?"

She sighs, and it sounds fatigued but content. "I think I'm going to fall asleep."

I turn my head to press one final kiss on her soft lips. "Sweet dreams, my queen. See you in the morning. And thank you for trusting me."

Gia's sweet face hovers, her eyes blinking up at me. It looks like she's waiting for me to say more. To say what she said to me the other night. But I can't. Not yet.

Soon, though.

Once I clear my heart and my conscience.

We meet Sawyer for lunch at the hotel in a bright, obsessively tidy restaurant called *Saltz*. The view is almost worth the overblown prices. Lake Zurich gleams like a postcard through the wall of windows facing east—pale yellow sun on calm water, mountains soaring over a bright green band of trees.

We're already seated with coffees and laughing at a Mr. Beast video on YouTube when Sawyer strolls in at eleven on the dot.

"Great spot." He takes in the pristine eliteness with a nod of approval. Give him super fussy over frumpy any day. "A little out of the way, but worth it. We could've hopped in the same taxi."

I said nothing about us staying the night. One less thing for him to pounce all over.

"Hi," he says to Gia, who looks improbably beautiful with cheeks flushed a gorgeous shade of orgasms-still-hitting-hard pink. We slept in hard, and she was still sore upon waking, so I let my tongue guide her over the edge while she fisted my hair. Every shift of her body beside mine reminds me of all the good things to come. "And congratulations," he adds. "The buzz is fantastic."

"Thanks," she says, her grin wide and unabashed. "It's been wild so far. *Sooo* good."

There's a moment of silence as Sawyer digests this version of Gia. A current of sensuality that's unmistakable. Her incendiary personality sanded down into this human-shaped container of demure sweetness.

He knows you have to be important to have enemies.

She'd checked that box, and staying in it was what Sawyer expected.

Before he can say anything, the waiter with hair as orderly as the row of chairs spanning the room marches over to drop my breakfast and asks Sawyer what he'd like.

"You already ordered?" Sawyer frowns. If I didn't know him any better, I'd say he sounded hurt.

Gia checks her chiming phone. "Time to hit the spa for my massage. FYI, they gave us a late check-out." She bumps my shoulder. Winks. "I texted the boys for a dinner hook-up."

"Cool," I say. "Meet you upstairs when you're done. Have fun."

She moves forward as if she's about to kiss me, then hesitates, gets up and wraps her arms around a startled Sawyer instead. "Thanks for coming. Appreciate it. Tonight will be a ripper."

She flounces away, and it's doubtful Sawyer will ever be able to match the look of genuine shock on his face. A good rule of thumb is to pull out the rug from underneath him before he does the same to you.

Harder than it sounds.

"Check out?" he repeats. "You're staying here?"

"Just for last night."

"That didn't take long." Sawyer's expression now broadcasts I-told-you-so triumph. "I figured you might wait at least a week."

I shrug, salting my eggs. "We wanted out of the bus."

"And?" He leans forward, all boys-club curious. Pantomimes some lewd act. "Is Gia in the sack like wrangling a feral bobcat?"

A flash of annoyance boils my blood. I want to smack him for that statement and refuse to dignify it with a response.

Well, not a kind response anyway.

"Fuck off."

A starched couple side-eyes us from two tables over with an air of moral superiority. Well, eyes me, specifically. Sawyer looks every inch the accomplished and well-compensated entertainment industry executive that he is. I look like a vagrant who accidentally wandered in among the rich and famous.

"Someone's got it bad," he teases.

I cut my bacon strip and fork a bite into my mouth. "Not another word. I'm serious."

"What's the bus mood?" he ignores my request. "This stuff can blow up the tightest band. Especially when she gets the golden treatment."

"It's fine," I lie. "They kind of knew what was brewing."

"Which means *you* knew."

I know what he's implying, but a noncommittal shrug is all he gets.

Sawyer sips his water, staring me down over the rim. "Does she know about your resurrection?"

"No." My eyes drift past his to the view of the snow-capped Alps. "I'm not convinced that's the right path. Plus, a reminder: my soul isn't yours to sell."

Sawyer gives me the look he's recently perfected—total pain in the ass. "Bigger men have fallen from the pussy effect. Lust only lasts so long. Do me a favor and think with your head, not your cock."

It takes every fiber of my will not to explode. If I give in to it, Sawyer wins the inevitable pissing match. He always wins. My older brother doesn't participate in team sports because doing so would one day distract him from the larger goal of his life: to be the last prick standing.

What I can offer on the flip side is a powerful look of disgust.

"Did it cross your mind that I might actually like her?" I ask, and the weight of that admission doesn't go unnoticed—even by me.

Sawyer considers me for a moment, like he figures I might deserve an actual, thoughtful answer. "Forced proximity, alcohol, and high times, JC. Vegas shotgun weddings are built on those very founda-tions. Touring relationships fall into the same category," he adds, as if my liking Gia is a flaw in my reasoning. "Who else are you going to like?"

I sympathize with any woman who dates Sawyer. The wine-and-dine fairy tale of everlasting love is a script to produce, not a life he actually lives. If a free blow job were on the line, he'd happily stick his dick through a random hole in the wall.

"Hell, maybe it's real," he muses on. "But ask yourself—if you didn't see her every damn day, would she still have that shine?"

Shine? I think. *How about glowing brighter than diamonds?*

This morning, on our private deck, Gia and I breathed the raw January air, bundled in robes, fingertips tracing each other's lips. The sun looked impossibly golden. Church bells pealed like angels. I'd never experienced the kind of peace that comes after everything has been said or doesn't need to be.

Holding on to Gia in a foreign city, in the gentle devastation of a new beginning, felt like a form of heaven. I refuse to let Sawyer diminish my feelings.

"What time are you coming to the show?" I ask, tired of speaking in his code.

"The opener sounds dreadful, so scratch that. I'll pop in backstage pre-show. And by the way…" He grins with a thumbs-up gesture. "Props. The reviews are smoking. You're magic on stage. Don't forget that. You can make a killing with the right tour. Six months on the road and, boom, fat bank account."

"It's not about the money anymore."

"Yeah, yeah," he says, carefree in his dismissal of me. "That's what all you creative types say. Gia's on fire right now, sure. But staying relevant? That's a whole different game in this market. And we both know you've elevated her to this level. Not saying it's entirely unearned…"

But he is.

For the record, I love my brother, but I do harbor secret fantasies about knocking him with my Les Paul, sending that smug attitude flying.

"Oh, do you remember Jordan Bettman?" he pivots, like he does, from one topic to another without preamble. "The guy running our LA office?"

"Vaguely." I imagine another fat cat in a suit. "Why?"

"He's retiring. Instead of the hiring runaround, I'm bumping Bettina to run the show in Vancouver. You and I in the City of Angels. I'll crash at your place until I get set up."

That jarring news makes me sit up straighter. Usually, Sawyer is as empty of surprises as a cover band. "Fun times."

A smile grows across his face. "Right?"

I throw him a thousand-watt skeptical stare. Wrong. Way wrong. I unfortunately witnessed Sawyer changing one day at the gym into sheer black briefs riding high in the back, digging into the crack of his ass. The front narrowed to a snug little pouch that made me squirm.

I'll take staying on the road indefinitely for a thousand, Alex.

Chapter Twenty-Three

GIA

Am I losing my edge? Getting soft and pampered, every whim catered to. A masseuse threw her entire body weight into unknotting my shoulders, and a crisply dressed blond served me peppermint tea in a dainty cup as if I were royalty.

But behind small, polite smiles, I wait for the question—how did a tattooed rock and roller stumble into their palace spa? It doesn't come, and the lack of judgment is a small relief on a day when nothing feels insignificant.

I sink deeper into the eucalyptus steam, hugging my knees to my chest, still in the depths of all this newness. I've never felt so intensely aware of my body in my entire life.

JC leaves me feeling feminine and wanting to be spoiled.

When he slid his finger up the center of me this morning, I was barely in control of the sounds leaking out of me. Then his tongue took over, and the world tilted into something startling and new.

"My queen," he'd said, his voice low and reverent between his fearless devouring. "Come for me."

Little old me did obey, for once. Twice, actually.

Now I'm thinking the most ridiculous thing.

That the man who peppered kisses down my torso and let his erection die a slow death in the name of my recovery, could maybe, possibly be falling for me. Gia from yesterday, uptight and riddled with doubt, feels like a lifetime ago.

Did I really spend six months flailing around like a headless chicken, pretending to be cool about JC? Too guarded to risk my own heart?

Yes, that was me. God, that's embarrassing.

I curl tighter in the steam, smiling to myself.

It's wild, tracing how we even got here.

Audrie, gutting the band. JC, all sexy sin, sitting across from me in the boardroom, my promised cargo delivered by Sawyer. Then our first gig in the tumbleweed town of Osoyoos, BC. Stars blanketing the sky, music rolling over my skin like thunder, our so-called stunt becoming crazy lore. JC sprinting across the stage, sliding between my legs mid-solo. The water I'd just chugged sprayed in a perfect arc from my mouth into his, defying every law of physics, but caught in hundreds of videos to prove otherwise.

My brain is nothing but fantasies of hot summer nights and the crowd going bananas when steam suddenly blasts from the faucets. I watch it rise, water transformed, suspended in the air. Feel the magic of that night dance on my skin like the mist surrounding me.

Then it hits me like a physical thing.

My breath catches, knocked clean from my chest.

Water falling, no one but me to catch it. Drowning alone in the magic.

The lyrics hit me all at once, and I feel dizzy.

Wait. Wait one hot minute.

That's not a metaphor. That's Osoyoos. That's JC catching what spilled from me.

That's *us*.

My heartbeat starts jackrabbiting all over the place. I press my face into both palms, not wanting to hide, but protecting myself from the possibility that I've got it all wrong again.

But my mind races, rewinding and recontextualizing everything through this new lens. I travel back to that afternoon in his studio, seeing his expression, so genuine, staring right at me when he sang those lines. And the sexual tension thrumming between us after he stripped his shirt off in the studio was so molten, it almost melted my brain.

Suddenly, all the other lyrics pile up in my brain like snowflakes in a storm.

We're strangers, every breath pulling us near. Then I'm alone in the shadows, wondering what's unclear.

I start pacing, doing laps on the tiles. My body doesn't know what to do with this energy. It all fits.

Slow down, Gia. Slow it down.

I stand still in the dense steam, taking the temperature of what I'm dealing with here. It's not a crime to write a song about someone; we'd have no music if that were the case. But it feels vaguely criminal for JC to be so stealthy. To harbor secret feelings and write a song about me? There's a nakedness to that. To unknowingly be someone's private muse.

Is that why he's holding on tight to the song?

I need answers. Not right now. Not with the sting of Brady's accusation still hovering on my skin like a stain. I'm not a scheming, cold-hearted bitch. Liking JC and his song are two separate things, living in different chambers of my heart.

Or are they?

I scan my soul for the truth and find it laughing in my face.

It's so obvious now, my ridiculous simpleton hack. The metaphor of JC giving me his song as a warped way for me to believe he was giving himself to me. And he's played along, humoring me, like the beautiful soul he is.

The truth is, a song never senses if I'm feeling frustrated and knows the right things to say to make me feel better. It doesn't push me to sing deeper, rawer, while I push everyone else around. It most certainly does not leave me breathless and high on orgasms.

And as Audrie said, a song has not once made me forget about my phone.

I breathe deep, smiling like a fool. A small part of me knows the real world waits for no one, and I need to step back inside of it. But this is not something to think my way out of.

And JC? He had better prepare for an interrogation, because I have finally figured it out. But first, the physical reality of him waits for me on the fifth floor.

Fuck, he is making me so hot.

Who knew losing my virginity would be this amazing?

♬

I hate leaving the hotel. When the taxi pulls away, I refuse to glance over my shoulder. Neither of us utters a word during the descent into the city, the patient, relentless raindrops pattering on the window. I lean onto JC's warmth, his arm snug around my shoulders, carrying the scent of us with it. I feel like a butterfly emerging from her cocoon, cautious about how far I can fly on my untested wings of womanhood.

But I'm one hundred percent certain something inside me has changed.

Thanks to him.

Sex with JC was even better the second time. I learned things. That he likes deep, punishing kisses and me on all fours, taking me from behind. His fullness slid into my body in long, smooth strokes that pulled moans and curses from him. He took his time, careful while going deep, every inch of him teasing that delicious spot inside me until the pinprick of light buried within me shattered into a blaze of white-hot heat.

He held me tight after, singing in a rich, low voice and stroking my hair.

Like he is now.

I sneak a glance at the classic lines of his profile silhouetted against the window. I want to challenge him on the song, the urge so thick, I can practically feel it pressing against my ribs. But I settle my mind, letting the memory of our lace-curtained kingdom sear itself into my heart.

Because there's more to come. More to look forward to.

Top of the list: a performance tonight guaranteed to scorch the crowd. Emotion pouring out of me, so sticky-sweet, bonding with every soul for two electric hours. Burn like wildfire so they'll leave wrecked and breathless, wondering what the fuck hit them.

And I'll give JC a grin with a touch of warning thrown in.

He is mine, whether he knows it or not.

Because he played his hand with that song.

And when it comes to Gia, give me an inch, and I'll take a mile.

Every time.

♫

Backstage before the show, JC and I have this brief moment of eye contact where it feels like he's thinking something he doesn't want to say out loud. During sound check, I sensed a transition in him. He texted furiously, his back turned. Claimed he needed a walk to help him "clear his head." Meanwhile, my brain was scrubbed clean of any thought other than his naked body.

He returned, shaking rain off his hair and kissing me, hot and open-mouthed. Thanked me again for the best twenty-four hours of his life.

None of that helps.

He's napping on a threadbare loveseat, and my mind drifts to how soundly he slept beside me on the flight to London. Curled up under his blanket, eye mask on. The soft sounds he made when I stroked his hair every time Queen Bitch Flight Attendant strolled past. How he kept a straight face when my hot mess of a suitcase tumbled into Heathrow baggage claim like a drunk late for the party, his sleek black TUMI luggage practically groaning in disgust beside him.

How his hands steadied me this afternoon as my body started to come undone.

Fuck!

The anxiety kicks in, a big knot in my stomach, like I'm waiting for something bad to happen all over again. JC acted a little strange last night, like he was spooked about something other than us. Why can't it be as simple as *I like you; you like me,* and *clear the decks*? Why can't he be humming to himself and throwing me winks?

"Yo. Can we talk?"

Brady sidles up to me at the craft table, eyelids smeared with the same rose-gold glitter highlighting his cheeks. For once, I feel prettier than him. Shagged into a perfect, beautiful woman, now stress-eating Lindt chocolate balls by the handful.

I shoot him a look of reproach. "Talk or talk shit about me?"

"C'mon, Gia," he says, shoulders slumping with his voice. "Cut me some slack. You don't think I deserve a second chance?"

He pokes my shoe with his moccasin. Does he expect a kind of delicacy after crossing a boundary? I know all his secrets and I've never thrown them in his face when we fight. There's the wrong side of the tracks, then there's Brady Bowen, the homecoming king of dirt poor. Stealing socks just to have a pair and surviving on food bank donations. His single mom slung burgers for chump change when she wasn't struggling with her mental health. The band saved him. Some respect is in order.

"Gia!' Brady presses again, patience of a gnat, persistence of a mosquito.

I feel the weight of observation, and sure enough, Tai scopes us out surreptitiously from the corner while pretending to read his novel. He tips his head in a gesture of *you know what to do.*

Tai and I had our own furious text storm after the Brady blowout. He always does his best to wrangle my hotheadedness, to varying degrees of success.

"The hall," I say in a tight voice, pointlessly indicating the door.

Brady follows me out. I spend five seconds trying to find the low-drama way to handle this. Band politics and unrequited love are a toxic mix, and this version of Brady—looking wretched and lost—is seven shades of shittiness.

I can't like him the way he likes me.

"How was the hotel?" he starts, awkward as hell.

"Next question."

He sighs dramatically. "I'm trying to make things better."

"How about not calling me a gold digger?"

He blinks, a red flush creeping up his neck. "I'm sorry. That was uncool. Never thought I'd be the jealous guy. Surprise."

I blink, caught off guard by his apology and the sincerity in his voice. He meets my eyes like he's ready to own the damage. We can either be crushed by the weight of this or adult our way through.

"Yeah, well…" I clear my throat. "Maybe I can relate."

He tips his head, giving me a funny look that takes me right back to our high school cafeteria on that rainy Monday when we first met.

Brady was drumming on everything back then—tables, trays, the arms of irritated jocks. Any freak naturally caught my attention, so I wandered over to introduce myself. He thought I was hitting on him and perked right up when I shared my intentions to form a band. Tai, Audrie, and I were already jamming together and needed a drummer.

Wouldn't you know it? Brady, the missing link.

I can't lose him now.

Brady waits a tactful amount of time before he replies, "Speaking of jealousy, you planning on diving off more bars in the future?"

He asks this very seriously, until his poker face dissolves with a smile. It's the best thing I've seen since JC was buried inside of me.

"You stupid ass." I grip him in a fierce hug, my throat tight, face smooshed against his pecs. He smells like a vanilla milkshake. "You know I can't do any of this without you."

For a long minute, we just hold each other, silently acknowledging our parts in the hurt. One day, Brady and Tai will introduce girlfriends and boyfriends, and things will change as we all adjust. The band soldiers on.

Brady pulls back first to gaze down at me. "Are we cool? Do you forgive me?"

"Yes," I say, meaning it with all my heart. "Unless you blow the intro to 'Blackest Nights.' Then I'll kick your ass."

With the hugest relieved smile, he leans in to kiss my cheek. "That's my girl."

Chapter Twenty-Four

JC

In many physical ways, my brothers and I take after our father: strong jaws just shy of arrogant, elegant noses that survived several punches to the face, and thick hair that defies neglect. But I cannot lie worth shit. Not like Dad used to, or Sawyer continues to.

It's all in the delivery, and Gia isn't buying my flimsy attempt at a cover-up.

"You wanna go hang with Sawyer and a bunch of bankers?" she asks, incredulous.

I tuck my phone away after pretending to text Sawyer. "Only for an hour. He has some people he wants me to meet."

Her eyes flash, sharp and assessing. We landed in the bar thirty minutes ago and are two shots deep, with more on the way. This does not track.

She tugs on the zipper of my leather jacket. "Can I come? I'll behave. I promise." Her eyes soften, like her voice. "Please?"

Her pleading crushes me. The show tonight was utterly transcendent—both of us in the zone. We should be deep into making out and riding the lust wave into the night. Brushing her off for what's coming makes me feel utterly miserable.

But I'm not dragging Gia into this, whatever old relic Amber plans to unearth from the grave of our past. During soundcheck, I felt Gia's eyes burn a hole into me while I cut a deal with Amber: if she no-showed at the concert tonight, I'd meet with her.

Naturally, she'd asked why.

I'll explain tonight, was my reply.

Amber kept up her end of the bargain. Now I need to face the music, guilt humming through me like feedback.

I tip Gia's chin higher, kissing her pouty mouth. "They will bore you to tears. Wait for me here?"

"K," she says, trying hard, I can tell, not to sound crestfallen. "One hour."

I weave through the crowd, all the dark shapes blurring into one. Flipping up my collar against the chill of the night, I tug my phone out and punch the Google Maps Link in Amber's last text. The red pin drop indicates another bar in the same neighborhood.

Perhaps too close.

Because not even ten minutes pass, and I'm facing the ruins of my evening.

I take a deep breath and push open the door.

What looks like an old factory on the outside smells clean and expensive inside, like everything in Switzerland. The light is warm and dim, votives flickering on pedestal tables topped with concrete. I scan the posh, middle-aged crowd, all cut from the same fine cloth, and find Amber sitting alone at the bar, backlit and in soft focus.

For a second, my memory stumbles into the murky past.

I see her behind the Ludwig kit, lit up from the stage lights. Twirling her sticks and ready to bring it on. Another lifetime ago, she took a swig of gin, and I took a hit of tonic. Our wet kisses created the ultimate messy cocktail—fuck the glass or the class.

Now she sips champagne from a long-stemmed flute.

She sees me and smiles, a quiet shine in her eyes. Fifteen steps feel like fifty, each one dragging old ghosts behind me.

The whole world feels like it's shrinking to a pinpoint.

"Hi," she says.

"Hey."

I swallow down the spreading lump in my throat. Neither of us seems to know what comes next.

She pulls the barstool out for me. "Thanks for coming."

I take a seat, my stomach a tight ball of stress. I've forgotten what it was like, getting to feel edgy all over. And is that scent—patchouli? I disliked it then and hate it now.

"I can't stay long."

"Your crew keeping you on a short leash?"

"No. Someone's waiting for me."

Her smile slides away. The space between us suddenly feels heavy, like I should apologize, but what am I apologizing for? I signal the bartender, suddenly desperate for the numbing effect of alcohol. He replies with a universal wave of *give me a minute.*

"Anyway, I'm here." I side-eye her. "What's up?"

Amber is looking at me closely. Not for the first time, I wonder if coming here is a mistake. "It's nice to see you in your element again," she says. "I love watching you on stage." She touches my hand, brow lifting on a smile. "I always did."

My breathing shallows, like the air is thinner. When we first met, Amber didn't qualify as a groupie in the strictest sense of the word. She was a musician looking for a band. But she set her sights hard on me. Tracked me at countless gigs before she zeroed in like a missile backstage one night, dressed to kill in a PVC catsuit. She'd heard my original drummer, Steve, was moving on. At the time, I had a thing for fauxhawks, and Amber was like a magical mermaid in a shoal of identical blonde and brunette wannabes.

Older, sexier, and spoke my language.

We definitely aligned horizontally, as often as possible.

Back then, I thought someone could understand every heartbeat of mine. Now I'm wise (jaded?) enough to know no one can fully understand. But some come nearer to it than others—some very near.

"Yeah," I draw out the word while shaking off her hand. "About that."

She waits for me to expand and elbows me gently when I don't. "Were you surprised to see me?"

I flick her a look. "Unicorns rarely make an appearance."

"Is that a good thing? Me as a mythical creature in your mind?"

She perks up, and for some reason, that bothers the shit out of me. Walking out of my life without as much as a goodbye does not warrant perk. It warrants a hard smack for cruelty.

The bartender asks what I want and I keep it simple—order a tequila neat. Tonight is already whirling in my mind.

"How many shows did you buy tickets to?"

"Why?" She leans in, trying to catch my eyes. "Are you offering me comps?"

"Listen." I square my shoulders and face her. "You in the front row, night after night, it's gotta stop. Our singer feels uncomfortable."

Amber stills. Her long stare knots my brain into a tangle, and I look at the floor for a painstaking minute while neither of us says a word.

"You and her," she finally says, her tone brisk. "The rumors are true."

"Nothing official."

Amber puffs out a small sound of disgust. "Sounds like a familiar line. Does she know about us? Is that why you don't want me in the audience? She can't handle the spotlight shining on someone else?"

Anger, sharp and hot, stabs through me. She has no business throwing that in my face. She fucked out of my life without a second thought. To materialize thirteen years later and have the nerve to belittle Gia's feelings?

"Do me a favor and forget about the rest of the gigs, okay? Let's not turn this into a sideshow circus." My voice rises, anger bubbling with it. "You left the stage. You left *me*. Don't make this weirder than it has to be."

Her mildly offended look warps into something far uglier. "*I* left for a reason. You remember? Our pregnancy—that involved you."

I imagine filling in the giant pause that presses against all four walls and the ceiling, resting our secrets inside one by one. And just like that, I'm backsliding toward the darkness I struggled to escape from a hundred times before. I think of our argument, the permanent negative space it created. My heart in tatters, lying to the world about why I killed the band, because my own child didn't make it into this world, and I was partly to blame.

Amber blinks. Not a single movement in a body that once moved so in sync with mine. "Or," she says, now fully on the attack, "maybe you wanted it all to go away. Funny how you said fucking nothing." She downs her champagne and slams the glass hard onto the counter. "And saying nothing is saying exactly what you were thinking."

It's a slightly unnerving experience to relive deep pain all over again. Can't recommend it. And it's true I didn't say the words she wanted to hear.

"I would've committed," I say, the words tight in my throat. "I just ... I needed time to process. I was nineteen. I didn't know how to handle any of it." I look at her, heart pounding. "But I didn't ask you to do what you did."

It comes out softer than I meant it. Regret laced in every word. Because the truth is, I didn't ask anything. I just froze.

And she stormed out and went on a bender. Miscarried two days later.

I remember the blood-red sunrise and her soft cries. And that my world became swirls and fragments, nothing making sense.

"Committed?" Amber snorts a laugh, ignoring the elephant in the room I just dropped like a bomb. "The only thing you wanted in your life was music. That's what I realized. Why have a baby with a man unable to love me the way I wanted him to love me?"

"Is that your excuse?" I scoff. "Because if it is, it sucks. I loved you with all my heart."

Her cutting gaze lands on mine. She looks like she'd prefer to be in another bar right now. Maybe a bar in another country. I'm wishing I'd never left Gia. She makes me feel space. Makes me feel everything. It isn't getting any easier to want her, but I miss her, and it's dark outside, and the air in here feels like toxic soup.

And Amber keeps tossing poison darts. "How does the role reversal feel? Or do you feel it at all? Older man, younger woman?" She laughs bitterly. "No one bats an eye, I bet."

At this point, I feel shamed and judged. And why should I feel this way? She soldiered on without me, as if, in losing me, she'd lost nothing. Too many nights, I dream about the child I'd wanted to hold, and wake up sweating with my sanity collapsing all over again.

I'm suddenly so tired, like I've aged two decades in a single night. I down half my drink in one burning swallow. "No one cared about that except you."

Time passes. Not sure how much. An entire sunset and sunrise's worth of slow, ticking minutes. My heart rises and falls and keeps falling.

Two lost souls staring into the bleakness they created.

I signal the waiter for the bill.

"What are you doing after the tour?" Amber finally asks.

"I don't know." I run an agitated hand through my hair. "And why do you care?"

She clears her throat, making me acutely aware mine is bone-dry. I feel this rolling seasick sensation that only ends when you step off the ship. I want to get outside of it all, feel like kicking holes in the world of my life.

And that's the moment Amber rests her hand on my shoulder. "Why don't you stay in Europe?"

There's a creaking sound above our heads, or maybe I imagine it— the universe slowly imploding. She searches my eyes, and I'm thinking the most incomprehensible thing.

Is she serious? After all this time?

"We were so good together," she adds, giving my shoulder a good, firm squeeze.

I open my mouth and close it again. I should do the JC thing and say something nice, not pierce her misguided ambitions with a dull blade of rejection.

But I'm done pretending it didn't hurt.

And maybe I've been secretly crafting the words in the blackest part of my soul for years because they spill out fast and clean and are nothing short of lethal.

"Whatever space I had in my heart for you … it's gone. You disappeared as revenge. I can't forgive you for that."

Time takes another drag. If Amber had any illusions left about us and what could have been, I snuffed them, figuratively, under the grind of a boot heel.

Her smile is the saddest thing I've seen in years.

"Typical JC," she says softly. "A poet to the fucking end."

A single tear slips down her face, leaving a wet trail behind. Then she slides off the stool, folding me into a hug. Maybe I've tricked myself into believing I can handle anything, but no man can prepare for a woman breaking down in his arms. And I don't want to be a spiteful, angry monster. Rubbing slow, consoling circles between her shoulder blades, I fight the drowning pull of her familiarity—her contours and scent, the little sounds. Force myself to remember that after Amber, I felt dark and never quite clean.

Gia and her chaotic brightness have illuminated the dusty attic of my heart.

Two complicated natures coming together in a beautiful, simple one.

She is who I need, and my caving-in heart knows it.

But when Amber ever so slightly maneuvers to kiss me, it's a place I've been before, comfortable and secure. I kiss her back. It feels like I'm suddenly free-falling, the ground rushing up hard toward me, and no parachute cord to pull. Then a tray of glasses shatters onto the floor behind us, the bartender yelling, "*Sheisse!*"

And it feels so very wrong.

Chapter Twenty-Five

GIA

Knives and bombs. Machine guns spitting bullets. Hell, give me that chick's throat, and I'll show you how much damage two skinny hands can inflict.

I'm alone in the shivery dark, lungs on fire from running. Lake Zurich stretches in front of me like an endless black stain under a starless sky. I feel echoey and empty inside, a toxic and creeping thing strangling my heart. A ticker tape spools endlessly through my brain with the word *lies* repeated over and over.

JC lied to me.

To my face.

To hook up with that front-row stalker.

How could he do this to me the day after we share our innermost parts? My legs suddenly feel wobbly, and I collapse on a nearby bench, bawling. Broken, ugly crying I don't want anyone to see or hear. Not a single cell in my body can pretend to have a Parisian level of nonchalance about JC and her.

My intuition screamed all afternoon.

JC acted jittery. Ditching me for Sawyer smelled worse than Mama's attempt at rack of lamb. He left me no choice but to follow him after he left me at the bar.

I had to.

I'm suspicious by principle.

The mental image of JC with her in the bar leaves no space in my soul for anything but venom, and I cannot work out what their strange drama is. Based on their initial body language, it was like two rival gang members stepping up to discuss turf wars and who could deal drugs where. Then, it almost got cozy. She smiled and touched his arm. I couldn't see his expression, but the line of his shoulders remained tense. Whatever he said near the end seemed to break her.

With my face pressed up against the cool glass of the window, I silently cheered, willing him to dump her blazered ass. Then I wanted to curl up and die.

The hug and then the kiss.

The goddamn KISS!

Some things you can never unsee.

I scream into the sky until my lungs burn and deflate. My survival instinct tells me to move, to put as much distance between him and me and all of Zurich, even if it means walking to our next gig in Milan. Ditch the bus and try to forget JC made my entire body ring like a bell.

How close *is* Italy? I tug my phone out to verify when a text lights up on the screen. The taste in my mouth turns rancid.

JC: I'm at the bar. Where are you?

I choke back a sob. Is he serious?

Hey, nothing mysterious is going on! Had to suck face with some rando.

I rip off a reply.

GB: Not there.

JC: So where?

GB: At the lake.

JC: By yourself?

I snort a laugh. That's rich. My fingers fly across the screen.

GB: Now ur worried about me?

GB: Mr. Chaperone.

I imagine his expression, hoping my scorn hits like a kick in the nuts. I jump out of my skin when the phone rings instead. Sinister Gia thinks, *piss off.* But if I learned anything from last night, JC has a relentless streak in him that borders on OCD. And these endless looping thoughts won't leave me alone.

After the third ring, I answer.

"What do you want, liar?" I yell.

Silence. The kind that tells me he knows I know.

"Gia." His voice is low and dark. "Where are you? We need to talk."

I want to scream *Who is she?* It physically pains me to hold it all in. But no. I will confront him with the ugliness. Watch him squirm like the insects Brady used to burn with my magnifying glass.

I squint at the tram station behind me, the sign visible in a cone of streetlight. "I'm at Bürkliplatz. The end of the Bahnhofstrasse. If you're not here in fifteen minutes, don't bother."

"I'm jumping in an Uber. Don't leave. Please."

Hunched on the bench, a thin cool breeze needles through my hoodie. I shiver, halfway to frozen. Numb everywhere, except for the smallest sliver in my heart that betrays me. It whispers all the good things, like JC's expressive touching and near-perfect tempo, the musician's instinct of what to combine for maximum impact. He wasn't one of Audrie's romance meatheads who mutter filth while drilling the heroine into a headboard.

He is fucking perfect.

Or he was.

Tears stream down my face, and I plug my mouth with two knuckles, holding down a throb of pain. What does she have that I don't? Other than she's so much easier to love, all soft skin and smooth edges. The curves I'll never have.

It sucks just thinking about it, so I think about getting plugged back into the music. The tour. What I can control.

In the time it takes for JC to arrive, I've run through every possibility. Firing him won't work, but I can force *him* off the bus. He's rich enough to limo between cities.

"Hey." JC approaches me carefully from the shadows. The words I want to say dissolve on my tongue as he sits beside me. "You're not cold?"

"I'm fine."

"Take this." He shrugs out of his leather jacket. The warmth of it on my shoulder, infused with its citrus scent, almost breaks me.

I slide away. "I said I'm fine."

He sighs, giant and somehow tight. "Gia…"

"How was your visit with Sawyer?"

He eyes me for a moment, then drops his gaze. "I think we both know I didn't see him."

All the red seeps out of my clamped muscles. I was convinced he'd backpedal or deny it. But something still feels broken deep down under my ribs.

"Who is she? And don't fucking lie to me, or I swear to god, I'll never talk to you again."

He blows out a long, dismal breath. "Her name is Amber Devlin. She was the drummer in my band."

My mind folds in around this information, before it triangulates on the photo of Read My Rights pinned to my bedroom wall, half a world away. JC with his sweet-ass Les Paul and beaming smile. Heath and Ari, bassist and keyboardist. And Amber, who I thought was the coolest thing ever—an older female drummer with a banana-yellow faux-hawk and Cleopatra-level eyeliner.

I stare across the abyss of night and nature. The dots didn't connect because Amber doesn't resemble her old self in the slightest. And of all the JC rumors floated over the years, not even one involved her.

"No one knew about us," JC says, reading my mind, "except the band and my father. He said it would kill our momentum if fans found out we were an item."

Something cold rips through my chest. "And she wants to get back together?"

He waits one second too long before he stumbles over a "No."

And I can't take it. His eyebrows pulled together, waiting for me to make perfect sense of it all.

"If you don't explain the kiss, I will stuff my pockets with rocks and walk into that lake."

"Jesus, Gia. Don't say shit like that."

He reaches for me, but I yank away, shuffling to the end of the bench. "I can say whatever I want. You knew who she was but pretended not to. And I can tell you're not telling me the whole story. What's it going to take? Because I'm fully prepared to drown if all I am to you is a giant fucking notch on your belt."

In the faint glow of streetlight cutting through the trees, his bleak expression shatters me. I don't realize I'm holding my breath until his confession jars it loose.

"She got pregnant. We," he quickly corrects. "Got pregnant. And it messed things up. She wanted to clear the air."

My head almost explodes. If someone aimed their flamethrower at me, I'd douse myself in gasoline to speed up the carnage. There's a secret baby. A mini-Trenton that binds them eternally. Just my luck, because how do I maim a mother in good faith?

"You're a father?" I'm so thrown, I can barely spit out the words.

"No," he says miserably. "I'm an idiot who handled it all wrong."

My nervous system teeters on the verge of collapse. I have an idea what he means, but I struggle to voice it. JC forcing a woman's choice?

"By *wrong*, you mean what?"

He looks past me. I brace for impact, a truck of information closing in fast to crash into me. "I was young and wasn't prepared. I didn't know what to say. And when you don't say anything, it must mean something. She took off and drank herself into oblivion." His voice catches before he continues. "Miscarried. We finished the last two weeks of the tour barely speaking to each other. She fucked off, cut all communication, and that was that."

I feel strangely bloodless. JC just righted the frame of his mysterious picture. This is the missing link, right here.

"Is that why you killed the band?"

His eyes flash around the park, looking for an escape route. Then they land back on mine with a flare of sorrow. He nods. A kinder, gentler soul might offer a consolation. Instead, I swing the conversation back to the black wool scraping over my heart.

"And there is nothing between you two?"

"God, no," he sounds truly mortified at the thought, "I haven't seen or spoken to her in thirteen years. Why do you think I've been climbing the walls all day? She reached out to my old bassist, sniffing around for my number. I agreed to meet with her on one condition: that she doesn't come to any more shows."

"She agreed?" Again, suspicious.

"Yes."

"And if she reneges?"

JC drops his head into both hands. "I don't know. What I do know is I have zero feelings for her. She caught me off guard with the kiss." He drags his fingers down his face. "And I don't expect you to understand, but I... I lost myself. For one fucked-up second, I thought it might heal us. But all it did was make me feel worse." He continues in a thin, stretched voice, "I've kept this locked up forever, Gia. I'm sorry you had to find out this way."

I stand there, fidgeting on the edge of this anything-can-happen evening. Sorry is one thing. What I need now is assurance. That Amber is a chapter in a book he's closed for good.

That he wants me.

"If what you're saying is the truth, then you need to take me down. Bend me over that bench, right here, right now."

He does a double-take, more shocked than anything. "How does that help? And forget it. Not a chance."

"Why not?" My voice spirals higher, and, Jesus, I sound like one of the Chipmunks on uppers. "Because you're thinking of her?"

"No," he says, his voice tight with something dark and unknown. "Because a) I don't fuck on demand. And b) You are worth more than that."

"But you fucked her in all sorts of places, right? Don't lie to me."

JC leaps to his feet and starts pacing, sneakers crunching in the gravel. "Do you really want to have this conversation?"

Yes, you idiot! is what I want to scream. *My heart drops like a roller coaster every time you walk into a room, and I can't handle it.*

"I want to know everything. How many women? Where, who, why. All of it. Now!"

I start pummeling his chest with my fists, and, yes, it's come to this. Full hysterics.

JC grips my wrists with both hands. His voice has the authority of a mid-riot prison warden. "Stop, Gia. No violence, ever. And if it means that much to you, how much detail do you want? That I've banged women in every conceivable position? Slept with so many that I've lost count?" His eyes pin mine with a desperate fury. "To what end? The past can't be changed. None of it matters."

I wrench out of his grip. "It does matter! You deny me when I'm asking for the same things you've already done."

His hand scrubs over his face once more as if he'd like to make this entire evening disappear. "Did it ever occur to you that I think of you differently? I will give you everything you need, Gia. But I will give it to you the right way. Not cheapen you with…" he flicks his hand in the general direction of the bench, "garbage requests." He rubs his forehead, like there's a mark he's trying to remove. "I'm sorry I lied. I wanted to figure this out without you getting hurt. We need to trust each other, Gia. If we can't, none of this works."

"Do you trust me?"

"Over time, I will, unless you give me reasons not to. Trust is earned, not brokered."

"So I'm right not to trust you. Not this soon."

"You're right to question me if there's a legitimate reason."

My eyes blaze onto his. "Tonight feels pretty fucking legitimate."

After a few seconds, he says, quite diplomatically, "Yes. You're right."

"And my ongoing paranoia is legitimate given your reputation."

The look JC gives me makes my stomach dip. It carries a gravity, like I've misjudged him entirely. "This might shock you, but give this concept some thought. That maybe I'd like to change. That maybe *you* are the change I want." He blows out what sounds like a tortured sigh. "I've spent the past six months agonizing over you. Do I tell you how I feel? Risk opening up? Not once did I think Amber would show up out of the blue. I tried to handle it and obviously fucking failed. But that doesn't change how I feel about you."

His voice isn't demanding; it isn't diminishing. What he says is merely a statement of fact. And how can I rail against that? A twinge of guilt ripples through me. He must clock it on my face because he dials his anger back a notch.

"Your fire can take you far, Gia, but you need to know how to control it. You can fight Sawyer, your mother, fight the entire goddamned music industry if you want to. But I'm on your side. You don't pick fights with me."

I feel an uncomfortable stab of resistance. "Because you're older and so much wiser?"

His pupils, furiously black as the sky, lock in on me before they slowly soften. "Because those are my terms if you want to be with me. And yes," he adds, "because I am older. Wiser, debatable."

And he disarms me with a crumpled smile. All my bravado and posturing, whoosh, up in flames. JC waits for some sort of reply, and it comes, eventually, after I patch my heart together and remember to breathe.

If you want to be with me.

"Do you mean that?"

"Yes."

It sounds like it's taken all his remaining energy to utter one word. I stare up at him as all the panic and confusion trickle out of my veins. "But I can't share you with anyone. I'm too territorial."

He takes a step closer and cups my face between his warm palms. "Gia, I have trouble sharing food. No way I'm sharing you." I suppress a tiny laugh, remembering how he swatted my hand away in the diner after I tried to pluck a fry from his plate. "And there is no stable of mystery women, okay? There is you. End of story."

His kiss lands tenderly, and it all comes out: the tears and want. I cling to him, afraid to lose the man who sees all my insecurities and likes me despite them. I'm blubbering like an idiot, and unless the shit burrito I ate for dinner is tearing my insides apart, I have no other explanation for what I'm feeling.

I have to say it.

Even if it's whispered in one battered breath against the soft cotton of his t-shirt.

And when I say, "I'm in love with you," he tightens his arms around me, holding me for an endless moment. I feel like I've stepped out onto a stage, stripped bare of clutter, and a single light illuminates the five words I uttered like an exhibit. My thoughts clatter louder and louder, more chaotic with every passing second, as all of Zurich remains silent, waiting.

But he doesn't say it back.

Chapter Twenty-Six

JC

It's always the same, right? The frustration that follows after-the-fact regret. Those moments in your life where you wish you could change what you said.

Or the things you didn't say.

I'm spooning Gia in her bunk, both of us naked as the day we were born. The rattle-hum of the bus vibrates beneath us, like one of those old motel beds where a quarter could shake up your night. She's asleep, her breathing slow and steady. Gia insisted we crash together last night, and who was I to protest?

She needed my atonement, and I needed her forgiveness.

We flew too close to the sun and almost torched the beginnings of us.

After two panicked laps when I returned to the bar last night, with Gia nowhere to be found, my heart cratered. I knew what had happened and kicked myself for being such an idiot.

When she tried to shore up her emotions at the lake, she caught a tear with her knuckle, but they kept on coming. It made me think how vulnerable she must have felt the other night, giving herself to me. To break in front of me, to be wholly at my mercy.

Tenderness crowded my heart: a sense of caring, duty even, of doing the right thing.

But can I deliver?

I've poured a lifetime of dedication into building up walls, but I would give a limb to know I was doing this right, or even just that I wasn't tearing them down horribly wrong.

The bus creaks and groans, cutting a wide circle. It feels like we're navigating down an off-ramp, leaving the Autostrada to motor into Milan. The motion shifts Gia's body, my morning wood now pressing hard between the curves of her ass. I feel my self-control crumbling, close to snapping like it almost did in the park last night.

Because it did cross my mind to do exactly what she wanted.

Turn that park bench into our personal fuck station, forget Amber and all the intensity, and light up Gia's body until she screamed.

Forget myself for being an idiot.

For not having the courage to express my own love.

"Morning." Gia's voice is slow and sexy, heavy with sleep. "I can feel you."

I brush a kiss against the curve of her shoulder. She smells like wet lake and sweet candy. "Hey. Can I get you anything? Water, coffee?"

"You know what I want?" she asks, half turning. "To cuddle all morning."

I smile back, more than a little relieved. "Even better."

She props up on both elbows, lifting her mouth for a kiss. I taste none of last night's bitter-cold accusations as her tongue twirls with mine. Just raw, morning Gia. She moves her mouth to my chin, dropping kisses along my jawline, before studying my face with a lazy smile.

"You're so hot with sleep crusties."

I wipe sand away, laughing. "My teen idol image just went up in smoke."

"You can idolize me."

Gia sinks back into the pillow with a demure smile. How beautiful she looks, stretched out on the bed like Manet's Olympia, hand over her privates, ankles demurely crossed. A flower in her hair and a satin bow tied around her neck are the only things missing. The explosions in my chest are more scandalous than Manet unveiling his art.

Despite our joking around, our connection feels different this time. Still physical and electric, but also serious. This is not some do-it-for-the-plot situationship. Our lives have become increasingly intertwined to the point that reversing feels impossible.

Not that I want to.

"What's the plan?" Gia asks, the implication clear as day in her expression.

I blink, trying not to look at her smooth pink folds tucked between her legs. I feel a rush of possession—to bury my face in that velvety skin and never come up for air.

"I thought we were cuddling."

Her eyes twinkle. "There's a box in the corner behind you."

I turn and bash my head on the top of the bunk. Softly cursing, I dig around until my fingers find the box of condoms.

Gia whispers, "But we have to be quiet."

I slant her a look. "I take it you're talking about yourself?"

She smacks me on the arm with a fiery "Jameson!" and I shrug back, trying not to laugh. I get lost in the breathtaking endlessness of sex, the peaks and valleys and ripe centers. I'm not a talker or a screamer.

Gia, on the other hand.

Well, as if her singing voice didn't give it away.

"Hey, I'm all for losing our minds, but I don't want you to be out five hundred bucks." I tip my head toward the sound of Brady and Tai snoring hard across the hall.

Gia laughs under her breath. "I'll use the pillow."

I settle between her legs and trail kisses up her inner thighs. She gasps and cradles both palms around my head, pinning me in place. I gently tease her clit with little flicks of my tongue, the smell of her sex filling my nostrils.

Her body tightens, and a soft, broken sound spills from her lips. I look up, catching her eyes in the dip between her breasts. "You okay?"

Her chin starts to wobble around the edges. Even in the low light, I can make out her stormy expression, like she's struggling with something I don't understand.

"Fuck me, JC. Make it all better."

My heart drops, brick-heavy inside me. She isn't asking for pleasure or forgiveness. It's redemption. Trust that I can fix what we almost lost.

We huddled in the cold last night, on the park bench more forgiving than Gia's endless string of questions. I parceled out bits from my past to appease her, without making me sound like an utter douche. And dealt with her fears about Amber.

"She caves inward, not outward," I'd told her, watching her breath fog in the cold. "If she had a vindictive streak, I would've seen it years ago. We have fuck-all in common now, and I plan to keep it that way."

Gia's jaw unclenched, her anger melted away, and we Ubered back to the bus, wrapped in the scent of salted tears, Old Europe, and a narrowly avoided disaster.

With the worst behind us, I want to erase this from my head; blip Amber out of existence. Our magical time in the hotel wasn't a puff of nothing—it was the start of something with Gia I'm not prepared to lose.

I wipe away a strand of hair that had found its way into my mouth and focus back on her. "I'm going to make love to you," I whisper. "We heal gently, okay?"

She heaves in a sharp, jagged breath. My throat goes tight, and for one agonizing moment, I want to look everywhere else except her face because I don't know what I'll do if she says no. The silence feels like a huge bubble around me.

Her fingers digging into my scalp are the only answer I need, but, true to Gia, she amends my question with the tiniest smile.

"Not too gentle."

♫

"Yo! Romeo and Juliet." Brady raps his knuckles against the wall. "Rise and shine."

My eyes snap open. For three blank seconds, that inevitable tour moment clouds my brain. Where am I? And…

"What time is it?" My voice is thick with sleep, everything one giant craggy blur. Gia and I floated off in a pheromone haze and crashed hard.

"Eleven," Brady says, his voice close but disembodied behind the bunk curtain. "And by the way, Tai and I accept all major credit cards. No backpedaling out of the fine this time."

Oh, shit. So much for the pillow being any help.

Gia stirs, rolling over so we're nose to nose. Dark, messy hair pushed back over her forehead, her eyes half-lidded, she makes a face, mostly amused. "Is he for real?"

I dust a kiss on her lips. My brain is still fuzzy from being ripped out of deep REM sleep. "Maybe I should offer a blanket payment," I say, speaking low. "Cover us for the rest of the tour."

"Payment before either of you leaves, please," Brady says, ever the taskmaster. "I got shit to buy in Milan. Versace's calling my name."

"Dude," Gia grumbles, singlehandedly defining a new term slangry—sleepy and angry. "Relax."

I chuckle at that, digging around for my boxers in the tangled bedding. This isn't the worst decision we've made on tour. Quite the opposite, actually.

"Three thousand," I tell Gia. "One point five each should shut them up." I find my boxers and awkwardly pull them on in the tight space. Ready for business in my finest SAXX.

"Offer them half that." Gia looks very put off by the initial figure.

I nod, pretending to reconsider. "Yeah, you're right. I have to buy you a bigger pillow, and that will cost a fortune."

Oh, to capture Gia's expression right now.

She jabs me with her foot but can't stop laughing. "I don't need anything bigger, Jameson," she says teasingly.

"Seriously?" Brady's voice teeters on disbelief. He's hit his threshold, assuming he has one. "You two are genuine perverts."

♫

PayPal accounts loaded, Brady and Tai make tracks for their Italian retail therapy. This Milanese soil must be blessed because it was shockingly easy to get rid of them. In the half-light of morning, I'm barefoot and shirtless, strumming my acoustic in the lounge. Happy as an A minor navigating a moody melody.

Gia wanders in, freshly showered, and my heart does a little flip. I like her in anything that shows off her legs, and the hem of her tight black dress falls mid-thigh as a counterbalance, I suppose, to the deep neck-line exposing the lace of her bra.

"Wow. You look great."

With a "Thanks, homeboy," she crashes into me, careful not to bang into the guitar.

I lean in for a kiss, only to be interrupted by my buzzing phone. It's on the coffee table, and we both lock eyes on the screen, a weird ripple in the air. The only indication that things are still creeping in the corners from last night.

I hold up the screen, and she squints at the text from Sawyer. "Is that the name of a restaurant or a person?"

"Sounds like he's rounding up the troops for a blowout dinner tonight. Did you pack a nice dress?"

She gestures at her black bodycon. "This semi-wrinkled one. Same one I plan to wear to lunch."

Gia's got relatives coming to the show tonight. Distant cousins from Bologna. She had to walk them off a ledge when they found out we weren't visiting. The consolation prize? A family lunch neither of us can miss. Saying no to Italian relatives is not an option.

"What time are we meeting them?" I ask.

"After sound check. They picked a place close to the venue." She nips playfully at my lower lip. "And what about this dinner tonight with Sawyer? He's dragging us to some ten-star place?"

"One Michelin star is his minimum," I joke.

"You know I'm not that kind of girl. And this," she points at her dress, "is all I have."

"We could *Pretty Woman* it," I suggest. "We're in the fashion capital of Italy."

Gia laughs out an incredulous "no way." Then, "You actually watched that movie?"

"At least ten times. But don't tell anyone. I have a reputation to uphold."

Her eyes flicker, then her smile slides away as quickly as it arrived.

Dammit. Wrong words. I wanted to steer this conversation in a meaningful direction. Like, where we see ourselves in five or ten years. The things we want that music can't give us. But how do I frame that Amber's reappearance stirred up my buried desire for a family without upsetting Gia?

And a conversation of that magnitude needs the proper air to breathe.

Gia, forever moving breathlessly fast, doesn't let the moment linger. She taps her fingers on my guitar like she owns the rhythm of my pulse.

"Speaking of upholding … is it time to negotiate?"

And there it is: the topic I didn't want to trigger.

"I was wondering when you were going to bring that up." *Hoping never*, I don't say.

"C'mon," she gives me a playful shove, "you know that song is perfect for us."

"What makes you say that?"

"I mean," she says, "our voices together. That song is begging for it."

"Sounds like *you're* begging for it."

Well, well. Stop the presses. I've made the great Gia Barlow blush. She scratches her neck as if she can stop the spreading pink.

After some throat clearing, she says, "If you weren't the most stunning human I've ever met, inside and out, I'd slap you."

"I don't think anything will ever stop you from slapping me. Or throwing things at me."

"Hey!" she protests. "I threw a pillow in the studio. Hardly a weapon."

"And a banana," I remind her.

She pouts, slouching against my shoulder, apology nowhere in sight. "Because you were teasing me."

I grin, having the best time putting Gia on her back foot, a place she rarely stands on. Sunlight slants in through the blinds, brightening the dark corners of the bus and her skin. God, she's beautiful. The human version of a hit single—rare and undeniable. I should do whatever it takes to keep her close.

Maybe even offer her my most personal song.

"So," I start. "If you really want a crack at this song, it's you and me. Right now."

She bolts upright. Smiles like they're offering a million bucks for the biggest one. "Bring it on." Her shoulders rock back and forth to the invisible melody. "You start, and I'll slide in."

Gia told me last year that she can memorize melodies and lyrics after one listen. After adjusting the guitar, I start finger-picking the chords. I sing the first verse; Gia comes in strong for the second. It's incredible, her innate sense. There are so many ways into a song, and she finds the right path just like that. We duet on the chorus, seamlessly finding harmony, like we've rehearsed it a hundred times. Listening to her sculpt the song the way I've only heard it in my head is irresistible.

No surprise, she makes the song better.

Sexier. More alive.

When we finish, the air hums with the echo of our voices. Gia, radiant from the inner glow she exudes after a performance, teases, "Gravity called and claimed copyright infringement. Stealing its thunder."

"Musicians never steal, remember?" I counter.

"Only hearts, right?" she flips back.

Her eyes land on mine in no uncertain terms. I get the drift. Why haven't I stepped up to the plate and confessed my feelings when she left hers strung out in the cold?

I hold her gaze until I can't.

"Talk to me about the lyrics," she says. "Who are you singing about?"

"No one specific. The universal muse."

I side-eye her, wondering if she can sense the truth lodged in my throat. Now's the perfect time to tell her she's the muse. So why don't I?

"Do you really expect me to believe that?" Gia pokes my arm, staring at me as if relentless eye contact will force me to answer, which it doesn't. "C'mon, sailor. What's it going to take? I will do your song justice. Pinky swear."

I tuck my hair behind both ears and pluck a few lazy notes. "Can you give me a few weeks?"

"As long as the negotiation table remains open."

"And if it doesn't?"

I see the hurt flash across her face and want to rewind to earlier, when I found her eyes deep with desire, with some other thing that didn't look destructive at all. Roots, not chaos. Belief in us. The thing is, I want to give her everything. My heart, my song, all of it.

But it's so fucking hard to trust anyone.

Through Tai, I learned she told Brady she wanted the song. Yes, she said she loved me, but what if she meant she loved what I could give her? What if I'm just the vehicle for her music career? I don't want to be the guy who falls in love again and puts the past on repeat.

Gia watches me in the heavy silence, brows knit together.

No need for words. The question is written all over her face:

What the hell is wrong with you, JC?

Chapter Twenty-Seven

GIA

Strutting across the piazza, I feel like a woman in one of those old-school Italian movies Nonna swoons over. The golden light of magic hour kisses my skin, and somewhere in the distance, scooters roar. The fantastical Duomo of Milan is almost enough to make me believe in a god, but I have my own—the one holding my hand and making every head turn.

JC's loose, flowing hair catches the last rays of the evening sun. He's on fire in a jet-black suit. So yummy, it makes my head explode. We're out as a pair, together, for the first time, and JC walks more slowly to accommodate the sky-high heels I'm navigating, lifting my hand to press a kiss against it.

My chest warms as his eyes sweep over me.

"You look stunning. Giving every goddess a run for their money."

"Thanks to you."

I'd better look hot. The beaded lilac dress I'm wearing weighs almost as much as it costs. A saleswoman in Rinascente (a department store for the ultra-rich) zeroed in on us immediately. Two young, slender types, one of whom could actually afford the price tags that made me a little green. I tried not to think about what Audrie texted me the previous day: that our Zurich hotel cost ten thousand francs. Every dollar JC spends on me now feels like a weight.

"I like spoiling you." JC leans in to nuzzle my neck. "I like everything about you."

My bright smile hides the prick of disappointment. Like isn't love, but it's moving in the right direction.

"Who else is coming tonight?" I ask.

"The boys. Shae and Sawyer. Mario, the promoter. Maybe one of his guys."

"So lots of shop talk."

He glances over. "Your favorite."

Is it wrong that I want to spend all my free time alone with JC? Flashes of him touching me, all the sweet, aching places, have tormented me all afternoon.

"I promise to be nice to Sawyer and eat all his precious tweezer food."

JC chuckles, his warm hand landing on my hip to stop me mid-stride. He tugs me closer, looking down at me like he's Edward the vampire and I'm Bella. Very serious. Very sexy.

My chin quivers, and I hold his gaze.

"I feel I can say this to you now," he starts.

My eyes are on his lips, I hear the words loud and clear, but my brain goes blank. I take a deep breath and try to settle down.

"Okay." It comes out slowly. "Spill the tea."

His hand touches the back of my neck. He lifts my chin with the other hand, and our eyes hold for a long moment. He's looking at me with so much tenderness, my heart aches.

"Have you ever heard that saying, 'You catch more flies with honey than vinegar'?"

Something happens in my chest. A crack. Not the kind I want. "Yeah. Why?"

"This industry is a people business, and you need people," he says kindly. I'll give him that. "The heights you want to scale require a team to lift you. Sawyer's trying his damnedest to make that happen for you."

My lips part, but nothing comes out. Does he think I'm difficult? Too rough around the edges? And maybe my silence radiates more than I think because he brushes the softest kiss on my lips, like that'll make it easier to swallow.

"All I'm saying is, sometimes you have to dial back the opposition."

Even though I know he's right, everything that makes him JC shines through at this very moment. My infatuation with him gets tangled in a wave of disappointment.

What he *didn't* say.

"I know. It's just…" I trail off, my gaze following two young girls skipping with balloons tied to their wrists. "I want it all so bad. I'm too impatient."

His warm hands cup my face. Nothing makes sense after what happened with the song this morning. He's holding something back, his shuttered expression when I asked about the lyrics a dead give-away. But how much more can I push?

"Have faith," he says. "You're so close to the top. But don't be reck-less with the people who have your back. Don't burn the empire before it's built."

He pulls my mouth to his. Kisses me, hot and filthy. It feels like sparks are shooting up my spine. The crowds milling in the dusky twilight start to cheer, egging us on. JC lets up his perfect tongue torture and laughs, taking a mini bow to all the applause.

I tug his hand, a flush spreading over my chest from all the eyes on us. "Hey. You're trying to steal the spotlight?"

He twines his fingers into mine. Winks. "As if."

Ten minutes later, he ushers me into a restaurant that makes me less mortified about the sum JC spent on the dress. To be clear: at lunch with my relatives, my basic black bodycon held up just fine. The rustic hole-in-the-wall had spaghetti sauce-splattered menus and an endless pour of cheap Chianti.

But this place…

The restaurant is typical Sawyer. Elegant and expensive. Dark lighting, so the prices on the menu don't make you pass out. A hostess wearing a beautiful, slinky cream dress walks us across the cobblestone to a private room in the back. As advertised, six people sit around the massive wooden table.

Mario and Luca, team promotion, with deeply Italian accents. Shae is in a blouse that doesn't look ironed beside the ever-impeccable Sawyer. Brady and Tai try to look the part in their thrifted designer duds.

Everyone seems to be having a good time.

Introductions fly back and forth as we take our seats next to each other, and a waiter—older, bald, possible member of the mob—appears to fill our glasses with wine. Sawyer leads the toast—*Salute* all around. I take a sip, and damn, this Barolo beats mouth-puckering Chianti.

Just as I'm starting to relax, Tai discreetly leans over. "Can we hang for a sec?"

"What's up?" I ask, speaking low.

The waiter circles the table, taking notes on the appetizers Sawyer starts to order on our behalf. His Italian isn't half bad.

"I'm going to show Gia the wine cellar," Tai announces to the table. "We'll be right back."

JC shoots me a quizzical look, and I reply with an uncertain shrug because none of Tai's earlier texts hinted at the intensity he's projecting. We walk single file past tables filled with runway-ready couples, the handful of people waiting to be seated.

In the darkest corner of the packed bar, away from the smiling clusters of drinkers, Tai stops. He looks like he's bracing for impact.

"Okay, dude," I say. "What gives? You're acting like a Russian spy."

Tai doesn't laugh, just shifts his weight from foot to foot, scratching the back of his neck. "I don't want to be the bearer of bad news…"

Suddenly, I feel my heart beating in my throat. "But?"

He coughs, glancing toward a row of cozy booths. "Brady and I got here early. Sat over there." He nods at the end booth with a half-moon bench. "Sawyer and the promoters came in a few minutes later. They didn't see us, and we didn't say hi. Figured it was business time."

"And?" It squeaks out.

"Sawyer was talking about how this tour is all about JC's second coming. A way to relaunch him."

Something shuffles around under my skin. For some reason, I know the worst is yet to come.

And bingo.

"Said JC's been writing songs. Plans to release an album soon," Tai says into the tense silence. "And that song you wanted? Sounds like it's meant for the solo project. Did you know about that?"

A pounding echo starts full force inside my head. *Can you give me a few weeks? Can you give me a few weeks?*

I stare silently at the wall, willing the words out of my head. JC had so much Italian love heaped onto him during lunch, cheeks pinched to last a lifetime. I gave him my trust. My body. Cashed in my V-card for him. And he's lecturing me about recklessness?

"Gia," Tai says gently. "Breathe."

I take a deep, steadying inhale. All this information is making me feel claustrophobic. But that doesn't stop my mind spinning back to the pre-tour meeting JC and Sawyer cut out of while we ate pizza. They camped out in Sawyer's office for a good twenty minutes. Suddenly, an entirely different picture emerges.

Trentons conspiring.

"He can do what he wants," I say. "We don't own him."

Tai rubs my shoulder with a sympathetic look. He knows how gutted I am. "I'm sorry."

My eyes start to prickle. That's why he's not giving up the song. All the fucked-up emotions of last night swarm on my skin, and a panicky thought hits me. Is Amber in on this? Resurrected as the drummer for JC's new band?

Tai flicks his gaze past me, eyes sharpening. "Incoming," he warns.

And—

"There you are." JC's voice slides through the crowd like a smooth four-bar blues riff. I turn, and he's suddenly there, haloed by the golden light spilling from the bar. Looking at me with so much *like* in his eyes.

"You stealing time with my queen?" he teases Tai. Makes no mention that we are nowhere near the wine cellar.

Tai doesn't miss a beat. "Just make sure you treat her right."

He claps JC's shoulder, slipping past us to avoid further conversation. Bonus points for how he handled this, because I feel sick to my stomach.

JC looks at me with that searching, quiet look. "What was that all about?"

"Tai just got some family news. Kind of heavy. He needed to talk."

I force a smile. JC studies me a beat too long, as if he's processing the weird tension and whether to address it. How easy would it be to put him on the spot and force him to acknowledge this thing? To say it out loud. But I don't.

He threads his arm through mine, walking us back toward the table. His warmth pressing against my side feels strangely numbing, even as he drops a kiss on my cheek, telling me how proud he is of me. How beautiful I am.

The entire time, I'm wondering how to get through dinner with this hanging over my head.

Good little Gia won't make a scene. I won't be *reckless*.

But if one more lie spills from his lips, I will torch this dress, throw his fucking trendy suitcases onto the bonfire, and watch the empire burn.

♫

Backstage before the show, the chaos in my head feels like the static on Nonna's radio when her favorite Sicilian station craps out. JC drops beside me on the sofa, getting all cozy, arm around my shoulder. He's changed into stage clothes. But is he Dr. Jekyll or Mr. Hyde? It's hard to look at him.

"You feeling okay?" he asks. "You seemed a little out of it at dinner."

A little? I drowned dinner in wine just to stay numb. Barely felt tethered to the moment. Ate listlessly when normally I hoover down platefuls.

My shoulders hitch in a tiny shrug. "It's been a long day."

"I liked hanging out with your family. Thanks for making me part of it."

He leans in for a kiss, but I turn my head so his lips land on my cheek instead. JC looks at me wordlessly, brows drawn. Let him think the worst. Let him feel what I felt last night, face pressed against a window, watching my entire world fall apart.

"I need to use the bathroom."

I stand abruptly, emotions rippling through me like an endless tide. It's killing me not to ask JC about his plans, but I refuse to create drama before the show. Relationship Armageddon can wait.

Head down and pulse skyrocketing, I crash into Shae, our miracle in cowboy boots. Prompt, friendly, and on our side as much as she can be as Sawyer's mouthpiece. She's weaving a little from all the wine she drank.

"Good news!" Her voice is jarringly loud in the empty hallway. "Just got word we have an extra special guest tonight."

A fissure runs up my spine. "Yeah, who?"

"The Italian prime minister."

I blink, unsure if this is real life or a random sitcom I'm now starring in. Politics? Couldn't care less. But Shae's expectant grin says this is where I'm supposed to shriek and clap.

"She's a fan. These Euro politicians don't rock out like ours do." Shae beams with pride. "Feather in your cap."

Jesus. If there's a hell, I'm living in it right here: pretending to care. "Amazing," I say. "I'll toss out some extra-special Italian just for her."

"Perf. Oh, and Sawyer approved a private meet-and-greet after the show. Major photo opp. Sounds like she has a wee crush on JC. But don't we all?"

She winks, and it feels like all my insides pool onto the floor. I mumble something that sounds like *thanks* and hightail it to the bathroom. Kicking open a stall door, I scream at the top of my lungs. I spent the evening in a smug dress, in a restaurant that amplified my impostor syndrome, and played nice to prove to JC that I could. Meanwhile, he's blabbing to me about not burning empires while secretly rebuilding his.

Off *my* thunder.

On my fifth "fuck," I calm down. Sort of.

I don't know how to be with someone I have these complicated feelings for. It's so rare that I let anyone in. But something in me has accepted him.

And I can't bring myself to believe the worst.

Ten minutes later, I'm still a hot mess, slumped on the toilet seat, when a text lands from Brady.

BB: Andiamo. Let's do this.

It's a struggle to stand. I feel weary. Older. I splash water on my face and trudge into the hall just as the boys and JC pour out of the dressing room. Tai and Brady have given me space since dinner, enough of it that JC's wounded expression makes me feel like shit.

I want to hate him. But I can't.

Not yet.

If he can convince me Sawyer is full of hot air, as he can be, we are good.

Maybe.

I walk like a robot, stiff with no rhythm, into the dense wall of darkness on stage. As soon as fans see our outlines, their murmurs of excitement explode into a welcoming roar. Brady, dressed in his flowy pirate shirt, whips them into frenzy, coaxing them louder with hand gestures before he settles behind his kit. Tai slings his bass over one shoulder of his Skinny Puppy tee and batters the crowd with a monster E chord.

JC finesses his pedals. Wah, chorus, and finally, distortion. The jacked-up crowd surfers in the front row cheer and high-five each other. They know what that means. Tonight, we're opening with "Bite into the Chaos." The classic of every dorm room party. It lights up the crowd and sets the tone for the show.

I feel looser, in my element. Ready to blow up the night. I face the crowd, scan the front row … and freeze.

There she is.

Haunted blue eyes, smooth, shiny hair, very blonde above the purple coat. Way too much cleavage on display for a cougar. Amber's smile almost looks soft, but something cold lurks at its corners.

I whip my head to face JC. He's in the zone, already escaping to the place where only music can take us. But he feels the laser beam of my eyes hit with full force. Like it's happening in slow motion, he turns to me first before his gaze pivots to Amber. His shock is almost comical. Did it ever occur to him that no matter how deep someone's crazy piles up, there's always more?

I'm dimly aware of the chanting as it slowly builds.

JC and Gia. JC and Gia. JC and Gia.

And then Amber blows him a fucking kiss!

Something inside me snaps. Later, I don't remember much more of this moment other than a crystallization in the pit of my stomach. Pure, white-hot rage takes over.

I grab the mic and scream, "Buona notte, Milano!"

The fans scream their approval while I signal Charlie, our guitar tech, to hand me JC's Fender Strat. He helps me adjust the strap, hands me a pick, and peels off enough cable to connect me to an amp. The entire time, Tai, Brady, and JC are giving major WTF looks.

Where is this change-up coming from?

I toss my hair back and address the crowd. "I've got a little surprise for y'all. A new song. Let me know what you think." I strum an A minor, sharp and purposeful, and turn to the boys, shouting: "It's A minor, F, C, E. Follow my lead."

Across the stage, I can see it dawning on JC—I notice the tightened control in his eyes and his mouth. Then he marches over, invading my space with no time to defend it.

"What are you doing?"

I breathe out, let the shakes subside. Either JC lied about telling Amber to stay away, or she gives zero fucks. Either way, I suddenly feel helpless, like they've pushed me here: an animal reacting just to protect myself.

"Why is she here?" I demand.

Someone in the crowd yells, "Are you two dating?"

I laugh nervously into the mic. "We sure are. He wrote this song for me. Tell me how beautiful it sounds."

JC stumbles backward as if I kicked him in the guts. Time stalls; sound evaporates. The chaos in my head screams louder. This is his song. I should wait. I should ask. But the moment is cresting like a wave, and if I don't ride it, I'll sink.

And Amber doesn't get the satisfaction of watching me drown.

The lights begin to change from white to a deep cherry red, touching the ocean of humanity with a rose-colored light. I could still stop this. It's not too late. My relatives are here, expecting greatness. The Prime Minister too, seated with Sawyer, who praised me earlier over carpaccio as slimy as his smile.

And maybe it's a trick of light, my imagination spiraling out of control, but Amber's eyes, a bright crippling blue, are suddenly all I can see.

I start strumming and feel the dangerous energy rushing out of me like I slit a vein. Four thousand phones are poised to capture this moment, and I know this is wrong, ambushing him. But I can't stop. And JC's glorious melody gets reduced to a skeleton, because I'm the only one playing.

JC stands motionless, a shadow in the dark.

Brady and Tai—unwilling to cross a line they don't understand.

And my oh-so justified vindication, meant to land like a fist against bone, swerves into a meaningless void. My fingers fumble. The lyrics tumble out of my mouth, and it feels like I'm singing my own obituary.

Based on JC's reaction, a funeral feels appropriate.

He whips off his guitar. Slams it into the stand.

And storms off the stage.

Chapter Twenty-Eight

JC

I'M STUMBLING DOWN THE HALL BACKSTAGE, SOAKED WITH FEELINGS OF all kinds, painfully alive with them. My heart is beating uncomfortably fast. I need out. I need space—to put as much distance as I can between me and this night of living hell.

Gia, of all people, singing my song?

Stealing it.

And the cold in her eyes, the accusation deep within them. Like I had any fucking control over Amber showing up.

The hall ends at a faraway door, and I kick the panic bar, rushing into the clear cold. I take a deep, ragged breath and stare into the shadows. The world suddenly seems bigger and emptier. And too quiet as the door slams shut behind me, the roar of the crowd muffled to nothing.

Right now, the fans are blissfully unaware this interlude isn't part of the show. But if we're not on stage soon, the mood will shift. One hooligan is all it takes to start a riot. Thing is, how do I walk out into the spotlight again? My soul feels tarred black. Gia is a traitor, not an ally. Not the woman I'm painfully, desperately in love with.

The door flies open with an explosive bang. Tai and Brady are practically falling over each other as they stutter to a stop. Their eyes sweep over me carefully, like I'm a vial of plutonium. Unstable, to be handled with caution.

"Hey, man." Tai raises both hands, palms out in the universal "easy" gesture. "It's cool. We'll figure this shit out. But can you move away from the edge?"

The raised deck we're standing on is a ten-meter drop onto the parking lot. How great would it be to jump, to end these intense feelings? But no. That dramatic finality is not how I deal with this.

I put space between me and the ledge, muttering, "I'm not that messed up," but they keep a respectful distance. Crazy might be catching.

"JC. Dude." Brady sounds out of breath. A winded pirate in his ridiculous shirt. "What's going down?"

I massage both temples, trying to ease the tension. "Sorry, guys. This is super screwed-up. Nothing to do with you." It comes out meagerly, like I'm not the once legendary songwriter with the aura of Kurt channeled through Bono with a side order of Bruno Mars.

"So this wasn't a pre-arranged stunt you two planned?" Tai's voice carries no hope. He already knows the answer.

And there's no time to reply, because Sawyer comes barreling out of the door next, a frazzled-looking Shae trailing behind him. His head is on a frantic swivel, from the boys to me. "Are you okay?" he asks, genuinely concerned, it seems. The giant dark wall of energy thrumming around me is unmissable.

"Not particularly."

"Where the fuck is Gia?" he barks. "I swear, I'm going to—"

"Right behind you."

Gia steps out, and there's a bold steadiness to her voice, like how a sniper might apologize to you before they pull the trigger. But that doesn't stop Sawyer from pouncing all over her.

"I just ditched the prime minister of *Italy*. Whatever insane explanation you have for why we're out here freezing instead of on stage, it better be good."

Gia folds her arms. "I'll explain once someone escorts the crazy lady out of the building."

Sawyer blinks. "Who are you talking about?"

Everyone bounces glances off each other. A creeping sense of déjà vu muscles around me. A parallel universe where, somehow, freakishly, two women who should never have crossed paths have spectacularly collided.

"Amber," I say tonelessly. "Amber Devlin."

Sawyer snaps his gaze to mine. The security light glares harshly into his face. "Your old drummer? What's she doing here?"

"She's his former lover," Gia cuts in. "Trying to become current. Or…" She pins me with a look of pure fire. "Sign herself up to be the drummer in your new solo act."

The air turns strange. There's a brief moment during which everyone looks at Gia and me. But my eyes lock on Sawyer, hoping I misheard that, that this can be something different from what it actually is. He swore not to follow in Dad's footsteps, but it's hard to fight against the weight of history.

"What the fuck is my *new solo act* all about?" I demand.

"Uhm…" Sawyer, the smooth talker, rarely at a loss for words, trails off like a fading sun just as a rising chorus of *boos* drifts through the door. It's a tone of pending chaos that Shae unfortunately knows too well.

"Friends," she interjects. "Appreciate that shit sometimes gets weird, but we gotta power through. The animals are going to freak out."

"I'm not setting foot on stage until I get a straight answer." I stare at Sawyer, both of us aware of the rough edge in my voice. "And if I don't, my ass is on the next flight home."

Gia flicks a tense look at Tai. "Tell him what you heard."

Tai's gaze drops to the concrete. "Gia…"

"Is anyone on my side?" Gia yells into the sky. "Spill or walk away for good."

That gets a guilty flicker of Tai's lashes. His shoulders hunch, like he's trying to make himself very small. "We weren't spying," he claims. "We showed up early tonight for a drink and overheard Sawyer's conversation with the promoters. To hype JC's return. Use our band as leverage."

I catch Sawyer's expression shift. "Is that true?"

He scrapes a hand over his hair, eyes darting between us. "I was, you know, talking up the possibilities."

Brady says quietly, "We heard it all, dude."

I'm conscious of some glittering thing in the distance before I close my eyes. "I told you the chance of my returning was zero."

"Then why did you even agree to this?" Gia demands.

I laugh, a losing-it kind of laugh, and turn to face her, looking small in the big quiet moonlight. "Let's talk about the real problem here. You played my song *without* my permission. That is artistic violation."

Gia pauses for a second, and I feel a moment of triumph at having nailed the betrayal so bluntly.

"And you don't think I felt violated with Amber blowing you a kiss?" she shouts back. She's white with anger, tiny fists balled at her sides. "You said you handled her. That she wasn't coming to any more shows."

"I had that conversation," I shout in reply. "And she chose to ignore it. What else can I do? Follow up? I told you I have no interest in her. She can fuck right off." I punch the words in hard to shut Gia up.

"Amber let me down, and I prayed to God you wouldn't do the same thing. Why do you think it took me so long to share my feelings? I have trust issues. And then you stab me in the back." My voice cracks, but I snap it steady to lay into her. "Whatever happened to musicians who don't steal from each other? Your disregard for rules and boundaries is the real problem. You have your kingdom, and you want to be the sole ruler. Just like your mother and Father Anderson said. Screw everyone else."

"That's not true." Gia squirms, all eyes on her.

I throw up both hands in frustration. "Of course it is! I mean, Jesus. You want to fine your bandmates for having sex, but you can do whatever you want."

"Hey, man," Tai cuts in, sensing we're veering off-course. "That's water under the bridge."

"Is it?" I snort a laugh. "To me, that's selfish."

"Me, selfish?" Gia has a stubborn set to her chin. "I haven't lied to you. You said you had no clue who Amber was, and then you're sticking your tongue down her throat. You might as well throw out a red carpet that leads to your bed. Give her a crack at another baby."

The words land like a bomb. Gia has a beautiful voice, even when she's unleashing fire and brimstone. But did she just say that out loud? This nightmare is suddenly everyone's.

"Baby?" Sawyer echoes. "You two were together?"

"Yes."

And with one simple word, the floodgates I've been holding on to crash open. "Couldn't share that news, or all the fangirls would revolt. How would Trenton Talent Management survive? The great Peter Trenton's son couldn't screw the business."

Sawyer stares blankly at me, like he's waiting for the punch line. Is this a joke he isn't in on? "Dad knew?"

"He figured it out."

More silence. And an endless amount of confusion on Sawyer's face. "Is there a kid I don't know about?"

"No," I say flatly, even as my heart pitches. "She miscarried."

The corner of Sawyer's mouth twitches. He's quick to put two and two together. "Is that why you killed the band?"

I spread out my arms. Might as well adopt a Jesus pose because it feels like a personal crucifixion. "The big mystery of JC Trenton revealed. Does anyone—"

"Shit," Sawyer interrupts. "Why didn't you say anything?"

"I told Rhys. He's the—"

"Rhys?" Sawyer cuts in.

"Can I please reach the end of my thought?" I shout. "Sawyer. Brother. I love you. But please, shut the fuck up! For once."

Brady and Tai shuffle sideways like crabs, out of the range of fire. Gia's eyes have slipped to mine, all nervous and concerned. I don't lose it. Not ever.

I catch another glimpse of something flashing above me on the roof.

Vague shapes, mixed in with thick layers of shadows. Someone with a phone? The hairs on the back of my neck rise.

I should pay more attention to that, but Shae makes a big production of clearing her throat.

"I'm heading inside," she says. "Fifteen minutes, okay? Not sure we have more than that."

"Get rid of Amber first," Gia says pointedly.

Shae adjusts her ballcap. "What does she look like?"

"The corporate-looking blonde. Stage left. Only freak show in a blazer."

Shae side-eyes Sawyer, who mutters, "Get it done with minimum fuss."

"And," Gia continues, spitting sparks, "tell her to stay the fuck away from the rest of the tour."

Sawyer whispers, "Jesus Christ," and sounds worn out. One minute, he's flying high with politicians, then he's dragged into messy band politics, which, arguably, suck more than actual politics.

Shae scurries inside, Brady and Tai jumping at the opportunity to exit stage left with her. Sawyer waits for me and Gia, but she waves him on. "Can you give us a minute?"

"No," I head to the door Sawyer's already walking through, "I don't want to talk. We have a show to finish."

I motion for her to get a move on, but she remains glued to the concrete. Looking very much like a twenty-year-old hit by a shit-filled truckload of her own doing. Somewhere beneath us, a bunch of roadies are laughing, their cigarette smoke stinking up the air.

"Can we hit rewind?" Her voice is the quietest it's ever been. "Forget this fuck-up. Sorry, times eight million. It won't happen again."

I shake my head at her attempt to brush this under the rug like it's nothing. "It has happened. And you put it in motion. Let's go."

Gia takes a tentative step toward me. "Is this because I said I loved you?"

I stare up at the sky, laughing. Of all things. If only it were that simple. "I think you've confused your love for my song with your love for me."

"I'm not confused in the slightest," she says, her voice gathering steam. "I'm fully lucid and above board, unlike someone else I know. Why didn't you tell me the song was about us?"

I sigh, feeling like I've reached my breaking point. "I planned to. Wanted to get through this tour first. See where we landed before I bled my heart all over the floor."

I turn to face her, looking deep into her eyes as she processes just how real and weighty my feelings are. "And are you really that blind, Gia? I'm so in love with you that it scares the shit out of me. But now that I know the queen can't handle the simplest request, fuck it. I'm out."

Her face registers this slowly. She starts chewing on her thumbnail and asks in a small voice, "Out of the band, or my life?"

I don't say what I'm feeling. I don't say anything, and she must know what that means.

She brushes past me with a brusque, "Fine," and yanks open the door.

Chapter Twenty-Nine

GIA

The bus feels too quiet when I climb on. Nothing but that soft mechanical hum as I move slowly, like walking into a trap I've accidentally set. Brady sits cross-legged on the sofa with his laptop while Tai leans against a cupboard, chewing a cuticle. They both look up at the same time.

"Hey," I say.

Brady closes the laptop with a *thwack*. Tai says nothing. The show ended a couple of hours ago, and I'm still reeling from being so thoroughly deserted by every member of my band. No one uttered a peep to me except Shae with an encouraging, *"Chin up. Focus on the next gig."*

I wandered the Navigli district of Milan alone, hoping the ancient, dark water of the canals and party atmosphere might steer me toward the right vibe.

How to handle this conversation.

"So," Brady starts, his tone sugar-laced sarcasm, "are we allowed to know what shit is brewing in our own band? Or is sharing now a fine-able offense?"

Tai winces. "Brady…"

"Just trying to figure out where the line is now. Since, apparently, we're on a need-to-know basis."

I glance at Tai, hoping for a little backup, but his gaze stays locked on mine—bruised, steady, and maybe worse than Brady's full-on attack.

"And what the hell were you thinking?" Brady sounds appalled and sickened. "Singing his song without asking."

My entire body wilts, cheeks hot with humiliation from being the idiot I truly was tonight.

"I fucked up is what happened," I say. "And this is my official apology." A sudden whiff of stale grease makes my nose wrinkle. The smell of their abandoned takeout on the table makes me acutely aware of the missing singular scent. "Where's JC?"

"Not hanging around for the apology blowjob, that's for sure," Brady scoffs.

I pin him with a venomous look. "Dude, that is uncalled for."

Brady lifts an eyebrow. "Is it?"

I start to say something, and then realize I can't find any words. I'm in the worst headspace. This tour promised so much, but it's delivering nothing but treacherous emotions and chaos.

Tai finally pipes up. "JC hopped a ride with Sawyer. We'll meet up in Rome."

Christ, I think, *another show to grind through.* How we pulled off tonight's gig is a miracle. I felt weightless, suspended in midair. Grabbed the mic and rambled an apology through the tepid, unsure applause. Four thousand sets of eyes flicked between JC and me, and we might as well have been wearing signs that said, "Lover's spat in progress." He refused to look at me, even as we slayed the choruses and the crowd went batshit.

The only saving grace? Amber hit the road on her own volition. Typical of an ex. Stir up shit and vamos.

Brady snaps my attention back. "What crazy power trip are you on, Gia? I respect JC for walking. I would've done the same."

Tai steps in to soften the blow. At least he doesn't look at me with disgust. "We're not trying to be assholes, okay? But while you two orbit each other in your own little galaxy, we're left holding the fallout when the supernova explodes."

Brady's expression hardens just a fraction. "And we're just the supporting cast in *The Gia and JC Show*."

"That's not fair," I protest. "I built this band. I've been grinding since open mics and garage sessions."

"And we've been right there with you," Tai reminds me. "We've bled for this too. But ever since JC came on, it's like your focus shifted. Your energy's different."

I expected this, but still find myself unable to suck it all up. "You mean professional? Because I'm trying to keep this shit on track while—"

"No," Brady cuts in. "He means obsessive. Controlling. We all know your sex ban wasn't about hygiene or harmony. It was about *him*. You didn't want to see JC get it on with some groupie."

The words land like a slap. Tai doesn't say anything. He doesn't have to. His stricken expression is an answer in itself. And JC ghosting me, not acknowledging even one of my dozens of texts, piles on the guilt. My shoulders slump. If you told me a week ago this is where we'd be, I wouldn't have believed you.

Brady, sensing the point has finally hit home, dials back his anger. "Look, we get it. He's a snack. *I'd* fuck him in a heartbeat. But we're all betting our futures on this tour. This is not the time for star-crossed lovers shit. I mean, Jesus. With the prime minister of Italy in the house!"

I don't reply to this. None of us pipes up with anything. But the air vibrates with everything we're not saying.

And leave it to Brady to save the best for last. "And, seriously, Gia, I said this before, but how does this play out? Think about your future. You're thirty-five, slaying a string of shows in Japan, and he's rolling into the drugstore for seniors' day discounts."

Something cold blooms in my chest. I know with a blinding certainty tonight is on me to fix. I overreacted. Lost it completely. But JC put this wild ache in me. He made me fall so hard. And Brady has no clue how deeply my love for JC runs. For him to minimize it with another swipe at our age gap pisses me off.

"And you two keep chasing anything and anyone that fogs a mirror," I snap. "How is that better?"

"What Brady's trying to say," Tai interjects, "is that *we* are your people. Thick as thieves. JC's filler, as far as the band is concerned. And..." He pauses as if thinking whether he should say what comes next. Brady tips his head in a gesture of—*go*. "You're worth more than him. He's yesterday's news stealing your front page."

I dig deep inside myself to find the strength not to fall for this. To get sucked into their jealous bullshit, like all the times before. They're gifted amateurs. JC's talent eclipses theirs, and they know it. And, yes, I was demoralized by the attention JC's been getting, but it has a reciprocal effect.

We are blowing up.

Thing is, maybe an explosion is what this band needs.

Just as I'm about to throw down the ultimatum we've been building toward, Brady beats me to the draw. "I pinged Kayla tonight, asking if she was down to start a new band. She's in. Say the word."

My jaw drops. It takes five seconds to process what they've done.

"You went behind my back?"

"How does it feel?" Brady asks, eyes colder than ice. He dumps his laptop onto the coffee table, gets up, and rallies Tai to join him. "C'mon, man, let's blow this joint. Give the diva all the space she needs to contemplate *her* solo act."

Tai shuffles to the door and pulls on a jacket. I can tell this is hitting hard. But picking fights is Brady's specialty. He thrives on combat.

So he can't resist one more uppercut to my chin. "If JC ever decides to talk to you again, I hope he rips you a new one."

I look down at my feet, at my black boots that stomped across the stage with so much fury. My heart aches to the point of imploding, and I let the tears fall only when the door slams shut behind them.

When our bus arrives in Rome the next morning, I'm climbing the walls. I tossed and turned the entire drive and sleep still feels hopeless. Before the boys wake up, I slip out and walk along the Tiber River, watching the water glitter in the sunrise, while last night spools like a worst-of highlight reel in my mind. JC brushed me off backstage without a word. Brady was genuinely hostile, and Tai offered nothing but an evasive shrug.

And today? It feels like Judgment Day with the entire world weighing in. Physics wasn't my jam, but Newton was right about the equal and opposite reactions thing. Our collective meltdown video is currently breaking the algorithm on TikTok's For You page.

Three million views and counting.

I want to strangle whoever scrambled onto the roof and filmed us. God, it's humbling to watch yourself acting like an idiot, the whole bad community theater aspect of it.

No wonder Sawyer summoned me to meet at his hotel.

I can tell from his snooty stare that the bellman manning the entrance of The Waldorf Astoria expects a grubby tour bus pauper to show some deference. But my insides are shredding apart, and one wrong word will push my teetering world over the edge.

I pump up my smile and waltz past him with both shaking hands stuffed deep into my pockets. First hurdle cleared. The second one won't be so easy. And the soaring, opulent lobby, crammed with one-percenters and their attitudes, makes me wish Sawyer and I were meeting at a sidewalk coffee shop, not some chandeliered billionaire haven that plays to his advantage.

He's on a call and waves at me from the lobby lounge. He shows up early for everything. JC says it's less about punctuality, more power play. He likes to survey the scene, get settled, and establish control before anyone else walks in. I'd rather eat spiders than attend this meeting, but I need to hit the reset button.

The press has gone mental. The long-buried reason for JC's disappearance is the hot gossip of the day, while a question mark hangs over the tour like a black cloud.

Not to mention, the conjecture of us.

And the number one headline screamed across the globe: *Has Gia Barlow lost it?*

I take a seat on the crushed blue velvet couch across from Sawyer's overstuffed chair. It feels like I'm at a parent-teacher interview about to be expelled. Or in court. I wonder if Sawyer rolls up anywhere not dressed like a defense lawyer.

He quickly wraps up his call and yanks out his earbuds. "That was the twentieth fire I've had to put out this morning, thanks to you."

"Yeah, things are a little crazy in my world too."

"A little?" He spits a laugh, running a finger down his exquisite silk tie. "That is a timeless statement of utter lack of awareness."

I flinch against my will. "You don't know the full story."

"Surprise, I do. JC told me everything." He and JC have similar piercing eyes, but the true-blue coldness in his gaze lands on my skin like early frost. "The legends in our industry know what it takes, Gia. Discipline, drive, professionalism. They aren't unpredictable wild cards who use a public stage to air petty vendettas. For all the industry expertise you claim to possess, that stunt you pulled proved you have the emotional intelligence of a teenager. We might, *might,* scramble out of the black pit you pushed us into by the seat of our pants."

I blow out a stuttering breath. "How's JC?"

"Gutted. Miserable. Blindsided." He pauses, as if thinking on a fourth adjective. "How do you think he feels? No one knew about Amber or why he killed the band. That was his own personal shame, now broadcast around the world. And to play his song without his approval?" He flicks his thumbnail against his index finger, repeatedly. "That is the ultimate betrayal."

The lashing, I'd expected. An audience, not so much. Two stuffy-looking businessmen with combovers drinking espresso in tiny cups next to the fireplace take in the unexpected entertainment.

"I know." I force myself to hold his gaze. He looks one step away from strangling me.

"Do you? I mean, do you truly understand the spectacle you've created?" A red patch on his neck, no doubt a Gia-induced rash, creeps above his collar. "You need to think long and hard about your career and where you want to end up. It's a fine line between the Boulevard of Broken Dreams and the Hall of Fame. You're one of the purest singers I've ever heard, but you can pave a highway to the moon with all the talented fuckups that never made it."

Sawyer's eyes flick to his phone again. Every few seconds, it beeps with new messages, and guaranteed every one of them is due to me. But one momentary pause from the speech of the century unclenches my jaw enough to stop my teeth from aching.

"You asked for JC, and I delivered him," Sawyer reminds me, back on track. "Do you understand how rare it is to be blessed with that kind of rocket fuel? Thousands of musicians would trade both their legs to play in the Royal Albert Hall. Give your head a goddamned shake!"

My insides curl into a tight ball. Being talked down to is one thing. A lecture from the patriarchy that embodies everything this industry needs to change?

"Dude, no need to get on your high horse. Give me some credit. I know how this business works. I know what to do to get what I want."

Sawyer breathes in and out slowly like he's calibrating his reaction. All the Trenton men have identical straight, narrow noses. Perfect for staring down at impulsive, impetuous women. "You're fucking twenty, Gia. You have no idea about the things you want."

I narrow my eyes at him. "I know I don't want to end up like you."

"You mean successful?" His goading tone shifts to patronizing in a heartbeat. "Watch your mouth. You are this close to losing everything."

My head spins from the truth of that. When I FaceTimed Audrie late last night to blubber and repent, she tried hard to boost my spirits. Sawyer is a picture of negative compassion. He pulls on his French cuffs in that irritated way of someone tasked with a bawling toddler.

"Here's what's going to happen," he starts. "This tour finishes without another drop of drama. When I say jump, you ask how high. Zero tolerance for insubordination. If you can manage that, our working relationship continues. One more misstep and we are done. Am I clear?"

"Yes," I say it quietly, for JC. He seemed so defeated last night. Before our return to the stage, it looked like he was trying not to cry.

"Then get upstairs and apologize. Room 304." Sawyer tosses an electronic key card on the table. He looks more fatigued than anything. "Never imagined you two together in my wildest nightmares, and do not break my brother's heart any more than you have," he warns. "I tolerate diva behavior to a point, because that's part of my job description. But you do not EVER fuck with my family."

As I palm the card, the espresso businessmen clear their throats and find someplace else to enjoy breakfast. I feel like a pile of concrete rubble. Heavy and broken. I can't bear the thought of not being around JC, not feeling his support, not seeing his smile. And if Sawyer thinks I'm going to cry and rock and wail and not own this, he can stuff it.

I push out of my chair and stand, throwing my shoulders back for the full five-foot effect. "I know it's on me to fix this. And I'll obey every one of your rules because I'm grateful for what you've done. But I'm not some stupid kid. Rhys told me you offered up JC to me because you were desperate to sign us. You didn't care about his baggage. And since you were willing to fuck over your own family member, spare me the hollow speech."

Sawyer watches my face for a long time, daggers in his eyes. But he knows it's the truth.

"JC is kind, decent, and smart. He understands me. He listens. He makes me feel worthy in an industry that values money over artistry. I can't ask for a better person in my life. And he agreed to work with me because *I* inspired *him*. Not for some shitty deal you concocted."

Sawyer laughs, like that's an absurd idea. "All that, and you still pull the shit you did last night? That's not how you treat someone special, Little Miss Sunshine."

Seriously? Sawyer, of the multiple divorces and moral high ground, accusing me of missing a sensitivity chip? Yes, I made a mistake, a very public one. But before he takes this any further, I reclaim custody of the raging wildfire in my heart.

"Even though it's not the reality you want to hear, I love JC. And I won't stop loving him because you, or anyone else, says I can't. I'm going to fix this, so you'd better get used to me hanging around."

Sawyer's face is wary and tired, waiting for the twist. After a long beat, he sighs and pinches the bridge of his nose. He looks pained. "God help us all."

Chapter Thirty

JC

ON MY BALCONY OVERLOOKING THE ETERNAL CITY, THE MORNING SLOWLY comes alive. Horns blaring. A hazy sunrise. Italian voices rat-a-tatting like gunfire off the sidewalk. I feel a step slow and sleep-deprived, my skin hot and itchy, brain fried.

Sawyer fumed nonstop on the drive to Rome last night, replaying every potential headline like a doomsday prophet. Then he pivoted to Gia's shortcomings, and something in me snapped.

I yelled, *"Shut up!"* and couldn't bear to see pity in his eyes.

After checking into the hotel, I stargazed for hours, wondering how the hell Venus became the planet of love. If the sulfuric acid lingering in its clouds didn't dissolve you, the atmosphere would crush you. Or incinerate you at 464 degrees.

The greatest irony? Anyone who's ever fallen in love knows that a one-way ticket to Venus might hurt less.

My buzzing phone pulls me from the outer space of my head. I fish it out of last night's jeans. It's Rhys. It's always him—showing up with honey for my tea, offering me a safe room to crash in when the Amber situation exploded years ago, and talking me through the wreckage again last night.

RT: Checking in. What's your status?

JT: Tired. Hating social media.

Sawyer has graciously forwarded multiple videos all morning, each more cringeworthy than the last. I feel inescapably on display, everything private inside me yanked out for the world to see.

RT: Did you and Gia talk it out yet?

JT: Sawyer asked to meet with her first.

RT: Asked? 😳 **Would love to be a fly on the wall for that showdown.**

I laugh, and it feels good to have my lungs do something other than collapse in on themselves. Trashing Sawyer is Rhys's national pastime, but I know it isn't easy being the guy in charge, the one who makes all the fun disappear.

And despite my love for Gia, she did cross a line.

I'm about to fire off a reply when soft knocks ring out on my door. Tension flutters through the room and my heart.

JT: Gotta run. She's here.

RT: Text me after, K? And hugs from Dani. We're both Team JC and Gia. No pressure. LOL.

I pocket the phone and rake both hands through my unwashed hair. My stomach is just empty enough to feel the full weight of apprehension. I fought against our simmering attraction for so long because maybe I knew we would end up here.

I cross the suite in a few short strides. When I open the door, the veil between the darkness of last night and this morning lifts. Gia stands there, cheeks flushed from the cold, and she has, even now, stunning eyes. Everything occurs there.

And something new lives in their depths.

Remorse.

"Hi."

"Hey."

She scratches at her messy ponytail. "Can I come in?"

I feel a ping of anxiety inviting her into my space. Nothing is the same anymore, but the presence of her is so familiar. It brings back the thousand small journeys that led us here.

I watch her scan the suite, the acres of golden carpet. "How did things go with Sawyer?"

She makes a face. "I haven't been banished to Mordor. Not yet. I'm on probation until the end of the tour. He said no one ever fucks with his family."

A soft ache pulses in my throat. For all the times Sawyer has driven me around the bend, to hear this is to feel the gates of my heart fling open wide.

"Probation seems justified," I affirm. "There are boundaries you don't cross. You don't hijack someone's music."

Gia stares up at me, her eyes two big moons on a sorrowful face. "I didn't—"

"You did," I interrupt.

She sinks onto the edge of the bed, head bowed. I can see her throat working, swallowing down whatever excuse she was about to offer. Whatever I'm feeling inside is barely recognizable. In my mind, before she arrived, I had it all worked out. What to say and how to say it. Now I'm standing in front of her, both of us with nothing and everything left to lose.

I start pacing, trying to shake off the nerves tightening around my ribs.

"I'm sorry," she finally says. "Can you forgive me?"

I stop in front of her, and she lifts her face. I imagine what she sees —dark circles, bloodshot eyes. JC Trenton, teen idol in crisis mode. Five seconds feels like five hours.

"I don't know if I should," I say, my voice gritty with tension. "Life is about lessons, and you haven't learned anything from yours. You're still terminating. Me. The boys. Brady texted me asking if I wanted to join their new band."

Gia blinks in disbelief. "Really?"

"Yeah. It shocked me too. Tell me if this is worth the power or the control or whatever it is your behavior gives you."

She immediately blurts out, "It's not worth it. Not at all. And I understand I need to change. I promise I will."

Her gaze of defenseless vulnerability sends me reeling. I take a deep breath, the warm air in the room thickening, settling into my lungs. The heat pulls me back to last August in the Trenton boardroom when we first met, sunlight spilling across her pale skin and the awareness blooming that she was tracking me as closely as I was watching her.

Now I study the contours of her face, those lips that make me groan every time they touch mine, and the realization lands hard. I'm completely in over my head.

How does this happen? To fall in love and be disassembled by it.

The urge to punish her, to teach her a lesson, starts to fade, but I shore up my melting defenses. "Part of me thinks you're just saying that so I do forgive you. And you'll slide right back into the same shitty patterns. I'm not doing this again. I can't." The last word comes out rough and Gia stares down at her hands. I feel both the physical pull drawing me to her and the rage for what she did. Why is this so hard? "I'm sorry if I sound harsh," I add. "I'm fucking exhausted."

Gia chews on her bottom lip and eventually asks, "Has Amber said anything?"

"We had a long call this morning. She apologized for coming to the show and we said all the things we needed to say. It actually made me feel better, finally getting it off my chest." At Gia's sharp intake of breath, I add, "And no, we're not getting back together. Ever."

Her voice turns small. "Does she hate me?"

"What if she does? You can't do a thing about it. And even if she did, who cares? She isn't your friend."

She digests that, me holding my breath, half expecting a tirade against Amber for showing her face last night after promising not to. Instead, she says quietly, "I'm glad you feel better."

My blood slows its breakneck trek through every vein, but the heartbreak is still there, little shards piercing my soul. Talking to Amber and finally getting closure made me confront what I'd kept sidelined for so long. And it might mean the end of Gia and me.

"One good thing came out of this, at least. Clarity about what I want." A tendon in my neck twitches, but I power through. "I want kids. Not tomorrow, but sooner than later."

Her eyes travel across my face. She senses it. "And I'm not the right person to do that with."

We look at each other for a long time, the weight of everything unspoken thick between us. I clear the lump in my throat, but my voice still sounds wrung out. "I'm afraid of not being enough for you when you finally realize what you want. And of having to start over again five years from now..."

I trail off, shifting my gaze from hers. A flash of shame passes through me. To be this emotionally naked in front of her. It's hard to breathe.

Gia reaches for my hands. Tentative at first, then more assured as she pulls me between her legs. "Hurting you kills me on a cellular level. There's no excuse. I just..." her voice wavers on the last word. "I wanted you so bad. I saw Amber and lost my mind. I'm sorry." She swipes her sad, glittering eyes. "I'm twenty and stupid and jealous. Messed up and fucking everything up. But I still love you." After a shuddering breath, she continues, "And I want kids one day too. I'll be a damn good mother."

The honesty in her voice punches straight through me. "I think you'll be a ferocious mother."

"How do you know what I'm willing to commit to if you don't bother asking?"

"Gia," I sigh, giving my head a little shake, "you don't fix hurt with a baby. And I can't ask you to throw away your career. I couldn't live with myself knowing I forced you down the same path as your mother. I already feel like I'm altering your trajectory."

"Who says I'm giving up anything?" she says. "*You* can change diapers while I rock the house."

It takes me a moment to recognize the change in atmosphere. She's looking at me like she's trying to read my soul and call bullshit at the same time.

"You know what I think?" She leans back, crossing her arms. "You're scared. Of me. Of my perceived lack of commitment. And maybe you enjoy this perpetual state of whatever it is, because it's easier. Because you don't have to risk your heart."

"Easy?" My jaw tightens. "You think any of this is easy? I'm surprised my phone hasn't gone up in flames from the nonstop texts. That is all you."

Gia stands abruptly, energy coiling around her. "Then what? Where does that leave us? Two people who walk away without trying? Fuck that." She kicks at the carpet with a sound of disgust. "There's no money-back guarantee with love, no quid pro quo. You dive in blind and pray you come up for air unbloodied and breathing."

Her eyes are two rings of fire, challenging me. She will not blink or wilt.

"I can say sorry a hundred times, and I know it sounds like BS, but I truly am. I hurt you; I hurt my best friends. Maybe killed my career. In the end, I did what I did because I love you. And if this ends here, then at least I know I fucking said it."

Our eyes linger on each other, and then we both look away. I'm aware of Gia's sweet perfume lingering in the room, but she's still the most beautiful thing in it. All the words I've held onto for weeks suddenly spill.

"Do you think I don't love you? I'm losing my mind over what you do to me."

Her lips part slightly, the rest of her face caught in stunned disbelief. "Then why haven't you said it?"

"Because I'm different from you. I keep things locked up. I'm careful. Maybe too much." I scrub my hands over my face, feeling grungy and beat up. "There's a lot I haven't told you about my past, but I grew up in a fishbowl, under scrutiny from day one to fulfill my father's expectations, not allowed to be just me."

She cocks her head. "What do you mean?"

"I had to live like a cardboard cutout in the shadow of my father. Be successful, but not more successful than him. The nepo-baby bullshit didn't help either. And when things blew up between him and Rhys, I lost my best friend. After that, touring was the only place I could breathe. My safe space. Then that implodes, and suddenly I've got nothing."

I blink away the tears that have been threatening to fall, and something stirs in Gia's face.

"I'm not a TikToker sharing every tear. What happened with Amber was private and painful for both of us. And I didn't tell the truth because it fucking hurt too much. You haven't been through this kind of loss yet, so maybe it's hard to understand why I kept it close to my chest."

Gia, whom I'd never categorize as a world-class listener, has, I can tell, carefully tracked every word. She guides me to sit on the bed, coming to kneel at my feet. Her hands cup my knees in a gentle squeeze. Wetness gathers on her lashes. "You loved, and she broke you. That's okay. But you're still here, still alive. And you're right, I haven't been in love. Not until you. But I feel like we're soulmates. Yes, we're different, but that's good. I kick your ass; you kick mine. That's how couples work."

She gives my knees a shake. "Don't be scared of us or let your past swallow you whole. Your scars are poetry. Turn them into music. Anything else is a waste of you. Please forgive me. I won't do anything like that again. And let me love you. Please."

I feel stripped raw. And Gia looks young, fresh, and so pretty at my feet, laying herself bare. Everything about her, her entire being is a provocation. She's softening me; I want to spend all day wrapped in her arms.

And she's right, I am scared. Because I'm older and know what commitment means.

And suddenly my mind spins backward to last December.

I drove Gia home during a snowstorm. Parked in her driveway, we kept talking as the hood of my car disappeared under a blanket of snowflakes. When our words dried up, she looked at me. The urge to kiss her threw my brain out of sync. But I let all my repressed feelings puddle onto the floor of my Porsche. I pecked her on the cheek instead, wished her a Merry Christmas, and drove home in a state of utter misery.

Pure cowardice.

I didn't trust the moment.

I feel my eyes burning. More than a decade braced against the world, and this spitfire slices straight through it. It's unsettling, intense, and liberating.

"Since when did you become the older, wiser one?" I dare to ask.

The smallest smile lifts the corner of her mouth. "Nice try. You're the old one in this relationship. Now and forever."

I smooth her hair back, thumb away her tears, and tip her chin up with one finger. "You make me want to risk it all, Gia."

I hadn't planned to say the words. But there they are, hanging in the air.

"I'm right there with you," she says, her voice equally soft. "I promise."

I let the silence settle between us. There are still questions and conversations to have, but for one suspended beat, everything aligns—our mistakes, our truths, our grief, our desire. Then her stomach growls, and it dissolves the last whisper of tension. We both sputter a laugh, touched by the absurdity.

"No time for breakfast," she admits. "I'm starving. Can I raid your minibar?"

Just like that, we're us again. Gia moves on fast, too fast sometimes. Maybe there's a lesson in that for me—to not marinate endlessly. But deep down, my cowgirl needs to learn something too.

"I have a better idea," I say, keeping my tone perfectly casual.

"I'll eat anything you put in front of me. Chicken feet. Organ meats. Not picky."

"Gia," I say quietly, standing and offering my hand. "You can order everything on the room service menu and charge it to Sawyer's room, but first, follow me."

She studies my face, trying to read my intentions. I can see her calculating. "What are you thinking?"

I expect her to push back, to question like she always does. But she reaches for my hand, lacing her fingers with mine. The momentum shifts into something inevitable and urgent, and we can't stay where we are, not for another moment.

Not with sound check in three hours and a lifetime of need scorching my blood.

Chapter Thirty-One

GIA

THREE ROOMS, TWO CHAISE LOUNGES, ONE GIANT BED, AND JC CHOOSES the bathroom like it's the only place that can hold what's about to happen. He shuts the door, clicks on the lights, and dims them until the walls of shimmering white marble glow like they're alive. The space is big enough to rehearse in, with a small audience. Towels so thick, you could fall back on them and sigh.

"Slumming it again, huh?"

I joke to settle my racing heart. A stillness has come over JC. His shoulder muscles are locked, eyes unblinking in the low light, something dangerous in the air.

"Can you take your clothes off please?" he asks.

A small breathless sound escapes my lips. "What about you?"

"Ladies first."

We've seen each other naked and done unspeakable things to each other's bodies. This feels different. Like I'm trapped in a room with a starving bear.

I tug the zipper of my hoodie lower. "Everything?"

"Yes, Gia. Everything."

He scratches the dark shadow of beard along his jaw, watching as my hoodie drops to the floor, my vintage Lilith Fair T-shirt with all the holes dumped on top. When I unfasten my bra, the fancy one, I feel oddly self-conscious slipping it off. All my natural stage exhibitionism is packed up and gone.

"Halfway there." JC's low, gruff voice is almost unrecognizable.

I fumble with the button on my jeans. It's so warm in here. But tell that to my diamond-hard nipples that JC's gaze tracks, his pupils huge and black, like my favorite rare vinyls. The hungry possession deep within them sends a ripple of anticipation down my spine.

I toe my sneakers off, wriggling my jeans down. Kick them aside with my socks. Nothing left but my red satin panties and an uncertain smile.

"Why in here?" I ask.

"I didn't shower last night. I'm feeling dirty."

Whoa. Did not expect that. And the bathroom makes sense now. A room built for purity, about to be defiled.

He chose it on purpose.

And, oh man, his voice.

Thick and musical, the sound of gorgeous disaster.

JC tips his head to the last scrap of fabric protecting my modesty. "Go ahead," he says, his teeth so pretty and white within that subtle smile.

I inch my panties lower and wonder where the hell this version of JC came from. Anchored in a very specific mission, with no vulnerability anywhere. Possibly dangerous. I can smell his masculinity, the promise of it.

JC closes the distance between us. He's lost in my face, scraping his thumb pad along my lower lip. "So much beauty spills out of here. The sweetest sounds that shatter me."

His touch unravels me, but I force myself to stand in place. If I get closer and touch him, kiss him, I'll never stop.

"My voice with yours is even better."

A deep, dark laugh. Borderline wicked. "Flattery will get you nowhere in here," he says. "A certain someone needs her fire tamed. Are you okay with that?"

Before I can answer, he sucks his index finger into his mouth. The glistening skin when it slides out makes my knees weak. The destination is crystal clear.

"Yes," I whisper like I've just agreed to another piece of pie and not what is certainly sensual terrorism.

JC nudges me backward until my spine presses onto the cloud of towels then kicks my legs wider with one knee. He skims his mouth over mine, maddeningly letting me chase until my teeth sink into his lower lip. If this is the game, bring it on. I'm ready to spar, ravage, and play.

"Oh, Gia." His rumbling laugh hums in the air between us. "You will not be in control this time."

And then he's kissing me roughly. Taking more than giving. He works his finger over me, then pushes inside me, all the way, knuckle-deep. I gasp, the sensation so intense, I can't even kiss him back.

Nothing but pure sparkle dancing all over my skin.

"JC." It spills from my lips in a desperate-sounding whimper. I clutch at his shirt, flexing my hips to somehow find another inch of space for him to go deeper.

"Fuck, Gia," he groans. "You make me think of all these dirty things."

He slides another finger inside to join the first, every pump of them driving a little deeper as I moan and writhe, my heartbeat racing until it's one endless throb. His free hand wraps around my waist, pulling me into him and his hot wall of muscles. Then he dips his head to my neck, his mouth nuzzling the curve of my ear, hovering until my body tingles and tightens. I can't see a thing through the dark curtain of his hair.

But I can feel everything about him.

"Why did you do it?" he asks in a rough whisper.

The world narrows to his voice, and then it explodes. "What? What are you talking about?"

"Why did you sing my song?"

My brain tries to file his words somewhere sensible and fails. I already told him why, sort of, but JC has that musician's instinct. He knows the layers that run deep beneath surface meanings.

His hand travels across my belly, sliding up and up until his palm flattens on my chest, holding my heartbeat. His dark irises flare as they find mine.

"Tell me the truth."

I blink, fighting through the resistance. The hardest swallow of my life dislodges the barren truth. "Because I wanted her to know you picked me."

He holds still. It's quiet, the silence oversized. Nothing but a barely audible *pop* when his fingers slide out in a smooth, unbroken gesture. He presses his forehead to mine for the barest second, then he pulls away.

"Thank you," he says. "I needed to hear that."

I breathe in his warmth, the citrus musk that will haunt me every night we're apart. My heart twists with inexpressible want. How can I not love this man? Even in dominance, he's unafraid to be emotionally raw. And maybe that's worth the humbling exposure.

"Okay," JC says softly, bringing me back. "Now it's your turn to undress me."

That flicker of a smile again, still not a whole one. I like the sweet version of him, but something tells me JC with a point to prove is next-level. I pull the T-shirt over his head. Unzip and maneuver denim over his hardness. His steady gaze melts into me, warming my bones.

And his almost nude body is fire.

"Good to know you're not above branded swag," I tease.

He smiles down at me, clearly proud of his very tented Fender monogrammed boxers. "I'm just a lowly guitar player waiting for Chanel to discover me."

I press my palm against him, huge and hot, beneath the cotton. All mine. "You're an idiot."

"As long as I'm your idiot."

He strokes my hair, slowly, lovingly, now that it's confirmed love goes both ways. Then, very casually, he tugs a towel from the silver dowel it hangs from. He folds it into thirds lengthwise and lays it between us on the glittering mosaic tiles.

"Get on your knees, please."

I try to laugh it off. "Are you serious?"

"Gia." His voice holds a warning in it, so I follow his order only somewhat reluctantly. He's said *please* and *thank you*. If this is a one-off lesson administered with respect, I can play ball. It's not in his nature to be cruel.

"I'll walk you through it," he adds. "Safely."

My pulse skitters, feeling it all—locked in the domain of his gaze and tight-jawed restraint. With unsteady hands, I release him from the boxers. His satin fullness stares me in the face, and I need a moment.

I need to be honest.

"I've never done this," I whisper.

He smooths hair off my forehead with the gentlest touch. "Good. I want to be your first everything. You know what's going to happen, right?"

"I think I have an idea."

"Beyond the physical, Gia."

Hard to come up with a snappy reply when his *physical* blocks out all light from the universe, so I let him win. "I'm a lousy guesser. Just tell me."

He looks down at me with a strange, serene calm that doesn't match the glint in his eyes. It feels like another day in detention hall for me, waiting for the other shoe to drop. God, the endless state of me. Forever in trouble.

Then he says, "I'm going to make you ache trying to contain me," and my entire body starts to shake.

Now he has my attention.

"Is that okay?" His deep voice vibrates off the tiles, like the lowest E string strummed on his Les Paul.

What am I supposed to say? Of course it's okay. Within five minutes of meeting him, I wanted this. I might not be on my knees on my own terms, but there's a reason for that.

I incline my head in silent agreement, a bit of my natural swagger fading. There's so much real estate. I need to figure out how this geometry will work.

"Start slow," JC suggests. "I'll guide you."

If that isn't the sexiest thing I've heard. And, seriously, if I can make it in the music industry, this is doable. Leaning in, I tongue him from shaft to crown. His musky scent and saltiness flood my senses, the pulse of his hips encouraging more. My fingers curl around his hard-on, and nothing feels familiar as I guide the length of him into my mouth.

For two heartbeats, I force myself to breathe. To just feel.

Then JC's fingers dig into my scalp. "Yes," he moans. "Keep going."

So I do. I try my best.

And I feel so powerful absorbing his power. His grip on my head tightens as he builds toward a crescendo, bitten-off grunts becoming low growling animal sounds.

It lasts a minute, maybe two, then he hisses, "Jesus, fuck," and explodes, his features twisted in a kind of rapture that borders on pain.

He rasps my name, but I can't find my voice at all, muted by one hard thrust after another. He's everywhere, filling space, time, and eternity, his breath catching between garbled groans.

Me? I'm in awe, a glow of pride flooding me.

I did that.

JC clings to me through the aftershocks, quivering and quiet. I'm not sure what expression is on my face, but I've never felt so thunderous before. His eyes slowly flutter open, attempting to focus on mine. I'm waiting for him to say anything other than heaving pants when he mutters "shit," staggers back, and then, boom—collapses onto the tiles.

Chapter Thirty-Two

JC

DRIFTING GENTLY TOWARD THE SURFACE OF REALITY, I FIND GIA KNEELING beside me, hair cascading over pale shoulders, pupils flecked with gold. A mythical nymph from some fairy tale who makes me feel everything.

"I guess I did alright, huh?" she asks.

I laugh, low and easy, my limbs liquid and floaty with dopamine. The last time I felt this out of my body owed a debt to some fine mezcal. And that was a decade ago. My hand reaches for hers, our warm fingers settling, grounding me while I'm still spinning in some faraway galaxy.

"That was … intense. And, yes," my voice comes steadier now, "nothing compares to you."

Gia brushes a kiss on my lips. So featherlight, and yet it ignites a fuse straight into my veins.

"Your side hustle was keeping me out of trouble, which meant you were basically set up for failure." She attempts a smile, but her mouth trembles slightly at the corners as her hand tightens around mine. "I don't want to make you feel bad, ever. I love you. In the deepest part of my guts. It terrifies me how much I come apart around you."

The fuzzy euphoria starts to lift, bringing my thoughts back into sharper focus. I caress her flushed cheek, falling prey to the still visceral memory of her mouth around me. But she means so much more.

"I feel the same way."

"You do?" Her voice curls with longing.

"Yeah," I murmur. "I do."

Sunlight pours in through the stained-glass window high above the sink, casting hues of violet, ruby, and sapphire across the tiles and her skin. We're inside our own private kaleidoscopic house of magic. Private and intimate. Gia waits, holding space for me to say more.

When nothing comes, she asks, "Do you need help getting up?"

I laugh, then immediately wince as dull pain shoots up my spine into my skull. Twice in one week, she's knocked me flat on my ass. What kind of wreck will I be in a year?

"That ended in disaster last time," I remind her. "I think I got this. Can you start the shower? Crank it real hot."

Gia steps into the walk-in and turns it on, keeping an eye on me. I want to stand, but I get the impression she might need to hold me up. Pride kicks in, pushing me to prove I can. I rise slowly, legs unsteady, still floating.

"C'mon." Gia tugs my hand. "Time to get clean."

She leads me into a wall of humidity where billowing steam blurs everything into a dreamlike haze. But I can see her so clearly. Water from the rain shower cascades down Gia's shoulders, tracing every curve, spilling down between her breasts. She reaches for the body wash, squeezing a trail over my chest, lathering me up. Her hands explore with purpose, skin more slippery, touch gliding differently. A low moan slips out. There's a specific intimacy in caring for someone else's body.

And the only thing better than Gia is wet Gia.

"We need to do this every day," I murmur, my words almost swallowed by the steam.

Gia lifts her eyes to mine. A long minute passes before she asks, "Will you finish the tour with us?"

"Do you think that's a good idea?"

"I think it's the only idea," she whispers back. "We need to be a united front. But I'll take the lead in making things right for you and the boys."

Oh, my sweet rebel with a cause. On the smooth column of her neck, the bruise I left behind last week has darkened into deep purple. We're leaving marks on each other, but I ache for a world where we play without drama.

Tonight won't be that world.

Not with the swirling rumors and my phone lighting up with interview requests. It will be that way every night until the tour wraps. With Gia at my side, I don't have to face this alone.

But I don't want to face it at all.

I rest my forehead against hers. Water echoes off the tiles, the drumbeat of my heart syncing to the rhythm.

"I have to say something. If I don't, we'll be hounded."

Gia studies me, all the gears grinding behind my tired eyes. "Don't be scared. Tell your truth. You did what you could at the time," she says softly.

I stroke her hair, wishing we had more time in the suite. Wishing we could live in this Roman holiday forever. I feel so fragile that, if she breathes on me, I might disintegrate. But Gia won't let that happen. Her belief in me is steadier than my own.

And she's right. The secret has sat in my mouth too long. I'm ready to let it go, even if I have to live with the fallout. Because men like me don't get the benefit of the doubt anymore. We get remembered for the worst thing we ever did. And who's going to believe a nineteen-year-old rock star decided, once he got his head straight, to embrace fatherhood?

No one.

"I'll be there for you no matter what," Gia says, reading my fear. "So just do it."

She stands on her tippy-toes, brushing her lips against mine. I can taste my salty earthiness on her tongue when it twirls and tangles with mine. We kiss and feel, give each other wings. I wash her hair with deep massaging strokes, and she soaps up my growing erection between us, both of us laughing.

Time slows to a crawl.

When the last of the lemon-scented lather swirls into the drain, we towel each other off and slip into matching thick terry robes. I'm stone-cold sober but feel intoxicated by her proximity. Even though I wanted her to learn a lesson, she turned that dynamic on its head. Gia was powerless to resist and yet somehow the one in control.

I suppose I'd better get used to that.

Her palms slide over my chest, her arms tightening around me like a vise. If the boys agree to push sound check, we have three more hours. But I'm in no hurry. And neither is she.

"Fuck 'em all, Jameson," she whispers with that fierce Gia conviction. "Fuck 'em all but us."

I breathe into her damp hair. I wish I knew what was happening inside my heart, other than it reminding me of hopes and wants.

And I don't feel entirely sure where my head is, but when I say, "Then let's give 'em a show, Regina. One they'll never forget," I'm as surprised as anyone to hear the edge of a grin in my voice.

♫

"Yo! Look who's back." Brady drops his phone and struts across the lounge, shirtless and grinning. He hugs me as if nothing in the world has ever bothered him. "The bus missed you, dude. Best-smelling guy in the biz."

"Thanks, man. Creed is my go-to."

"I looked that shit up," he banters back. "For five hundo a bottle, that cologne better come with a lap dance."

Hmm. Not the best analogy with his spangly stage things drying across what looks like many yards of dental floss strung between the bunks.

Gia steps in beside me. She's rosy-cheeked from the cold air and my thorough destruction of her. "Hi."

Brady pins her with a look. "Can't say I missed you much."

I can't tell if he's being serious, although I expected some static. That's why we pushed our sound check by an hour. We need time to discuss.

Tai exits the bathroom, hands stuffed into his jeans. Energy stand-offish. He eyes Gia, then chin-nods at me. "How you holding up?"

"You know, basking in the fame. The latest viral TikTok star."

He gives me a wry smile. "Shae said tonight's going to be mental. Hope you have a plan."

"We do," I say. "We talked and—"

"Talked?" Brady's eyebrows shoot to the sky, that lazy little smirk curving up the corner of his mouth. "You guys are giving major hook-up vibes."

"Seriously?" Gia sighs. "Can we not go there?"

Tai and Brady exchange quick, furtive glances. We could trade barbs all afternoon, but Dad always told me, before I face the press to read the room. I understand what's needed here.

"Well," I say. "We did shag like maniacs, and it was amazing. But then we talked."

Gia smacks my arm with a spirited "Excuse me?" but, hey, it was amazing. Atomic heat still pulses through every vein and muscle because we burned that bed to ash.

Brady whoops. "See? Don't pretend you're better than us. It's okay to have needs."

"I'm not any better." Gia's voice brims with earned self-recognition that I might take a sliver of credit for. "In fact," she clears her throat, "as of now, the tour bus sex ban is done and dusted."

Tai squints at her. I get the sense there are layers here that I'm missing. But I don't know him well enough to read through the murk.

"No more rules," Gia adds quietly. "I promise."

Tai nods with deliberation. "Considering you never followed your own rules, that's big."

"Guess there is someone in this world who can wrangle the Queen." Brady turns to address me. "Does this mean you're in the band permanently?"

The day hits me all at once—the roller coaster of emotions, the upcoming show, the weight of everything I need to fix. But Gia, after some convincing, agreed to the only conclusion that made sense. "No, actually. I stick around until the tour ends as planned. After that, you continue without me."

A fast twitch, like an electric shock, buzzes around the lounge, a tiny inhale of breath from the boys. Tai's cool composure slips a notch.

"Really?" he asks, suspicious.

"That's the other thing," Gia says. "Shoot me Kayla's info. I think she'd be a great fit."

Brady blinks, processing. "Wow. We kinda thought this was like … the end of the road. You two riding off into the sunset."

Ah. So that explains Tai's energy. He thought we were staging a band coup. But the tight line of his shoulders still hunches close to his ears.

"What about all the shit from last night with your ex?" he questions. "How's that playing out?"

Over the next twenty minutes, I lay out the plan. Sawyer's arranging an interview to appease the media, and it happens with Amber involved, because this is the ending of our story, and she needs a voice in it.

Collectively, I explain, we keep our mouths shut. Play every show like it's business as usual. And make it clear the Pop My Cherry chapter for JC officially ends after the tour.

When I'm finished, Brady blows out a breath. "Shit. You mean it."

"That's cool," Tai says, reserve still embedded in his voice. "But is your ex playing ball? She sounds a little whack."

"We spoke twice today and cleared the air." I feel Gia stiffen beside me and huddle closer to her. It took a little more convincing for her to be comfortable with Amber and me doing a joint interview. But I promised we wouldn't be in the same room together. "And," I add, "I told her security will escort her out if she makes an appearance at any future show."

Tai nods again, but not in the way of someone agreeing with you. Maybe he thinks I don't have the balls to handle this. Truth be told, without Gia's support, I might not have.

"No violent tendencies?" Brady asks.

"I'm pretty sure we're good."

Amber wasn't violent. She was kindhearted and sweet until life threw her a bitter curveball. She loved animals and children and, in spirit, was one herself. There is a reason why I fell in love.

Tai shifts his gaze from me to Gia. Cautious, as is his nature. "What about at the meet-and-greets? The fans will hurl questions."

"Get used to throwing out *no comment*," I say. "The less oxygen this gets, the better. It's my mess to tidy up."

Brady scratches his epic bedhead. Seems oddly deflated that we're not throwing down headlocks or outrageous terms. "Fair. Gotta be honest though, I was low-key hoping you might stick around."

"He'll be sticking around me," Gia declares. "Play your cards right, and I might share."

She looks at me with that crooked-tooth smile, and my mind flashes to her on her knees, tonguing me from root to tip before slipping me into her mouth.

She blew my mind empty.

Bless her enthusiasm and white-hot innocence. Less expert and all the sweeter because of it.

I pull myself back to the here and now. "And in the spirit of sharing, I've got some ideas for ending this tour on a cracker note."

I know before Brady claps his hands and asks, "Is it too early for shooters?" and before Tai smiles for real—yeah, that landed.

They just needed to know I wasn't leaving them in a pile of shit. That I've got their backs. That nothing will blow their band up.

Reading the room.

Dad would be proud.

♫

It's funny how a month can feel like forever, until suddenly you're scrambling, wondering where all the time went. We're backstage in Barcelona, dripping in sweat, laughing, smiling, and gearing up for the mother of all encores.

The final show of our tour feels night and day to the uncertain energy we faced in Rome. We were all a little on edge, unsure how the crowd would react. It's not every day a band blows up on stage.

But we muscled past the hecklers, and once we cleared that first hurdle, every gig got easier. Bigger and wilder. Even crazier after *Music & The Muse* dropped the interview with me and Amber.

I didn't expect the tide to turn the way it did. It's a crap shoot when you lay yourself bare, warts and all. A few trolls tried to take me down, but fewer surfaced than I'd feared. And Amber owned her part, bravely stating she had to live with the decisions she made. I respected her for that. I wished her well and made the boundary clear—we were done.

Our lives might've been different with different choices, but like Gia says, you can't edit the past.

The only way is forward.

And here we are, moving toward another milestone.

I peel off my sweat-soaked t-shirt and swap it for its identical twin. Brady's hovering again for the skin show, but at least he tries to frame his obsessive staring as observational.

"Bro, how many black and white T-shirts do you own?"

"I'm in my Steve Jobs era. Streamlined. Less shit to manage. You should try it."

He grins, scraping back his blond bangs. "Nah. I'm still in my glitter and spandex era." After a pause, he comes in for a slightly awkward bro-hug. "Just wanted to say, it's been dope having you around. You're the real fucking deal. Respect."

"Thanks. Appreciate that. And you guys will take the world by storm, one step at a time. Keep chasing the dream."

Tai saunters over, his shirt and tie somehow still impeccable after two hours of craziness. "Speaking of chasing—dibs on the blonde hottie with dreads, front row."

"Pace yourself, brother," Brady warns him. "Tonight's party is wall-to-wall models and actresses." Addressing me, he says, "Thank your man Rhys for the tix."

My brother's connections from his influencer past keep the invites flowing. Tonight's after-party he scored us tickets to is some celebrity-studded affair the boys are panting over.

Me? I'm hot and bothered for one person only.

My head is on a swivel for our North Star, but Gia must still be primping in the bathroom. "How do you guys feel about the encore?"

Tai answers with a devious smile, "Those mofos won't know what hit them."

I'll leave all the pomp to the journalists after the fact, but *incendiary* is the goal. They left it to me to choose tonight's songs, and we're sending these kids home floating.

If *I* come down from cloud nine.

Gia slinks in, wowing us all in a tight black catsuit, tousled hair, and…

"Heels?" Brady does a double-take.

Gia spins. "Too much?"

I loop an arm around her waist. She's transformed again, and every iteration she comes up with melts my heart. "You're the right amount of over-the-top."

Shae barges in, sees Gia, and smacks a hand against her chest. "Sweet baby Jesus, girl! You are serious as a heart attack. Is this your work, Trenton?"

I shake my head. As if. My basic wardrobe doesn't hold a candle to Gia's she-jaguar era. Thank god we have hotel rooms tonight. No bunk could contain either of us.

"Well, it's time." Shae holds the door open. "Last call." She's acting like our tough general, but her chin wobbles slightly beneath the smile. She notices me noticing, and swipes a finger under both eyes. "I hate this part," she admits. "I always cry."

"Awww." Gia slides in to hug her. "You killed it. Thank you so much for everything."

I follow Gia and the boys out, confirming with a sniffling Shae, "Two mics up front?"

She smacks my ass, not going down as the softie with me around. "What do you think this is, Trenton, amateur hour? Go kick some butt before I kick yours."

Mounting the stage stairs, I can feel the air as thick as the anticipation. The chanting crowd senses it—something special's coming. My mic lined up next to Gia's is a dead giveaway. And then she appears in her first and only costume change of the tour, waving like the queen she is, thousands of voices merging into one throat-shredding scream of approval.

Phones light up like a galaxy of stars. I can feel my heartbeat in my fingertips.

We are on.

Behind his kit, Brady cracks the opening beat. I slide in with the guitar. Before I even hit the mic, a shockwave ripples backwards through the audience—the opening chords of "Need You Tonight" are unmistakable.

They erupt, jumping and grabbing their friends, screaming the lyrics with me. I lean into the sexy vocals, channeling Hutchence (everyone says my voice sounds like his) while Gia struts across the stage, making me and everyone else sweat with her raw moves. She was already a hot stage actress, but I'll take credit for coaxing out the full vixen. London Gia wasn't shaking her booty during choruses. Wasn't grinding behind me like an after-hours showgirl.

Damn.

Never sang a song this turned-on in my life.

We don't stretch the ending. The real kicker's coming.

And what happens next is one for the history books—mine, anyway.

I breathe the final line into the mic, my voice oozing desire because Gia is one of my kind.

Without giving the audience time to catch their breath, the house lights blare on. At the same time, mesh netting in the rafters unfurls, and a blizzard of silver confetti rains down.

Brady hammers that first drumbeat.

I howl the iconic, *"Hey, Hey, Hey, Hey—"*

And the crowd loses its mind. Until the day I die, I will never again experience the screaming wall of sound that explodes in my face.

Because no one on earth doesn't love "Don't You (Forget About Me)."

It's chaos. Strangers making out at the front of the stage. Others crying. We are responsible for the conception of at least five babies tonight.

So much love. So much energy.

Tai slays the synth track as if he were born in the '80s, and Brady's big drum riffs tumble through my bones. Gia and I ham it up, bringing one of the greatest love songs ever to rom-com life. She marches past, me pining, begging her to look my way.

And the finale! A sea of arms waving like metronomes during the world's biggest sing-along.

There are no words.

When we finish, the fans refuse to let us leave, showering us with endless applause, begging for more. I fling guitar picks while Tai and Brady crouch at the front, shaking every hand they can without getting yanked into the pit.

Me? It's hard to describe the weird sense of time distortion. Two hours have passed, but it only feels like five minutes. I'm sweat-soaked, heart pounding against my ribs, the roar of the crowd washing over me in waves. Feeling invincible yet vulnerable at the same time, because I can't capture the magic, this moment in time, and it's already slipping away.

But I feel a profound sense of gratitude—for the crowd, my band-mates. For my beautiful Gia, clinging to me and bawling tears of joy.

We both know this kind of magic happens once in a lifetime.

And even though this is her moment, I just want to stay in this noise, this light, this love.

Savor every second before the curtain comes down on the finale of JC Trenton.

Chapter Thirty-Three

GIA

"Gigi!" Audrie shrieks. "We made it!"

My bestie barrels into me, rocking us back and forth in a fierce hug. I'm still flying high from the rush of the show, and her girl-love brings me back to earth.

"You looked *so* hot tonight," she rambles drunkenly in my ear. "Best show ever!"

Wrapped in her arms, my throat thickens, both eyes starting to water. Shit. I promised myself I wouldn't cry. In the tiny, sensible, and mostly ignored corner of my mind, our final show was a lay-up. Me, the picture of poise. Not a vibrating hot mess crashing like waves against JC, my rock. Nothing can match the insanity from our first electric gig, but we tried.

We all bled for this.

I pull back, wiping mascara-streaked tears off my cheeks. "Thanks for coming. You two must be beat." And then I remember: duh, private jet. Paul Schlitzmann whisked his bride-to-be to Spain before they take off for Italy tomorrow. He's behind us, shaking JC's hand, acting like the CEO of our backstage.

Audrie giggles, "No, but yes," leaning in to whisper scandalously, "You're looking at the newest member of the Mile-High Club."

My hand flies to my mouth. "No!"

I drag her into a corner, craving every morsel of gossip she'll let me share. Am I thrilled they crammed our show in as a stopover? Not really. But this is her new life—pearl earrings, not fake Zara, designer heels where sneakers used to be—and I need to represent.

"So." I grin. "How was it?"

"Killer!" she gushes. "I mean, I was kind of worried the flight crew could hear us." She side-eyes Paul, who's bringing Wolf of Wall Street vibes in pleated slacks, beige cable-knit cardigan, and penny loafers. Amusing JC with their *tour-Tuscany-for-a-wedding-venue* mission. "He likes to talk dirty," she adds.

I stifle a laugh. That does not track. "Did you pick a date?"

"Paul likes Villa Cora in Florence," she says like this actually means something to me. "But they might not be able to accommodate August. You'll love it. It's so pretty and private."

And expensive is what she doesn't say. Gia from a month ago might've felt a pinch of envy. But my man spoils me with the riches of the erotic variety and keeps *his* trash talk to a minimum.

"Yo! Time to cel-e-brate!" Brady and Tai swoop in with fistfuls of plastic glasses overflowing with champagne. Brady shoves one into Audrie's hand and plants a sloppy kiss on her cheek. "You look like an executive assistant. Where's the briefcase?"

"I'd kiss you, but I'm not sure where that mouth has been," she fires back.

"All over Europe," Tai assures her. "And back." He shoots me a smile. He knows Brady will get over his crush on me and is helping him along, one man and woman at a time. And good for him. Guys need their buddies.

I wave JC and Paul over. JC loops his arm around the curve of my waist, tosses his impossibly shiny hair and smooches me on the lips. "I'm in love with tonight," he says, beaming a smile. "So in love with you."

My heart flip-flops. It smells like old shoes and good times in this bare concrete room, *Eau de Backstage,* but it feels like I've sprung up overnight, fully grown into a goddess. JC has opened up the unthinkable possibility: that I can fit against his smooth edges and still be me.

And did he ever pull out all the stops tonight! Full meltdown from the crowd with his choice of tunes.

"Guys!" Brady interrupts our second torrid kiss. "Can you keep your hands off each other for one second and help me out here?"

JC gladly relieves him of two glasses fizzing with champagne and hands one to me. I wink at Brady, who gives a little shake of his head. But his smile lights me up inside, just like the day he caught me staring at him across the high school cafeteria.

We've come so far since then.

And tonight lives inside me forever: standing shoulder to shoulder on stage, bound with sweat and adrenaline, the house lights hitting us like a sunrise. Pure, deafening love washing over us.

There are no words to describe musical ecstasy, but I have things to say to the wonderful souls who have created that magic with me.

I raise my glass, first to Audrie and Paul. "It means the world to have you here. You know how much I love you, A."

Then to Tai and Brady: "And you two. My dearest friends. My freakshows. My—"

"Jesus, girl," Brady cuts in. "Why are you going all end-of-the-world on us? I'll be the same asshole next week."

"Yes," I say. "But you're *my* asshole."

JC spits up the sip of champagne he sneaked, choking on laughter, as Tai grimaces. "You might want to rephrase that before the Grammy speech."

Paul soaks it all in with an amused smile. He might look like a Harvard Dad, but at least he rolls with the punches.

"Seriously," I say, voice catching, "you're all idiots, but I love you. Thanks for putting up with me."

Brady tries to gulp down his drink, but JC blocks the glass with his hand. Startled, Brady looks up at him fondly and kisses his knuckles. "Finally! You've come to your senses. I knew it was only a matter of time."

"Dude!" Audrie roars. "Inside voice!"

"It's okay." JC grins and slowly reclaims his hand, taking it all in stride. "All I wanted to say is props to the one and only Miss Gia Barlow." He lifts his glass. God, he's gorgeous when he smiles. "Thank you for the wild ride."

"Rub it in, why don't you?" Brady mutters. He tosses back his drink, eyes ballooning with a drank-that-too-fast expression. Then he lets out a belting burp that echoes off the walls.

Tai can only groan. The father to his eternal trainwreck son. "Forever classy, Mr. Bowen."

Audrie smirks, steps forward, and promptly dumps her champagne over Brady's head. The sentiment catches fire. One by one, the rest of us join—Tai, Paul, me. JC brings it home with a flourish, grabbing the bottle of Cîroc and spraying it like a victory lap. The cold stickiness coats my skin while our shrieks and collective laughter fill the room.

Our loveable showboat pretends to be offended, but we all know Brady loves the attention. When he shakes his dripping locks and asks, "Which one of you lucky souls wants to lick this off me?" I shake my head, pulling a slow grin.

Here we are.

Is there a better way to end our last show?

As Tai chucks a towel at Brady, JC slides beside me. His warm palm circles the small of my back, the steadiness I didn't know I craved.

"Nice speech, Miss Barlow," he murmurs. "Almost made me emotional."

"Almost?"

"You'll have to try harder next time." He leans in, brushing his lips against my temple, barely there, but enough to make me feel it in places only he knows.

"And what about you?" I ask, throwing it back at him, just as playful.

His smile is pure mischief. "I'm not done with you yet. Not by a long shot. And the night's still young."

♫

An hour later, we're on the outdoor patio of the W Hotel, a warm wind whipping around us. I'm nestled in JC's arms, his heartbeat slow and steady against my spine. Waves crash on Barceloneta Beach, the beach-front promenade a curl in the dark, spooling along the shore toward the city.

We dropped into the party, did a lap, and JC is already champing at the bit to leave. He has plans.

"Finish your drink and then we blast?" he whispers into my hair.

I burrow into his warmth and murmur yes. The glitzy crowd was fun for a hot minute, but the bedazzled outfits and too-cool-for-school bros wearing sunglasses at night are not my scene. Still, I need one last inhale of Spain. The end of our long, strange trip that gave my life and my heart a different shape.

I can't lie; it's been amazing and brutal, learning how to be a better person.

I take a deep breath and release it slowly. "Thanks for the upgrade."

JC nuzzles my ear; I can feel his smile. "Can't have rock and roll's next big thing slumming it in economy. What would the press say?"

"Guaranteed, I'm going to rock business class like a pro."

"How will this new Gia handle bitter flight attendants?"

I laugh out loud. "The same way I handle you: with authority."

JC turns and kisses me until I'm woozy, pressing me so close I can feel him already swollen and ready for what's to come. I shut my eyes and pretend, like I sometimes do, that I discovered him. That no one else holds a single claim. That I own him in the way Boomers believe Bob Dylan is theirs alone.

Mine, all mine.

When he pulls back, his eyes are dancing. "Not tonight," he says, his voice tender, flirty, and so very dirty.

The possibilities crash over me like a breaking wave.

I can't wait for what he has in store for me.

And there's so much left to learn about him.

I tip back the last of my wine, and we head inside, assaulted by a wall of thundering house music. JC holds my hand tight, shouldering a path past the chocolate fountains and rosé towers. The party is this weird mash up—half nightclub, half industry conference. Booths line the far wall, staffed by film and TV studio executives with teeth white as piano keys, smiling and hyping their shows. Actors work the crush of obsessed fans oohing and aahing and angling for autographs.

Trying to get out of here is like Grand Central Station at rush hour.

JC bumps up against a wall of Asian muscle, does the Canadian thing and apologizes, then stops moving altogether.

He's still as a statue, his gaze locked on the woman in front of us. She's one of the most beautiful Asian women I've ever seen, but my brain tries to make sense of the cropped ash-blonde wig and what must be blue-colored contacts.

For a second, my heart disintegrates. I see the old JC—the player. Is she another girlfriend from his past, another Amber with an axe to grind? Because the way his body goes tight, the way he looks at her, this isn't just shared history.

It's unfinished business.

This woman, a delicate China doll, signs autographs for a group of besotted fans. Every movement is languid and classy, speaking to well-bred manners and private schools.

One of the fans gushes, "When does the next Scarlet Shen movie come out?"

The woman, Scarlet, tinkles a laugh. "March. The month I move to Hollywood."

Another fan squeals her approval. "We *so* need more Asian representation. Do us proud."

JC, who's been listening in, tightens his hand around mine like a vise grip and blurts out, "Jasmine!"

It's crazy what you can see in a flash. Scarlet pretends not to hear him, but a little muscle works along her jaw. And her eyes flicker—not toward him but because of him.

Then I notice it: a black mark on her neck, beneath the curl of her ear. Strange. Nothing about her perfect poise screams tattoos. I can't make out what it is in the murky light, but it's like a man in a five-thousand-dollar suit sitting down and crossing his legs, and a hot pink novelty sock with a clown face grinning up at you.

More to her than meets the eye.

"Autograph line starts there," the Asian muscle grunts, jerking his chin at the mob of fans waiting patiently between velvet ropes.

Ignoring him, JC shouts her name a second time. This time, everyone hears. Everyone looks. Like a swan deciding to acknowledge you, Scarlet slowly turns her regal head. The frozen look in her eyes says she was quite happy living life without ever seeing JC again.

His breathing shifts, short and uneven. Angry, if I didn't know any better. "Where the fuck have you been all this time?"

Something changes in her face. She touches the emerald pendant necklace draped around her neck, and I notice the faintest tremor of her hand. "I'm sorry. Do I know you?"

"You know me, Rhys, *and* Sawyer."

Holy shit! It suddenly dawns on me who this is. Jasmine King. Sawyer's old girlfriend. The one who disappeared. The one Sawyer never talks about. No wonder JC looks like he's seen a ghost.

"Back away." The bodyguard chest-bumps JC, then lifts his shirt to reveal that he's packing. "We don't want any trouble."

"Let's go," I whisper urgently. Guns are a real reason to get the fuck out of here.

I drag JC out to the elevators, him stumbling behind me in a silent daze. The change of scenery, the sudden quiet, snaps him out of the dark cloud that settled over us.

"Sorry," he says absently. "She's the last person I expected to see." He smiles, but something is radiating off him, his sweetness curdled into something dark.

"It's her, right? Sawyer's Jasmine."

"Yeah," he says in that slow, thinking voice I now recognize. "Now Scarlet Shen." I can see his mind working overtime, trying to piece it together. He whips out his phone and promptly gets lost in a minute-long Google session.

He eventually looks up at me with a blank expression. "It doesn't make sense."

"What?" I crane my head for a look.

Glossy photos of Scarlet/Jasmine fill his screen. I tap to read one of the articles. She's the go-to actress of every famous Hong Kong auteur. Has built quite a reputation.

Now I understand JC's confusion, even before he says, "They're in the same industry. How does Sawyer not know?"

I search his pale face. "Are you going to tell him?"

"Yeah, of course. But not tonight."

He hammers the call button for the elevator, mouth clenched from the intensity of the encounter. In one way, Jasmine has me wondering. She exuded power—an inner strength that went beyond confidence. The kind of vibe you don't mess with. Dark, a little wild. And I always watch the eyes; they usually tell the truth. Hers were cool, detached… until they weren't. For the briefest second, I caught a flicker of something held down.

A bird trapped in a gilded cage.

"Hey, sorry." JC hugs me tight, muttering into my hair, "She threw me off. But not enough to forget it's all about you."

His words defuse some of the tension, but not all of it. If there's one thing I know about JC: he protects his brothers like worker bees protect their queen. I'm dying to know more and have this knot of questions inside me give the slightest bit, but smart enough to keep my mouth shut.

But he's true to his word.

True to *his* queen.

Back in our hotel room, he undresses us both, his kisses crawling down my neck into the hollow of my collarbone. I arch into him, begging for more. Then his fingers glide between my legs and dance along the thin wet fabric separating us. He groans, peeling my panties off slowly, taking his time to guide them over my ass to let them drop on the floor beside his boxers.

He kneels in front of me, mumbling, "Oh, Gia," and my eyes flutter shut from the heat of his breath on my trembling core.

My fingers tangle in his hair, every inhale of air burning my lungs. "Am I making you emotional yet?"

He looks up with a wicked smile and says, "Almost," before his head dips between my legs, and I hold on, fighting not to scream as he circles my clit, licking and sucking. It's too much, too hot, too fast. I try to wiggle away, but he holds me tight, his mouth working me, until all I feel is my body about to blow apart.

"Fuck! JC. Slow."

Just as the last shred of my control is about to unspool, the pressure relents. The bright electric stars behind my eyes fade into blackness, the entire room spinning as JC staggers to his feet, cups my ass, and carries me blindly to the bed.

He fumbles with a condom, roughly spreads my legs, and buries himself in one dominant thrust.

I gasp and feel myself clench around him.

"Shit," he hisses. "I can't go slow. Sorry. Not this time."

His lips brush against mine for a deep, bruising kiss before he finds a steady rhythm, picking up pace as he exploits every angle, rolls his hips to go deeper, on a one-man mission to chase away every shred of worry from earlier. I dig my nails into his back and hang on for dear life. The climax builds like fire in my belly, moans ringing out so loud he reaches up to cover my mouth with his palm.

His eyes find mine, and so many things pass between us as the ache crests, my fists twisting in the sheets, every muscle pulling tight, before the cascading waves of pleasure consume me. His own release powers through him, and then we're both falling through light and shattered shadows, crying out each other's names.

Chapter Thirty-Four

JC

Easter
Vancouver, B.C.

AT THE DINING ROOM TABLE THAT HEAVES WITH ENOUGH FOOD TO FEED Bolivia, David Barlow says the evening prayer. Gia squeezes my left hand, Antonia Barlow holding my right. I poke an eye open to keep watch on Gia, head bowed, grateful for the meal. Saying grace is still new for me, but I have many things to be thankful for.

David's acceptance of me, for one.

He's a guy's guy. A hearty beer drinker in plaid shirts who watches Hockey Night in Canada and smells overwhelmingly of drugstore aftershave whenever he bear-hugs me. Cranks Rush and Genesis while he cooks. Twenty years married, likely another forty to come.

We're tight.

Antonia? *Slightly* different story.

The initial shock of Gia moving out to live in sin with her recently scandalized failed chaperone gave rise to stern questions about my intentions. To me, loving Gia is the most natural thing in the world. My now and forever. But our age gap (or rather, her social circle's view of it) remains a point of contention. Plenty of opinions, shared weekly.

Funny, considering she was barefoot and pregnant at nineteen with Gia.

Still, if Gia in my bed means Sunday dinners deep in Burnaby, praying to a god I don't believe in, that's a sacrifice I'll make ten times over. Whatever we have together, it's going to outlast all the noise.

Prayers done, Antonia hands me a platter of eggplant parmesan. "So," she says. "Any progress to report?"

Gia rolls her eyes. "I told you, kids are in the five-year plan. Not the five-month plan."

"Toni," David warns. "Let them be."

Antonia purses her lips, retreats. Unchecked, she'd rant and rage, maybe ground Gia if she still could. And as she silently piles food onto my plate, doing what moms do best, I understand. This shift in dynamic must be tough to swallow. She held the upper hand before the tour. Now her daughter is a bona fide star—not a cabaret casualty like Mama, but a headliner, living debt-free and in luxury with a handsome, rich boyfriend.

Ha.

"It would be better if you were married." Antonia throws a look at me, then at David, who, best guess, is concentrating on pouring wine to avoid eye contact and the ruin of the world. "I only want the best for Gia."

"Wow!" Gia exclaims. "You said my name right."

I nudge her under the table—a gesture of *don't push it*. Their relationship has slowly inched toward improvement, with Gia stepping up and asking her mother's opinion on songs, and Antonia holding back her criticism. At times, both still circle each other like alpha wolves, waiting for the other to strike. When we moved Gia out in February, Antonia stood like a sentry in the bedroom, eyeing me like some no-good pirate whisking her daughter into sin.

Not the smoothest start.

Anything to keep the peace is the name of the game, and I get the sense that an extravagant wedding is the only thing that will put me firmly in her good books. I found out from David their shotgun vows at City Hall with Antonia pregnant did not go over well with her family. The expectations are high for Gia.

"My mom is keen for us to get married, too," I say, the first thing all evening that elicits a small hum of approval. The moms have met twice and hit it off. Ideally, their budding friendship fast-tracks my welcome into Antonia's still-wary heart.

"First, we need to record our next album," Gia explains for the tenth time, or so it feels. "Then we tour again. Then maybe, after that…"

Antonia silently does the math. "At least two years until I see a grandchild?"

Gia shuts her eyes with a helpless-sounding sigh. She prefers her mother hiding out in the kitchen, rustling up meals, and not rehashing the same topic, week after week. Me? I can live with the parental pressure because I'm dying for us to get pregnant. Until then, the greatest gig I could ask for: all the practice. My blushing virgin has overcome her initial shy debut, and she makes love to me like a dream.

Sometimes rough, always deep and messy.

She's my favorite song on heavy rotation.

I take a swallow of pinot grigio, Italian, of course, and smile. "I'm trying my best to move things along, Antonia. Rest assured."

Grinning, Gia leans over and kisses my cheek. "Every day you try. Sometimes twice. You work so hard."

Dave chokes on a laugh while Antonia falls silent, scrambling for something to say. Did we just drop a reminder in her G-rated imagination on how babies get made? Should I tell her how I was making omelets this morning when Gia wandered in without panties and draped herself over the butcher's block? How wrapped up we were in each other, we didn't notice the kitchen smoking until the fire alarm went off.

I don't. No need to stoke her fire.

She fizzles out on her own, and we enjoy Easter dinner in peace.

♫

By the time we pull into Coal Harbour, the city's bathed in soft twilight. The days are getting longer. Spring is around the corner. Everything feels a little magical.

Our new home. Our new life together.

Not even a minute inside the condo, and Gia flings her leather jacket onto the couch, oblivious to the fact that some mystery man keeps hanging it in the closet. I won't lie—there's been a few hiccups to navigate, the usual new-couple stuff. I like my private time in the bathroom, unlike Gia, who barges in to take a whiz and chatters away while I floss. She insisted on cooking dinner last month, but after Mom gamely ate the crunchy rice cooked in a frying pan with no lid, a box full of cookbooks arrived.

To her credit, Gia has made great progress. I'm confident our kitchen won't blow up anytime soon. Because, let's face it, if Gia can love me, she's capable of anything.

A wild, natural woman with a soul as big as Texas.

Gia throws her arms around me and mutters, "Sweet Jesus. Thank you for your endless patience with Mama."

"I'm just a king serving his queen."

"I think you mean *servicing*."

Her laughing grin widens as Gia grinds her body up and down my zipper. All the low-level gray frustration inside me turns golden bright. Our bedroom is a quick walk down the hall, no stairways to navigate. I scoop my bundle of sexual magnetism into my arms, pitying any man who isn't me.

Her eyes bright with joy, she looks up and asks, "What are you doing?"

"A little of this, a little of that."

"Nothing you do qualifies as *little*."

I smile back, informing her, "We have four other frying pans to destroy."

Gia snuggles into my chest, cheeks flushing an adorable pink. "I owe you for that."

I nudge open the bedroom door and gently lay her down on the soft silk duvet. Our eyes meet, and I feel the blood rush south.

"Do tell."

"You like it when I'm on top, right?"

The sight of her sly grin makes me laugh. "That, my love, is a throwaway question."

Her hand finds mine, and she places both between her legs, putting her whole life into my hands. I'm getting used to having to think about exactly nothing to keep up with her.

Before the sparkle gets too bright, I murmur, "I bought more condoms. They're in the bathroom."

"We ran out already?" Gia laughs and rolls off the bed, me starting the silent countdown in my head. I figure nine seconds and just hit seven when she returns.

"What's this?" She shakes the gold-wrapped box that most definitely is not condoms.

My voice turns soft. "I got you something."

Her eyes very wide, she lowers herself onto the side of the bed. Something is up. But what? We agreed to wait a year before I officially asked for her hand, and the gift is bigger than a ring box.

"It's a gigantic pair of toenail clippers, in case you're wondering."

She elbows me hard in the ribs. "It better not be!"

"Open it and find out."

Very carefully, very unlike Gia, she undoes the red velvet bow. Unsticks the tape from the golden paper. Spins the plain cardboard box in one hand, looking for any identifying mark. In the meantime, I've settled beside her. Thighs touching. Lightning inside of me.

Gia opens the lid, her mouth forming an "o" of shock. "Oh my god! What?"

She lifts the custom-made tiara into the light. Weighing the heft of the twenty-four-karat gold in her palm, she admires the centerpiece jewel, an enameled skull and crossbones with two shining red eyes.

"Are those real rubies?" she whispers.

"Red, to match your lipstick."

She turns the tiara over in her hands. Watching her, I realize maybe this is what it means to love someone truly; to overcome the complexity of opening your damaged heart and brave the unknown, guns blazing.

"JC," she says, all choked up. "This is beyond beautiful."

"That represents part one of my two-part commitment. If you'll be my spicy baby mama, I'll be your Mr. Mom."

Gia looks at me, smiling, so happy in her bubble. "We need to agree on one thing, though. We have to name our kids something cool. That they won't have to shorten."

I trace the fine structure of her jaw with my finger. "Like Vladimir?"

She laughs. "No. A pretty name for a girl, like Lily or Georgina. Maybe Randall for a boy. It sounds strong."

"Randall?" I exaggerate a shudder. "That sounds like a tech geek or a McDonald's manager."

"Hardly. He'll be the spitting image of you. Are you ready to be the proud father of a male model?"

A thrill shivers down my spine: *Father.*

In another life, that word would be unbearably heartbreaking. But it's like I survived the biggest test of spirit and soul and was blessed with a prize worth more than gold.

The moment swells my heart.

"I have a couple of names to run past you."

Gia sets down the tiara and runs her hands through my hair. "Lay them on me."

I take a breath. This is big. Not having Gia prod things out from the depths of me. That I can be vulnerable without needing a crisis to force it.

"Micah for a boy. And Everly, if it's a girl."

Something moves across her face, something like shock. Then she starts chucking every pillow off the bed, sending the remains of my elegant gift-wrapping flying. Lifts the duvet, searching. Scans the room.

"What are you doing?" I ask, genuinely confused.

With both hands parked on her waist, she asks, "Where are you hiding it? Your copy of *God's Gift to Baby Names*?"

Ah. I smile to egg her on. "You know I'm a wordsmith."

"Jameson!" Her voice turns scolding. "You did not just pull the two most perfect baby names out of your ass."

"Wanna see what else I have up there?"

She pauses, lifting a brow. "Is that an open invitation?"

"Kidding. Absolutely not." Little Miss Handsy pushed the envelope last week. In that context, *No* will never mean *Yes*. Not even a *Maybe*. "But is it too early to put in a request for a boy? If we create a mini-you first, I'll be outnumbered."

She gives my erection a playful squeeze through my jeans. "Hush. Or I'll bless you with triplet girls. And Everly Trenton sounds so pretty. When did you come up with that?"

Truth is, I've sat with those names for years. At times, they've haunted me. And Gia senses some thought went into them. Just not how much.

"I thought of those names … a long time ago."

Her grin falters, tenderness takes over her expression, and I know she sees me clearly in this moment, without the haze of great sex and greater music.

"I love you," she says, her voice like smoke. "I love that *I* get to be the mother of your children."

I can tell from the weight of the silence that follows where her mind has traveled to—a small reminder that Gia is a normal, jealous twenty-year-old. It's healthy for her claws to come out, and I never want them to retract fully. To be clear, I encourage nothing. Flirty JC is a relic of the past. But for my own stupid pride, Gia's possessiveness is a good thing. It means she loves me. Without that, I might as well pack up, move to Nashville, and be a goddamned country singer.

"So," I scratch my chin, "your competitive streak is still alive and well."

Gia shrugs, nonplussed. "I hate her irrationally. And always will. You can't take that away from me." She pauses, then adds, as a sweetener, "But I'm making an effort with Sawyer."

"You two are finally bonding."

"Like Crazy Glue."

Shame for Sawyer. I suppose it's his destiny to have not one, but both of his brothers' girlfriends indifferent to his charms. And in the case of him and Gia, separation is a good thing. Nice not to have to break up two heavyweights constantly going at each other. Sawyer packed up for LA last month, living in my Hollywood apartment until he finds his perfect mansion.

And I've stopped asking about Jasmine King. That instant blank look he gave me when I mentioned running into her said everything about how much he hates discussing what happened.

Still … I'm keeping an eye on her.

Gia nudges me. "Hey, you."

"What?"

She studies me. Knows every lie I tell myself. "Where you at?"

"You know, somewhere between totally in love and terrified."

She smiles and plunks herself into my lap. "You'll be a great dad. The best ever. Full respect, because not many guys would feel comfortable, or even step up, like you plan to. I'm forever grateful."

I pluck the tiara from the rumpled duvet, tucking it into the crown of her hair. Her eyes, dark and shining, level on mine.

"Well?"

"It's perfect," I assure her. "Suits you to a T."

Preening a little, she says, "I'm wearing it at our wedding. With the poufy skirt I mentioned."

I ruffle her hair because I know she loves it, even though it once drove her crazy. "I'll buy whatever dress you want, as long as you're marrying me."

Her arms loosely drape around the contours of my body and pull me into a devouring kiss. Tongues and torment, friction and rhythm, diamonds in my veins. Needing her as she needs me. I can smell that she's wet where I need her to be, and no part of me wants to remain clothed.

But she pushes my greedy hands away, breaks our kiss, and I try to decipher the glint in her eyes.

"I have all sorts of ways to say thank you," she says in her girly voice that means trouble, "but can we listen to the song first?"

I mock-groan. My song, the never-ending negotiation song. The master recording landed in my inbox while we were eating spaghetti in Burnaby. It was my mistake to tell her.

But I can negotiate equally hard.

"We listen to the song once," I sound very much like a soon-to-be father, "and then *I* get to do whatever I want with you."

She grins and, for once, miraculously, doesn't counter.

"Deal."

♫

In the studio, Gia listens intently, and the shine in her eyes tells me something immense is moving through her. My song about our intense connection is pure grandeur, made more divine with her contribution. We both know we've created something extraordinary.

When the last chord fades, she's breathing slow and shallow, her face inches from mine. "It's so good, right? Our voices together." She squeezes my hand. "Will you finally tell me the name?"

"You can't change it," I warn. I might be a modern man letting my woman run the show, but I'd insisted on naming and publishing rights. If Gia wanted in on the writing going forward, she had to play the game like a pro.

"I know!" she says. "But I'm dying. The boys wanna know too. And Kayla. I promised I'd involve them in every decision."

Gia pinky swore to be a team player with the band, and so far, so good. They all have a voice in songs and direction, even if Gia's remains the loudest.

"In that case…" I let the moment build until she looks ready to kill me. "'My Cherry Duet.'"

Her mouth quirks. The silence stretches so long, it feels like it's tugging on my bones. Did I make a misstep? In the low light, her eyes turn into a deep, dark ocean I fall straight into.

Then she grins. "It's perfect."

It really is. The mix. Our voices. The name. It had to be perfect because it reflects my love for her.

I wink. "As perfect as me?"

Gia hauls me out of the chair, laughing as she pins me against the wall, her body flush to mine. She loves this: keeping me on my toes. It's her constant, her heartbeat, her purpose.

Forever unpredictable.

"I love you more than any song, you idiot," she whispers.

Our mouths close over each other's in a torrent of kisses, and we're wild, lost kids, on fire and desperate. Her hands are in my hair, the thump of her heart against my own. We barely make it out of the studio before we're stumbling down the hall, falling back into bed, my intended slow, careful process of destroying her quickly turning into something more feral. Gia takes charge and rides me shamelessly, flexing to give me all the right pressure until every muscle releases and a white-hot flash of oblivion rolls through my body like electric thunder.

Nothing feels sweeter than her in this moment. Not spring, or the endless possibilities just around the corner.

Her feelings for me are not linked to a song.

They're all about *me*.

How amazing is that?

♫

After I return the favor and push Gia over the edge, she collapses into my arms and falls into a deep sleep. I lie in the dark, listening to the sounds of midnight and her soft breathing. Somewhere outside, down on the walkway, a woman laughs.

I like the sound of happy.

It feels good to have someone by my side with so much ahead of us. Too much time was wasted, alone and restless, and yet so full of life. Now we have inside jokes and code words. Routines and rituals. I scratch Gia's back in the morning, knowing just where that unreachable spot between her shoulder blades is. And she guides me out from the tumble of my chaotic thoughts that still swirl from time to time, chipping away at my years of self-protection, all the little things forced on me.

Growing up in a household that prioritized entertainment in the same way others value God, my love of music was always tangled with my father's. I had talent, that special ear, but I felt like I owed him to be the musical success he never was. Killing my band was painful, but it also brought relief. To shrug off that pressure.

Now I make music without expectations, writing songs for the woman who leaves me flush with more feelings than I can pinpoint.

Stroking her tousled hair, I glance up at the ceiling. High above us, tucked into a corner, are the touchstones Gia snuck in. Two glow-in-the-dark stickers peeled from her old room and pressed into ours. Steady Saturn with its protective rings. A comet blazing beside him.

I smile, big feelings blowing up my heart. The blaze of Gia—you can see her from space. It doesn't surprise me anymore how completely she dazzles me. She was fierceness personified that night at the Troubadour, and I felt the beginning of something I had no way to explain. I was helplessly drawn to her, the pull far beyond the passing fascination of other women. She seemed to operate on a higher level than everyone else.

Up in the stratosphere.

My shooting star.

I pull her closer, breathing her in. The stickers wink down at me, and just before I drift off to sleep, the thought lands. Tomorrow I'll tell Gia, and she'll absolutely call me an idiot. Maybe throw something at me. But she is my version of heaven, and some things are worth saying, even if they're cliché.

Our love was written in the stars.

Thank you free bonus!

I hope you enjoyed *My Cherry Duet!*

Reviews are the lifeblood of an indie author's success. I'd be honored if you took a moment to post a review on any of the sites below. If you're not comfortable putting your thoughts into words, a star rating works just fine.

Amazon

Good Reads

Book Bub

♫

What's coming next? Book three in the Trenton Troublemakers series! Starring the inimitable Sawyer Trenton and Jasmine King, the mercurial daughter of a Hong Kong billionaire. Their story is one helluva ride. Title and tropes revealed in my newsletter in summer 2026. Anticipated publication date: March 2027.

Thank you free bonus!

♬

Save 25% on future eBooks by buying direct through my Rowan Rossler Shop. All eBooks delivered immediately through Book Funnel. Signed books also available, mailed with love & bonus swag!

Scan to Shop!

Curious what songs made the *My Cherry Duet* playlist? Of course you are! Scan the QR code below.

My Cherry Duet Playlist!

Also by Rowan Rossler

THE HUSTLERS SERIES

The Cruiser (book 1)

The Challenger (book 2)

The Closer (book 3)

This jet-set romance series stars three BFFs navigating dreams, desires, and all the beautiful complications of falling in love. Glamour, spice, and sexy drama. Pack your bags and follow your heart!

THE TRENTON TROUBLEMAKERS SERIES

My Grape Crush (book 1)

My Cherry Duet (book 2)

Book Three (coming soon)

Three brothers and the fiery women who tangle with them star in a trio of interconnected but standalone romances brimming with sibling drama and shameless fun. Trouble always comes in threes…

Acknowledgments

This time, before I thank the people who helped bring this book to life, I need to thank music itself. It's as essential to me as breathing—and some days, more so.

It took me until my fifth novel to write a rock and roll romance, but *My Cherry Duet* is undeniably one of my most satisfying stories. I love writing big feels and JC's backstory was particularly rich and emotional to explore. Pairing that with the collision of two artists at different points in their careers and exploring how the relationship to risk gets viewed through different lenses, added a fundamental layer of tension.

Early on, I gave up trying to funnel my deep love of music into the narrative and let Gia and JC do the talking instead. (Always the smarter decision to let characters lead!) This is their love story with music and each other.

Full credit to my father for introducing me to the power of music. Growing up, music was always cranking in our house, Dad grooving to jazz beats with a glass of wine in hand, or slumped in a chair, overwhelmed as Richard Wagner blasted out of the speakers. He's still rocking out at 88 years old, and I send him Youtube links of singers and bands he might enjoy. We share that special kinship all music freaks understand.

On a personal note, setting the story against the backdrop of a European tour allowed me to indulge my two favorite pastimes: concerts and travel. My parents are from Europe and my father worked at Air Canada for thirty-one years, so we were always on the road as a family.

I've also seen close to five hundred shows, on all corners of the globe, and I still get a chill every time I'm in the front row, the lights dim, and the musicians walk out in front of the monitors. Live music is ritual to me, a sacred exchange of energy between performers and audience. That exquisite high of a pinnacle show, like Pop My Cherry's finale in Barcelona, is one of life's greatest gifts.

I'm fortunate enough to call several people in the music business good friends. From corporate managers to tour managers to musicians, they freely spilled stories and tidbits for this book. Thank you Kuba, Rock, Mary, Robin, and Rob for sharing.

A hearty shout out to those who weighed in on early versions of this story to make it better. No book gets written without editors and beta readers, so thank you Krista and my swat team of Betas. You're the best!

Last, but never least, a huge shout out to all the booksellers, my street team, and my dear readers! Without your support, none of this would be possible. Grateful for every one of you!

Love,

RR

xo

About the Author

Rowan Rossler is an Amazon Top 100 bestselling author and travel junkie living in Vancouver, BC. She loves bringing bold and flawed characters to life in her contemporary romance tales. If you're a lover of sultry moments, sexy drama, and heartfelt emotion, Rowan is your one-click author.

A lifelong book lover and former financial planner, her pivot into production inspired her to put pen to page. If she's not writing, you find Rowan stage left at a concert, cooking, whipping her abs shape, or enjoying la dolce vita on one of her many travel adventu

CONNECT WITH ROWAN: